Three Parties

Three Parties

A NOVEL

ZIYAD SAADI

HAMISH HAMILTON
an imprint of Penguin Canada, a division of Penguin Random House Canada Limited

Canada • USA • UK • Ireland • Australia • New Zealand • India • South Africa • China

First published 2025

Copyright © 2025 by Ziyad Saadi

All rights reserved. No part of this book may be reproduced, scanned, transmitted, or distributed in any form or by any electronic or mechanical means, including information storage and retrieval systems, without permission in writing from the publisher, except by a reviewer, who may quote brief passages in a review. No part of this book may be used or reproduced in any manner for the purpose of training artificial intelligence technologies or systems.

Hamish Hamilton, an imprint of Penguin Canada
A division of Penguin Random House Canada
320 Front Street West, Suite 1400
Toronto Ontario, M5V 3B6, Canada
penguinrandomhouse.ca

The authorized representative in the EU for product safety and compliance is Penguin Random House Ireland, Morrison Chambers, 32 Nassau Street, Dublin D02 YH68, Ireland. https://eu-contact.penguin.ie

Publisher's note: This book is a work of fiction. Names, characters, places and incidents either are the product of the author's imagination or are used fictitiously, and any resemblance to actual persons living or dead, events, or locales is entirely coincidental.

LIBRARY AND ARCHIVES CANADA CATALOGUING IN PUBLICATION

Title: Three parties / Ziyad Saadi.
Names: Saadi, Ziyad, author.
Identifiers: Canadiana (print) 20250148498 | Canadiana (ebook) 20250153572 | ISBN 9780735250963 (hardcover) | ISBN 9780735250970 (EPUB)
Subjects: LCGFT: Queer fiction. | LCGFT: Novels.
Classification: LCC PS8637.A2255 T47 2025 | DDC C813/.6—dc23

Cover design by Emma Dolan
Cover images by Emma Dolan except: (vase) © Anatolii Frolov, (birthday cake) © FARBAI, both Getty Images
Book design by Emma Dolan
Typeset by Terra Page

Printed in Canada

10 9 8 7 6 5 4 3 2 1

Penguin
Random House
HAMISH HAMILTON CANADA

To the indelible among us

CHAPTER ONE

Firas needed the flowers to make a statement. All of it needed to make a statement: the food, the music, the decorations, the favors, even the guests had to have some purpose, some thematic relevance that couldn't be forged or fouled. Every element of his party would serve as a clue, a pinpoint on a map across his lips whence his secret often spilled in drips of jargon throughout hurried breakfasts and quiet suppers. Those inclined to do so would partake in the journey, and those less inclined would have the journey dropped on them like a brick house. His secret would come out, that was certain, but the precise manner in which it did would remain a mystery until reality blended with surreality, Time stopped spinning its merciless hand, and all the mind's senses fizzled to a hum, for in that moment his unprotected heart would be the only thing in existence.

He wondered if the clues would be enough to lay the cobblestones to his destination, or if his parents would be too preoccupied, perhaps even too dim, to notice the path at all. They had much on their minds in recent years, as did his sister, as did his brother, each member of the family an island in an archipelago, viewing one another with familiarity and little else.

When he awoke that Sunday, his room displayed a strange new motif that he could only describe in his groggy morning state as *askew*. As though he'd woken up in the middle of the night and rearranged everything with a faintness that denied him any memory of it. A newfound intimacy had developed among his possessions: the Tustin solid wood armoire three inches closer to his bed, the occupants of his floating shelves—books, landscape paintings, souvenirs—huddled in a secret meeting. The velvet ottoman on which lay his prayer rug, unfurled once a day to give the impression he ever used it, now tucked itself into the corner to allow for the emergence of its oldest friend, the streak of caramel staining the wall despite a decade of attempts to clean it. Even this everlasting emblem now struck him differently. But it could not be refuted that this disorientation was much less the fault of the picture than it was of the viewer, whose perfectly fixed head and perpendicular gaze were no match for the upturned mind behind them, viewing not only the whole room from a different angle, but the whole world from a different angle, looking for all the stains along its path and finding beauty in them. Today, after all, was to be a beautiful day.

He marched downstairs, expecting a half-hearted birthday wish from everyone, only to find Suhad alone in the kitchen cooking breakfast. The smell of frying bacon meant their parents were out of the house, and the awkward contortion of her body, obscuring the stove, meant they were scheduled to return any minute.

"Where are Mama and Baba?"

Her head jerked up like a rabbit startled by a breaking twig. "Oh, it's you," she sighed with relief. "Mazen had a session this morning. They should be back soon."

"They booked his session for *today*?"

"Um, yes?" Her upward inflection portended the oversight, made more blatant as she slid the bacon onto a plate of eggs and toast and sat down to eat. Fork in one hand, smartphone in the other. No eye contact whatsoever, even as she sensed him gawking.

He went to the fridge to retrieve the ingredients he'd bought the day before to make himself the commemorative birthday breakfast of banana chocolate pancakes he'd long enjoyed, beginning back when Mrs. Tullinson lived next door. Myra Tullinson was a sixty-year-old widow with pink streaks in her hair and unabashed laugh lines who'd just been empty-nested when the Dareers moved in. Firas was nearing adolescence, but he still possessed his most childlike features, including the ruby cheeks and helpless eyes that made her instantly fall in love. She doted on him constantly, buying him clothes he didn't need and toys he was too old to play with. She taught him how to cook and decorate, and the fine art of appreciating beauty, natural and man-made, and thus set him on his path to a career in architecture. On his fourteenth birthday, she asked his parents if she could steal him away for the morning to spoil him with a special breakfast. They agreed, so long as Mrs. Tullinson didn't strain herself. By his nineteenth birthday, she had gotten sick and could no longer make the pancakes for him, but she insisted on inviting him over and teaching him the recipe. That was the last birthday they ever shared. Firas continued the tradition, making a more flaccid version of the treat in the years since. When he opened the pantry, however, the chocolate chips were gone. An entire bag, disappeared. He felt that asking a question to which he already knew the answer was tacky and tactless, so he simply made do with buttermilk pancakes because buttermilk pancakes were delicious in their own right and today was to be a beautiful day.

While the batter simmered over the griddle, Firas stepped outside to check the mailbox, almost expecting to find an anonymous birthday present. Instead, he found one hand-delivered note, addressed to him personally, which he snatched just before rushing back to the kitchen to flip his pancake. Watching it closely now for fear of burning the other side, he checked the contents of the fridge to ensure that the food items required for that evening's four-course meal had not suffered the same fate as the chocolate chips.

As he sat down to eat, he thought about his next task for the day. The flower shop opened at eleven o'clock on Sundays, and he would head over as soon as he finished his breakfast. That would give him enough time to prepare the dinner and the setting, after infusing his day with the vigor of a promising start. For what could be more promising to a beating heart than the ambrosial whiff of nature?

The syrupy pancakes slid down his throat and he thought of Mazen in his room with the chocolate chips. Nibbling on them like a royal servant testing the king's meal for poison. On their own, the chips tasted odd, a hint of sugar and cocoa assaulted by a barrage of flavored fats. But Mazen wouldn't have minded. Mazen never minded the little things, which made him the ideal guest and the first, among a periodically winnowing list, that Firas invited.

"OH MY FUCKING GOD!" Suhad slammed the table with an open palm, as though her exclamation lacked emphasis on its own.

He didn't dare ask, nor did he need to. "DJ Shiv is making a cameo at the Grind tonight!" She didn't look at him when she said this, because she wasn't saying it to him. She wasn't even saying it, but simply willing it into the universe as if the text she'd just read weren't real enough.

A strip and a half of bacon still lay on her plate. Firas asked if he could have one. She didn't hear him, so he speared the full strip with his syrup-speckled fork and crunched on it with three quick, successive bites. She noticed it barely, her eyes studying the same text over and over as though its meaning would change if she dared to look away. It was only when she shoved the last half strip into her mouth that a sensation, something in the realm of an alarm, diverted her attention to him, because when the scent of bacon began to waft out of the room, a new one took its place.

"Are you wearing cologne?"

He was. A musk-like concoction that Mrs. Tullinson had bought him when he turned sixteen and officially became, in her own doe-eyed decree, a man. He wore it only on his birthday, since nobody, least of all himself, cared much for the smell.

"I wear it every year."

The light inside her head finally ignited, followed by an apologetic wince.

"Happy birthday . . ." The wince persisted, but, as her eyes shifting back to her phone made clear, only because of the cameo that now began to feel less real. The Dareers were not close, but they believed in formality, relied heavily on it, understanding, as the water around them stretched out, that none of them would be able to navigate their household without it.

She cleared both their plates from the table and began washing the dishes in the sink. "How should I dress tonight?"

Firas had initially planned to go grand, have the guests dress as ceremoniously as possible, as though they were attending the wedding of a couple so elite that half the guests knew them only by association. But as he readied the invitations—handcrafted on coated paper, gilded Baskerville against periwinkle blue, a bold summons ("You are called upon . . .") capped by a soft, playful dare ("Will you miss out?")—it occurred to him that turning his party into a grand ceremony would not enhance his big announcement but undermine it, suffocating it beneath a mountain of anticipation, an atmosphere of puffery in which the product sold is nothing like the product advertised.

"Casual," he answered.

"Can I bring a friend?"

This was another issue he'd considered, one that kept him up every night since he decided to throw the party in the first place. At times, he even debated abandoning the idea, or canceling it once the idea materialized into the physical world and the RSVPs rolled swiftly into his mailbox. The guest list was the most curated element of the party, with each attendee playing a distinct role: the neighbor who replaced Mrs. Tullinson for help in the kitchen, the cousins from Sterling Heights for comic relief, his fellow interns at the architecture firm for moral support. An unexpected guest could lead to unexpected events. He imagined animosity between longtime rivals that exploded into fistfights, or the sabotaging of meals to undermine his culinary repute. More than animosity, he feared charisma, the life of the party who might steal his thunder, toppling his nerve and cackling so hard that Firas would be sent cowering into the corner for peace of mind that never comes.

"Sorry, but I just don't have enough food for any more people."

"Oh she wouldn't eat! I wouldn't either."

"There's also not much space in the house . . ."

Sensing his unease, she nodded, then finished washing the dishes and went upstairs to her room.

The invitation was for half past seven, which meant it was for half past eight, with several guests likely to arrive closer to nine. It was then that dinner would be served, some of it in the dining room and some of it on folding tables in the living room. His mother would forbid anyone eating on her sofa, a peach English roll-arm the likes of which she'd spotted in an interior design magazine whose origins were never known. He wondered if anyone would show up at all. Twenty-four of the twenty-six invitees had RSVP'd *yes*, with the other two texting excuses, feigning disappointment, and offering rain checks that were likely void.

He was always more grateful for people who declined right off the bat. With these invitees came the element of certainty. Rarely does a person RSVP *no* and show up anyway, but so often do people RSVP *yes* and then don't. Firas had at least two contingency plans for every part of his daily life, be it for unreliable bus lines to his regular destinations, for restaurants too crowded to make it back to class on time, or for his assignments, which he saved on flash drives and copied/pasted into emails each and every time he made an edit. If his workplace had a change in management, he secured job interviews before the new, potentially monstrous boss even started. Where a contingency plan could be formed, he formed as many as possible. Yet in the event that every single guest who was expected to arrive would, with only an hour's warning, change their mind, he had no contingency plan whatsoever. His special effort to form a plan for disastrous circumstances, no matter how unlikely the disaster, was a tool he had acquired at the age of twelve, when he was to have his very first birthday party in America. The guests were all the boys in his class, as his parents were still unaccustomed to the notion of mixed-gender parties, a custom eventually quashed upon his brother's first step on the ladder of adolescence. But between the day Firas's invitations were handed out and the day his party was scheduled to take place, something happened. He overheard the sound of his name, caught in a whirl of snickers like a gazelle surrounded by a pack of hyenas, circling their victim for what feels like eternity to make the eventual pounce more rewarding. The boys planned not to show, despite assurances to the contrary, leaving him to discover the truth only when everything was already set up to receive them. The following day, he had his mother call the boys' parents and inform them that the party was canceled. No explanation was given to them by Firas's mother, nor was any explanation given to Firas's mother by Firas. He managed to avoid disaster that time, but only with the help of fortunate circumstances—the honor of being trusted by his sprightly teacher Mrs. Robbins to deliver a note to the principal's office—that led him past the bathroom whence the snickering emerged. But good fortune rarely strikes its bolt upon the same person twice. What would he do in the case of disaster on the night of his twenty-third birthday? The announcement itself might end the party, but what of everything that preceded it, everything that could prevent the announcement from taking place and rob the party of its primary purpose?

He wondered why he hadn't come up with a contingency plan this time around. Perhaps it was newfound audacity that enabled him to finally relinquish his control over his world, a budding faith in humanity to return the many kindnesses he'd been supplying now for years. He smiled at this thought, prided himself on the courage it took to submit oneself to the will of the universe.

But he could not smile for long; soon enough the truth arose, slyly at first, teasing him from the back of his mind, then inching closer and closer to the front the more he dared to ignore it. There was no courage in his decision, no pride rightfully taken; his failure to plan for a disaster was born, in fact, out of a secret desire for it. Disaster would serve as his excuse, his reassurance that he was indeed courageous, but simply unfortunate, that surely the party would have gone perfectly were it not for the fire, the earthquake, the asteroid, the plague, the uninvited plus-one. Because the only disaster that truly mattered on this night was the inevitable fallout from his announcement.

His mother, a soft-core denialist of evolution, would harken back to verses in the Qur'an and sermons she memorized off YouTube, and a sense of doom would overtake her. His father, a man whose most precious value was his standing—already slithering from his grasp with every passing day without a job—would rage at the public display, and even more at Firas's exploitation of it to stifle a scene. Each guest had their own individual purpose, but collectively they were all meant to shield him from repercussions, delaying them until the very end of the night when the announcement would be stripped of most of its sting. Perhaps the reactions of others may even influence those of his parents. Perhaps not.

His sister may finally notice him, but only through the ephemeral glow of learning a new fact about someone you'd always assumed you knew fully. She, too, might resent the gathering crowd, the gaudy display, the discomfort that comes with being placed just left of center. Most of his parents' attention was dedicated to Mazen, but Suhad accepted this as a necessity. It seemed very unlikely to Firas, impossible even, that his case would be viewed as the same.

And then there was Mazen, whom Firas seldom understood yet always admired. Admired him for his unobtrusive manner that often made you forget he was even home. Admired him for the simple way in which he viewed the world and all its chaos. How would Mazen react?

Firas's twelfth birthday—a sushi dinner at a restaurant in Dearborn to substitute for the canceled party—culminated in tears, shed in the bedroom that he and his brother shared in their family's old apartment. They had twin beds, Firas's closer to the window, the moonlight zigzagging through the branches of a venerable oak tree and making his wet cheeks glisten, and Mazen asked him what was wrong. Firas, lying on his side with his back to him, wiped his tears, closed his eyes, and drifted to sleep without a word. He never cried in front of anyone again. He would not cry tonight.

As Firas rose from the kitchen table, the front door opened and closed. Windbreakers rustled along the rack, shoes thumped against the wall. His father bolted past him towards the bathroom, while his mother, her skin somewhat ashen, her eyes concentrated on her phone, went up the stairs, not noticing him. Then Mazen drifted into the kitchen, gray-eyed, hair parted to the left. Brown smudges encircled his mouth, which curled up at the sight of his brother. He gently deposited the chocolate chips on the table in front of Firas, and from the sight of the bag, twisted one inch from the bottom, it looked as though Mazen had left him two dozen chips.

"Happy birthday, Firas."

Today would be a beautiful day.

CHAPTER TWO

Regal lavenders and prickly cacti. Hypnotic chrysanthemums and thunderous sunflowers. Bashful lilies of the valley and uninhibited birds-of-paradise. And of course the rose, which shrugs off one's admiration the second it gets it. Firas never tired of visiting the shop, which effortlessly created an experience for its customers in the most sensory form of the term, most notably and surprisingly through its sound—that mild but unmistakable stir of nature. Today, however, he heard not nature but an unusual buzz. He wasn't quite sure what it was, nor could he decide whether it was ruining his enjoyment, but he chose to focus instead on the flowers and the cheery staff. The staff added much to the ambience. Firas couldn't know, however, that the buoyancy he saw in them seldom occurred in his absence. It was he who inspired them, the disgruntled nonunion employees, to smile the genuine smile that obscured long, underpaid shifts. Firas was, in fact, the flower shop's perfect client. Yes, he often lingered, but he was courteous, self-sufficient, and never one to drop in without intending to buy at least one flower, because such a missed opportunity, such a waste of nature, was the stuff that clogged the very flow of life. This was his philosophy as the surrounding flora burst, its petals and perfume sashaying all around him, lulling him into the only comfort the world never ceased to provide. He was not there to waste space but to relish it, to thank it for its service, for releasing him from his mind and body and allowing him simply to exist. He absorbed the ambience more than ever on this day, as he readied to buy the most important arrangement of his life: red poppies, which would flow towards orange butterfly weeds, which would flow towards yellow Carolina jessamines, which would flow towards green envy zinnias, which would flow towards blue forget-me-nots, which would flow towards violet irises, which would finally circle back to the poppies.

This particular arrangement would strike the staff as odd given Firas's usual shrewd eye, his understanding of how each color bled into the other, how each perfume melded into the other. He imagined how painful it must be for dandelions to rub up against thistle flowers and how suffocating for jasmines to gasp next to gardenias. He always endeavored to return to them the comfort with which they supplied him, lightening his daily burden. But today he would be selfish. Though beauty would thrive, the day called for practicality more than anything.

Firas had thrown dozens of parties before, his organizational skills and vigilance proving to be a most fitting asset. Most were done as favors for friends, and some were paid jobs. He questioned, a few years back, in the phase of post-adolescent ennui that often preceded terror when the collegiate finish line emerged, whether to become an event planner instead of an architect. But the idea of planning other people's celebrations served only to remind him of the lack of his own. He had, until this day, never thrown a party for himself. There remained the sting from his twelfth birthday, occasionally popping up at the most inopportune moments to forbid him from making the same mistake again. But it wasn't merely that. There was also the spotlight that came with being the party's subject, with being the king for whom the throne was built. He never minded mingling with other guests, never minded the excessive, sometimes backhanded compliments he received for the parties he threw, because the attention always reverted to the host, or at least the most drunken guest the host eventually regretted inviting. Were he to slip into the role of host himself, however, all eyes would be on him. And with eyes came stares, with stares came thoughts, with thoughts came questions, with questions came stuttering, bumbling answers that revealed nothing but the sheer determination to hide. Questions had already arisen.

"Since when do you have birthday parties?" his mother asked.

"Yes, I thought you were done with all that," his father added.

"I just thought I'd try something different this year."

"But why?" chimed Suhad, the nuisance of it all ever audible in her tone.

"Why not?"

His father explained: "A change of behavior usually reflects a change in circumstances." Then Firas got nervous, trapped in an interrogation room closing in on him, under a dangling light bearing down on him, facing federal officers towering over him, sealing his lips to prevent the truth from erupting only for the truth to pour out of his armpits and forehead. He debated calling the whole thing off, nodding along with them that the idea was so ludicrous it should be expelled from the family's collective mind, which veered as often as possible towards consistency. Because while it seemed, understandably, as though something had changed, nothing really had. It was always the same for Firas: the same impervious caramel stain on his bedroom wall, the same halal breakfast to please his devout parents, the same trip to the architecture firm where he mostly conducted research, the same lunch he could barely afford just so he could eat it with the trust fund interns who might one day be his employers, the same lumbering journey home punctuated by trips to the flower shop often enough to keep him chugging along but seldom enough to avoid having the trip sucked into the monotony. It was not change that inspired the party, but addition, a surplus of sameness that overflowed and now required draining. Upon this draining, he felt alive as he hadn't in a long time, and it was a feeling so vague, so distant, he was sure it'd been abandoned across the Atlantic on his family's journey here.

"Remember your twelfth birthday when you had to cancel your party because nobody would come?"

Mazen could always be counted on to bring bluntness to the table, to steer the Dareer family outside the realm of comfort precisely when they needed it most. Over the past couple of years, his social skills, ingrained in him as early as he'd learned to ride a bicycle, had been thwarted by a loss—a forfeiture, in fact—of his filter, and of any desire to regain it. This bluntness, for what it was worth, was powerful enough that it rarely felt the need to make an appearance, the resulting taciturnity marking each phrase he uttered with particular importance, even when it served no purpose and made no sense. In this case, however, his rude, awkward question, which, in any other circumstance, would have destroyed his brother, did serve a purpose. The rest of the Dareers retracted their inquisitive fangs, letting the wounded eldest do as he pleased, a belated consolation for the failed party and subsequent despair that his parents never fully acknowledged.

His friends all posed the same questions. And although some were perfectly satisfied with *I just thought I'd try something different this year,* others insisted on more information. They poked holes into answers that seemed to him holeproof, responding to every generic *Why not?* with answers that demonstrated the depth of their knowledge of him, depth he never imagined they had, considering the superficiality of their interactions.

"Because you hate being the center of attention," said Howie, one of the trust fund interns.

Firas couldn't deny it, nor did he want to. What he wanted was to know how exactly Howie had picked up on this fact. Howie, who was unequivocally the least intelligent of the firm's five interns, deduced a core part of Firas's character based on things Firas had never mentioned. If Howie could tell this about him, then surely the brighter interns could, too.

And if they could figure out this trait, what else had they figured out about him?

At certain moments during their lunch hours, Firas struggled to change the subject or downplay "the anomaly" (as he would come to name his surge of courage), and when the spotlight scheduled for the night of his party made its way over to him beforehand, he dodged it with his own set of questions, bouts of defensiveness about his friends not being supportive, about making him feel like a stranger to them and to himself, digging their nails into the new ground he was trying to walk across rather than moving out of the way so he could cross it. So they'd relent, offer apologies and encouragement, knowing he was hiding something and gushing with excitement because they had a fairly good idea what that something was, then reeling back their excitement so as not to scare him off, all the while offering subtle drops of wisdom about abstract concepts like superego and self-actualization, terms Firas wasn't entirely sure they understood.

The buzz pervading the flower shop seemed to grow louder now. But it hadn't grown louder; Firas's perception of it had merely grown sharper. Everything about him had grown sharper recently. He had begun to notice things he'd never noticed before. Not with his eyes or any other physical part of him, but with something beyond his consciousness, a bell going off whenever a moment needed to be had, a feeling needed be savored, a flower needed to be sniffed. A bell he had acquired only months before, upon his graduation, when the horizon before him seemed to be dwindling while the horizon before his peers expanded. Not professionally, of course, for he had obtained his internship before any of his classmates had, a prestigious one at the city's top firm, and his grades were impeccable, his degree unburdened by debt due to the scholarship he'd earned. Professionally, his options rolled out before him like a carpet to an award ceremony in which he was the sole nominee in every category. But personally, he had shrunk. Firas, whom Mrs. Tullinson watched grow with pride, had begun reverting to the nine-year-old who fled Gaza starving for a sense of identity, his parents quick to force-feed him the American dream despite its indecipherable taste. Personally, he was not a man. He was something Mrs. Tullinson remembered her own son being before his harrowing downward spiral. Bryan Tullinson frequently deprived himself of life's pleasures and was outraged when life nonetheless inflicted upon him its miseries. He grew up to fight strangers in bars, vandalize his workplaces, manipulate his girlfriends into staying, and narrowly avoid drug trafficking charges almost every other month of his adult life, and eventually left his mother with the unbearable realization that no parent wishes to have: her son's death—a drowning on a camping trip while swimming in a drunken stupor—was a blessing. The only thing worse than seeing your own child suffer is having to witness that suffering manifest outward and spiderweb into a vast network of suffering that continues to spread and makes the world and the people in it a little bit worse every day. Firas saw a bit of himself in her son, in his creeping resentment towards the world. He had never met Bryan, only heard about his many troubles, only saw him in old pictures above the fireplace whence he watched Firas spend time with his mother, whom he likely took for granted when he was alive, and it was then and there, on the rustic wooden floor of her living room where they played board games into the late hours of the night, he believing himself to be indulging an old widow and she believing herself to be indulging a lost youth, that Firas realized he had spent more of his life in the company of Mrs. Tullinson than he had with his own mother. It sobered him, this revelation, for his elderly neighbor had become a bigger part of his life than any other, even the parts he loved. Yet somehow it seemed obvious and natural for him to orbit her so closely. She reminded him of his Teta, the way she always used to lower her voice to a purr to ease his and his siblings' nerves after her volcanic screams traversed from one end of the refugee camp to the other. "Wala yhimkum, habayeb albi," she always assured them when they worried. Mrs. Tullinson had this same ease about her, this ability to bestow peace of mind onto others at the expense of her own. He knew she would have approved of his party plan. One winter night, a few months before his last birthday with her, he and Mrs. Tullinson were drinking spiked apple cider together in front of her fireplace, the first alcoholic drink he'd ever had in his life. As they danced around the subject of her deteriorating health, a subject preceded by mild objections from Firas about her incremental drinking habits, she seemed to imply that he should throw himself just such a party someday. Ever since her death, that night had rung its bell incessantly in his head and now here he was in the flower shop on the very day she imagined for him.

The buzz, though not growing louder, persisted. It began to grate his nerves, this inexplicable noise he'd never heard before, intruding on a day that could scarcely afford spontaneity. For a second, he wondered if it was in his mind, but it couldn't be, for it was far too palpable, far too determined to get him to *do something* about it. He wanted to. He wanted to investigate the source, because another noise, a voice, this one indeed in his mind, often encouraged him to explore new things. Missed opportunities had become a pervasive fear in Firas's life in the years since Mrs. Tullinson's death. Just as he saw in himself Bryan's creeping resentment towards the world, so too was he forced to confront his own complicity in it. He never skipped classes, he never attended concerts, he never went clubbing, he never took drugs, he never had a threesome, he never broke the sacred rules of twenty-firstcentury America as scribbled on the scrolls of the twentieth. He never had fun. There were moments of joy, certainly, whether in the flower shop or on Mrs. Tullinson's living room floor or in the office break room surrounded by friends. But something was amiss. That spark he witnessed when he observed the social gatherings of others—an air of community, a passion ignited out of a shared experience, a secret whispered from ear to ear until those with firsthand accounts became legends whose special bond crashed through generations, cultures, laws of nature and science. This was connection of a spiritual kind, the tests organized religions preached about, promising they would irrevocably alter one's life should one fail and succumb to temptation. Nobody forbade Firas from attending concerts or clubs, no one promised him the meaning of life in a string of polite Sunday brunches. Despite their religious conservatism, his parents trusted his judgment and worried only if he stayed out all night without calling. And so to counter this abundance of caution and restraint, Firas had taken some risks in recent years. Calculated risks that just barely satiated his need for those special moments, marked by a prerequisite discretion that often bothered some of the men he shared them with.

He hovered by the entrance, where the buzz was loudest. It was coming from nearby, mere blocks away. As he opened the door to leave, a voice beckoned to him from behind the cash register.

"Not buying anything today?" asked the smiliest of the staff members. His inquiry was tinged with concern, as though he was personally responsible for Firas's break from his customary purchase.

Firas gazed wistfully at the flowers he planned to arrange, to divide into bouquets of six, one for each foursome set to arrive. He wanted to buy them, but he couldn't resist being lured away in that moment. He had left so much territory uncharted that every single event happening around him, no matter how separate from his own identifiable interests, needed to be experienced until more lessons were learned, more feelings were had. Forcing meaning into his days just for the sake of it and hoping somehow it would make him a better man.

"I'll be back in a minute."

The cashier's smile began to wane as he struggled to convince himself that Firas's response was more than just a line from a customer too cowardly to say *no*. Before he could reply with an overzealous *Not a problem!* and a thumbs-up revealing his thorn cuts, Firas was already out the door and heading down the block.

As he reached the corner, the buzz became a roar. An outdoor concert, perhaps? No, this was something livelier, a roar that stemmed from something deeper. A protest? No, this was a joyous roar. A soundtrack accompanied it, electronic music that he only recognized from his brazen brushes past nightclub entrances.

He continued walking and began to see droves of pedestrians striding with purpose towards the noise, like open-mouthed doomsday believers heading for the hill on which their prophet stood with tablets and promised salvation. Firas followed their gaze, tripping and bumping into people along the way and stopping to excuse himself, until finally he reached the end of the block, where the full spectrum of colors and sexuality exploded into the sky and every outfit in sight became both the most and least significant feature of its wearer. The music throbbed like a heart buried in the middle of nowhere, its pulse reverberating throughout distant lands, ignored by the masses but loudly, undeniably *heard*—and never again unheard.

How could he have forgotten about the parade? It was one of the catalysts of his party! He had been debating when and how to finally do the deed, and suddenly it was announced that the first pride parade in Detroit since SCOTUS legalized same-sex marriage the previous summer would be held on his special day. He could only interpret this as a sign from an ingenious force of the divine world that his parents had tried—and failed—to engender a belief in since his youth. Strangely, however, Firas had no intention of actually attending. Not merely because of his tight schedule (it was already quarter past noon and the parade had only just set off), but because this was far from a calculated risk; this was a premature public display of his ties to the community, one that a simple *I just happened to be passing by* would not suffice should he run into the wrong acquaintance. And yet, he couldn't help feeling that this happenstance had beckoned him to revel in the event so that he could know, with every fiber of his being, that he was making the right decision.

"This is your first time," said a nearby twink. Firas studied him closely, his parted auburn hair, his cut-up denim shorts and tight white tee, even his heels, which hovered over the back of his sandals as his toes lifted him up for a better view of the parade from the back of the crowd.

"Huh?"

"I said it's your first time at a parade." His smile was cut with encouragement that came off to Firas like pity. "I can always spot a newbie," he added. The twink was dashing, but in a generic way, like a model from a department store catalogue forgotten as soon as the page is turned. "What's your take so far?"

"My what?" Firas was suddenly devoid of thoughts. He was no stranger to gay men, but his interactions with them thus far were always mired in secrecy. The sheer openness overwhelmed him now.

"Are you enjoying it?"

"Yeah. I am."

The twink's grin widened. "This is my fifth," he said. "I came out right at the end of junior high." This surprised Firas, who fancied him older. Not because of his looks, which were ageless, but because it rarely occurred to him that people younger than he was would already be further along on the journey. "What about you?"

"What about me?" Firas asked, still thrown off-balance.

"When did you come out?"

"Today." He had no idea what prompted him to say this, but he liked that he had said it. It was a pull from the future Firas that suggested this version of himself was not simply *going to* exist but already *did* exist and was just waiting.

"Congratulations!" The twink patted Firas's shoulder, then turned back to the parade. "They really went all out with these floats, huh?"

Firas peered at the procession of floats, ignoring the corporate logos reminding him of the capitalistic exploitation that often ensnared these parades, conditioning sexual honesty on promotional duties. As he took a moment to assess them, measuring each float against the one preceding it, he was ready to choose as his favorite the Busch float, on which a giant beer can made of rainbow-colored balloons was tipped to the side, trickling down a stream of brown balloons into a shot glass composed of black balloons. Then a dark horse emerged from behind to claim the title: the Tiffany's float, on which a male dummy knelt before another male dummy to bestow upon it a large diamond ring composed of gold and white balloons. Suddenly no other floats seemed to exist.

A profound roar arose from the crowd.

"What's going on?" he asked the twink.

"Probably a celebrity or something. I wish I had a better view." The twink bobbed his head left and right, hoping to see the oncoming car past the sea of waving arms. Firas was hardly curious, always the only one of his friends who never followed celebrity gossip, who never kept up with the trendiest shows and films. He would never recognize names like Kardashian or Teigen or Denzel, and in some cases he failed to even recognize them as names.

The car was drawing closer to his part of the sidewalk.

The sea of arms waved more frantically, desperate for acknowledgment from this mysterious celebrity Firas could not see. The roars reached an octave he never imagined possible. The sun was scorching now, and sweat trickled from his armpits down to his hip bones.

The car was drawing closer.

He didn't know why his feet were teetering, or how the twink began to annoy him simply by existing, but on some level, he saw each of these factors, blurred at first like the road outside a rain-soaked windshield, then creeping into focus like the dissolution of a dream before the strike of reality, then sharp and unmistakable like the drill of early-morning hangovers, as obstacles to something big, something urgent that needed to be addressed, a sudden attack on his psyche that dragged him back to the deepest, darkest hole of his childhood that, for whatever reason, took the form of his parents' den, which leaked toilet water from one of its corners and reeked of mold and regret.

The car was drawing closer.

This must be someone important, after all, this must be someone worth the trouble it takes to see them. He couldn't miss out on such an opportunity, not today, not here and now. He brushed past the twink and headed farther down the sidewalk, quickly realizing he was going in the direction opposite the car. He whipped around and rushed right back, his head turned sideways, bobbing up, down, left, right, from behind the sea of arms that now seemed to loom larger in the air. He kept tripping and bumping into people again, this time ignoring them even as they demanded apologies.

Who is it? he thought, *Who is this mysterious person in the car?* But the question was too stubborn to be spoken out loud, because the fact of the matter was that he didn't really want anybody to tell him, he didn't want the answer handed to him, he wanted to *take* it, to be the one who gave it to others, he *needed* to be that person, to finally be the one ten steps ahead of everybody else, the one who no longer watched younger people bypassing him in rides he never got and celebrating with pride he never felt and basking in the spotlight he was always too happy to dodge until the day finally came when he realized that now it's too goddamn LATE—the hand of Time has fallen.

He was trailing the car by a few inches, its deliberately slow progression now matched by the speed of his maneuvering around all the people getting in his way on the sidewalk, like some hapless character in a 1980s video game. But the closer he got to the car, the more pedestrians got in his way, placing the car farther and farther out of his reach until—

"OH MY GOD!"

A six-foot-five drag queen in a flamenco dress now drenched in some unfathomably sticky soda.

The collision had knocked something into Firas's head, for the words and events that came to pass in its aftermath were distorted to look and sound and feel infinitely worse than they actually were; so when the drag queen calmly informed him of the effort she had put into the design, Firas heard *Do you, fuckwit, have any idea how long it took me to make this dress???* And when she politely but firmly expressed the importance of being careful when walking along a crowded sidewalk, he heard *Are you blind or just a dumbass?* And even when she coughed, merely coughed, as humans tend to do, Firas heard the roar of a lioness demanding that he apologize.

He did. Or it felt like he did. He couldn't be certain, for his mind was still firmly on the car, the purr of its engine growing fainter as it continued down the street, but still reverberating in his ear beyond the drag queen's voice. A crowd of onlookers soon began to encircle them. And while, as with any circle of people with two points of reference, some stood nearer to him and others stood nearer to her, Firas had no doubt whose side every single one of them was on. On one side, he heard grumbles, scoffs, curse words, and felt a shove from a shoulder behind him. On the other he witnessed gentle strokes of the arm and offerings of napkins dipped in Evian. He dared not scan this crowd for support, the risk too substantial for a reward too negligible. Then suddenly, as the drag queen's breath seemed to puff in and out of her nostrils like a bull about to strike the matador, it occurred to Firas what was really happening to him. Another bout of clarity struck, sharper and crueler than the most punishing of hangovers, and he realized that this event, this happenstance, was not a sign from the divine to encourage him on his path to his party. It was a prank. A carrot on a stick he was doomed to keep chasing until either he or the stick finally broke. The universe was taunting him, letting him know that the entire day he'd been planning for months (*years*, when he really thought about it) would not be beautiful at all. It would be at best a missed opportunity and at worst an explosive crash whose consequences forced him into place even as he begged for mercy, for liberation, for *progress*.

"I'm sorry." The words whistled out of tense lips, barely audible.

With her head lowered to see where to wipe the dress, the drag queen's response was muffled, which made the possible variations of it all the more limitless, leading Firas to hear a string of words that would inevitably come to haunt him.

Gays like you always ruin these events.

The drag queen tossed her empty soda cup onto the ground and marched off. The onlookers dispersed, at which point Firas noticed that among them was the twink whose congratulatory warmth had now vanished, not even in a slow fade to make for an easier withdrawal, but simply *vanished*, replaced by hot rage, as though Firas were the amalgam of every playground bully who ever robbed him of his self-worth.

Soon enough the drag queen's voice was echoing in his head. *Gays like you always ruin these events.* The remarks that cut the deepest and fester the longest are the ones whose prick stems from each segment of the phrase, adding up to a sum far more painful than its parts. The first segment: *Gays like you.* He was othered by a group that was already othered, making him doubly othered and quadruply alone. The third segment: *ruin these events.* A man who prided himself on his ability to throw the best parties, parties that were not only festive but also perfectly fitting of both the occasion and the person marking it, was now the man who *ruined* the party, casting doubt on an essential part of what made Firas Firas. And the middle segment, often the most noticeable and acrid: *always.* The word implied a vicious cycle, a life sentence to a crime he had no knowledge of committing but was sure he'd committed because the more seasoned members of his community said he'd committed it and nothing in his arsenal of information could be drawn upon to refute that claim. He was marked.

Now seemed as good a time as any to return to his haven. He hurried back down the block whence he came, at first hanging his head in shame, then, realizing that walking without looking was precisely what had led to this shame, keeping his head up and his eyes vigilant.

When he arrived back at the flower shop, a burden had been lifted. The burden of memory, which he could eliminate altogether if he simply kept his focus on the long day ahead. But the only thing that could ever truly lift such a crippling burden from one's memory was the sudden drop of an even bigger one.

"You came back!" exclaimed the friendly cashier, with a smile so wide and a sigh so desperate it was as though a loved one had just returned from war.

"Yes," Firas mustered. "I'm ready to make my purchase."

"Well I hope you weren't counting on those envy zinnias and poppies."

"Excuse me?"

"Somebody just cleaned us out. I saw you eyeing them earlier. Hope you weren't too set on them."

Gays like you always ruin these events, the voice echoed in his head. Except now the voice was his.

CHAPTER THREE

There was never any sweating when they made love. There was panting, there was moaning. There was the curling of toes and the rolling of eyes and the rush of the mind leaving the body to spare it from trifles like introspection or logic. But even on a hot early afternoon such as this, neither of the young men could muster up a sweat.

Tyrese Pule caught his breath faster than most lovers. This was due in part to his impeccable stamina, owing to a daily ninety-minute cardio regimen, the first half of which took place in the park, and the second half in a gym rife with middle-aged women who ogled him unabashedly. Mostly, however, it was a lack of exertion. Tyrese refused to strain himself in bed. His priority, it struck Firas, was to establish a consistent rhythm. Thrust, thrust, pause. Thrust, thrust, pause.

When he came too close to cumming, there would be a brief moment (though it felt uncomfortably long from Firas's spread-eagled POV) in which Tyrese called his soldier back to base. Yet Firas took no offense to this mild, sometimes clumsy cadence, for he saw it merely as misguided tenderness. Tyrese's kisses, too, were slow, steady, and even a little hesitant, as though he were unsure he had permission. But their thoughtfulness was unquestionable, given as often as possible, with his eyes—serpentine, as if spiked at birth with some metamorphic potion—wide open, for he knew how much Firas loved to see them up close. And he loved, most of all, holding Firas's hand during sex, and certainly long after. It was a duty Tyrese felt needed to be done, and he never failed to do it. He never failed to provide the comfort of dependability, even in circumstances that did not require it.

But on this day, Firas found little comfort in Tyrese's company. Their chemistry was compromised, and Firas was unsure which of them was to blame. Had he been able to avoid this encounter altogether on this day, he would have. Had he been called into work, as was recently often the case on Sundays, he would have gone there rather than here. But his stop at the parade demanded a distraction, and the alternative to here was nowhere.

As with most of his former lovers, Firas met Tyrese in college. An enviable meet-cute at the library in the farthest aisle from the front desk, perfect for a private conversation about an Indonesian history book that both Firas—an architecture major—and Tyrese—a finance graduate—could easily pretend to have read. Not long after vague assertions about the

2004 tsunami and historical inaccuracies about the Dutch East Indies did this private conversation veer towards the mention of a certain professor whom each young man had once known intimately.

"I didn't realize Professor Markum taught Greek mythology," he told Tyrese. "I had him for Urban Design and Planning."

"Yeah, he's really versatile."

Firas, his parents' friends always noted, was much more mature than most men of his age. He respected and obeyed his elders, he looked after his younger siblings, he worked much harder than any of his employers deserved, and he single-handedly led the initiative to install speed bumps on his street to prevent accidents. Yet upon the utterance of the word *versatile*, even in the most innocuous of contexts, Firas turned into a giggling child. He could hardly control his laughter, which often furrowed the brows of the oblivious heterosexuals around him and occasionally brought his sanity into question. The upside, however, was that it outed him in the safest way imaginable, a secret code communicated to his ilk that immediately revealed he was one of them. Not all gay men understood this laughter, but in the right circumstance, the right gay man understood instantly. Tyrese thus took solace in the fact that his mild flirtations were not in vain.

Although he wished that he could give Firas a kiss right then and there, Tyrese detected the recoils, sporadic and subtle as they were, that accompanied each compliment he gave him. So instead he invited Firas to his apartment, where, shortly after achieving near-simultaneous orgasms, they got to trading stories about their mutual acquaintance. With Tyrese, Professor Markum was rather sheepish, his tongue twisted and eventually subdued by White liberal guilt so as not to offend. That guilt did not extend to Arabs, however, so with Firas he was much less his demographics, much more himself. Firas really liked Professor Markum, who was not his first lover, but unquestionably his most formative. Here was a gay man who was open about his sexuality, took confidence in that openness, handled questions with ease even when they were mired in intrusiveness or ignorance. A gay man who had a burgeoning career as a college professor, who drew the respect of his community, who was not grappling with drug addiction or some deep-seated psychological trauma. Here was a gay man who represented *hope*. In this older man, Firas could see possibility, that beautiful realm in which fantasies become reality and tensions melt away as though they'd never even existed.

"He's a rich White guy," Tyrese said from the edge of the bed. "And his family is mostly rich White lawyers and doctors."

"You think that makes it easy?"

"Of course not. But you're looking at the wrong map."

Somewhere in the back of his mind, Firas knew this to be the case. False equivalencies and the false hope they inspired would only lead him down a most troublesome path.

"Not to mention the fact that he's fucking a bunch of his students," Tyrese added. "Trust me, we're not the only ones he's taken advantage of."

"I don't feel I was taken advantage of."

"You will."

The conversation reminded Firas of a realization he'd once had from within the closet. As far as he could tell, the act of coming out involved eight different stages:

1) The Self: The first stage, as one would expect, is the most crucial. Until the Self acknowledges its homosexuality, said homosexuality is merely an abstract concept. A dance between the genetic and the hormonal across the floor of the environmental. An idea with no origin and no destination. Abstract material becomes raw material.

2) Strangers: Those lacking names make the best confidants. Often they also lack faces, reduced to appendages with which homosexual acts are committed and homosexual identities are confirmed. A convenient people for practicing the art of slipping off the mask without slipping off the mask.

3) Acquaintances: The intersection of sex and conversation. A lowering of guards in which personal information is inevitably required (though given at minimum), and an opportunity to dip one's toe in the lake of intimacy is presented.

4) Friends: The point of no return. Those who knew you as one thing now know you as another. Some sever ties, some let them loosen slowly (either out of respect or out of embarrassment), some will walk a tightrope, viewing it as their journey just as much as yours. Some will shrug and ask you to pass the ketchup.

5) Co-workers: Similar to Stage 4, but with the added bonus of workplace discrimination and potential job

loss. Worst-case scenarios include sexual harassment. Best-case scenarios include a forced friendship with Kenny from Accounts who just went through a breakup and wants to paint the town pink.

6) Family: High stakes. The first group to which one is a member can also be the most fragile. Whether positively or negatively, foundations shake. Exceptions are limited to families with a sense of reality about their children.

7) The town: Out and about. Drag shows, dyke nights, Tony Kushner stagings. City Hall protests and diversity fellowships.

8) The internet: The endless discharge of social media. Photos with same-sex partners, tweets about bear culture, bios flaunting that one article from *The Advocate*. The viral Instagram marriage proposal. Your sexuality now belongs to the world. Godspeed.

Firas was still only at Stage 3, a fact Professor Markum not only knew but regularly inquired about. They would be lying postcoital in bed, Markum's chest hair banging its ritual drums until Firas's head floated over and buried itself, and Markum would ask if he'd told anyone yet. At the time, Firas thought it sweet, these weekly check-ins from a man he admired and idolized professionally and personally. He'd whimper *no* and Markum would embrace him tightly, Firas ever so grateful for the sympathy. Yet in talking to Tyrese, it occurred to him that perhaps these check-ins had less to do with Firas's mental and emotional well-being than they did with Markum's circumstances. He and his husband had recently married (a shotgun wedding, he often joked) and he was inches away from tenure, and the revelation of his after-school sessions with what, by then, had averaged one student per semester would derail both. His sympathy felt like a warm, tender embrace even without the physical manifestation that accompanied it. But was it? When Firas really thought about it, his mind sifted through vague memories of ostensible reassurances like *Probably for the best* and *No shame in that*, which he knew to be false and knew that Markum knew to be false, but still made him feel better in the same way they would in any other instance of failure or rejection. *My wife just left me . . . Probably for the best. I can't afford air conditioning . . . No shame in that. I ran over a jogger this morning . . . A little discretion never hurt anybody.* In these moments lurked the hidden benefit of silence: Firas's Stage 3 was Professor Markum's alibi.

His relationship with Markum lasted approximately four months, after which Firas abstained from men—the ill-fated New Year's party the sole exception—for a period of two months that ultimately paved the way for the man at the edge of the bed.

"I wanna give you your present now!" Tyrese said with much earnestness. "I'll be right back." Tyrese was at Stage 6, and how impressed was he when Firas informed him of the party, a bold leap over Stages 4 and 5 that even Tyrese could not have imagined taking. Tyrese's coming-out journey, in fact, proved rather benign. At least as it pertained to his parents, a young Methodist couple just outside of Atlanta who adopted him when he was six months old. They were loving and generous people, forsaking the option of having their own child in favor of providing a home for one who'd been dropped off at a fire station. They informed Tyrese of his adoption once he reached his early teens, spinning a common tale so intricately that Tyrese could not determine how it arrived at its conclusion: the Lord wanted them to have him. Their devotion to God and the local church was the driving force of much of their kindness. But their attempts to instill it in their adopted son failed repeatedly, for the hole they hoped to fill with religion (a convenient, if not convoluted, solution to any identity crisis) was filled instead with a relentless search for his birth mother. This would be an exhausting task for anyone, let alone an adolescent boy, but he took it on nonetheless, because Tyrese's parents and the local church in which they had ensnared themselves associated homosexuality with fire and brimstone. In his search for this anonymous woman whose existence he had just learned about, Tyrese hoped to find an explanation for his sexual deviance, and eventually, God willing, a solution for it. Years of searching through online databases, phoning clerks at the adoption agency, accosting firefighters to dig through their faded memories of the fateful night they'd found him, all led to nothing more than an increase in determination.

But this determination eventually imploded.

Although his school spoke little, if at all, about America's history of slavery, Tyrese nonetheless came to learn about it. Throughout his informal education, he encountered the tragic fact that even if he found his biological mother he would likely never know where exactly he came from. As he grappled with this realization, he soon came to accept everything in his life, from the identity of his birth mother to the reason behind his sexuality, for what it was: a mystery not meant to be solved. On the one hand, his parents were relieved to see him give up his search. In the years since they'd told him about his adoption, Tyrese had hardly spoken to them. This was not an act of resentment or vindictiveness of any kind; he was simply too busy searching. On the other hand, his abandonment of the project felled them. They were first-generation Americans, having emigrated from Botswana three decades prior, and thus had no real understanding of his plight. And the idea of "not knowing" was something they normally would have relished incorporating into their gospel. Yet they found it difficult to do so, suddenly, given that Tyrese seemed genuinely unbothered by it. So unbothered that they began to be bothered by it themselves. The purpose served by religion could be fulfilled elsewhere, it turned out, and with arguably much less exertion. And so it happened that the day Tyrese informed them he was gay, they had only to voice practical concerns (communal ostracism, work discrimination, hate crimes) before eventually conveying their support.

Firas was only familiar with the last part of this story, the happy ending he could not help but envy from Stage 3. Although sometimes he considered himself at least partially at Stage 4, a couple of his past affairs having evolved into friendships. The first of these was the first of all: Anton, a thick-accented Russian on a student visa who applied to as many universities in the West as he could afford to; eventually he settled on the University of Michigan because the young man on its brochure reminded him of the porn star who made him realize the truth about himself. "It is a major sign!" he had argued in response to Firas's shock that he turned down a full academic scholarship to Yale. "This is where I must go to make my gay life happen," he said. "I saw it in brochure man's eyes." Their first night together, in Anton's oddly pristine dorm room, bore the trademark clumsiness of virgins, along with the dejection that trailed not far behind it. Their subsequent attempts allowed them to figure out the mechanics, but it was only upon the climax of the ninth attempt that anything beyond the technical demands of intercourse was achieved. And once they achieved it, they couldn't stop achieving it. Once they deciphered their own bodies, their g-spots, their fetishes, their limits, their lack of limits, the sheer significance of their flesh to another, the serene, unmistakable discovery that they could make a fellow human being feel ecstasy while trusting them completely, courageously, ethereally, to whisk that feeling right back to them, when that moment finally arrived, the whole world opened up to them . . . and they crumbled. The tears of abandoned children, the wails of buried youth. It surprised Firas how much he needed it. It surprised him how much it was in and of itself a requirement of the individual and not simply a criterion to be met as registration into society. It surprised him that his soul had been craving it even more than his body had. And it disappointed him when, a mere four months into the affair, it devolved into mundanity.

The chasm between the boys grew and grew until each of them straddled the edge of friendship with benefits, made less precarious than it often was by the fact that neither of them particularly enjoyed the other's company. Anton was a headache-inducing chatterbox who kept forgetting, somehow, that Firas wasn't Russian ("Oh, apologies for the Runglish, I will do better"), and Anton thought Firas was cold and dull like a knife that'd been used in all the wrong ways. He saw his introversion as indicative not of a reluctance to talk but of a lack of anything worth saying. "You are empty vessel. Someone must fill you," he would posit as he slinked his briefs back up his legs. The word *someone* implied that Anton himself was not the man for the job.

Nonetheless, they found solace in each other, the indelible soft spot that comes of being one's first, and often spent time together musing about when and how they would finally come out. Firas had no idea at the time and could hardly imagine doing it at all. He predicted it would be whenever a serious relationship came along. No, not serious—official. A paper trail of governmental documents, vendor receipts, a pre-nup if desired, and his handcrafted invitations in bulk. That would have delayed his coming-out well into his thirties, after he'd started his own architecture firm. Anton was different, more eager ("It is like with Band-Aid, do it quick!"), determined to do it as soon as he switched from a student visa to a working one and his parents inevitably asked why he was bothering to stay with the godless Americans he'd always mocked with them back home.

"What job do you think you'll get with a philosophy degree?" Firas once asked him.

"Not sure. Might get PhD and teach."

"Don't fuck your students," Firas joked. But Anton didn't laugh. The very thought almost scared him.

"No way. I will be good Russian boy in America."

Two years later, his academic career folded and he was forced to return to Saint Petersburg. He'd spent so much of his time on (and off) campus experiencing gay culture that he neglected his schoolwork, only delaying the inevitable by a year because a certain professor of Creative Writing, Personal Finance, and Intro to Statistics had given him just enough A's to scrape by—an assurance of silence under the guise of sympathy, which, unlike Firas, Anton deduced right away.

The boys lost touch shortly after that, but Firas still kept in contact with Cetan, the wiry insomniac from his Freehand Drawing class. Cetan was a middling student, aimless and in love with aimlessness. In his senior year of high school, he made an arrangement with his parents, who'd given him a choice between college five days a week and church every Sunday. The only other option was a boot out the door. Cetan was already at Stage 8 when they met, and his relationship with his parents was, to Firas's delight, disastrous not in a tragic disowning-a-gay-son sort of way, but in a comic this-kid-is-a-lazy-jackass sort of way. It filled Firas with hope how quickly they accepted their son's sexuality, with their reservations and cringes limited to the photos he frequently posted of himself sporting gold-painted nipple tassels. The Aung family saga was not much different from that of the Dareers. They too had fled their country when Cetan was younger, from a fear, deemed irrational by Cetan's obstinate father, of the attacks on the Kachin Independence Army. "There will be a permanent ceasefire agreement soon!" his father argued as Cetan and his mother packed their bags, followed by a chorus of "See, what did I tell you?" throughout ceasefire talks with the Burmese government, and then finally a profound sigh that drifted across the Pacific when the Tatmadaw attacked again. They were religious, too, as much as Firas's parents were, and raised by conservative parents of their own. As far as Firas was concerned, the situations were comparable enough to vindicate his optimism.

"You're not seriously comparing them, are you?" asked Cetan with raised eyebrows.

"Well, why not? It's not that different."

"Bitch, there's like a million factors you're not thinking of."

"Like what?"

"I don't know, there just are."

"Look, I'm not claiming it's the same exact situation, but there's a lot in common there, wouldn't you say?"

"Again, I don't know. I mean . . . damn, girl. The history of Myanmar is way different from Palestine."

"What does that have to do with being gay?"

"I DON'T KNOW! I'm just saying, these factors make a difference. Everything from your mom's heart attack to your dad getting laid off makes a difference."

Firas knew he was right, and he thought long and hard about it as he sucked him off. Their interactions thenceforth involved little to no talking on the subject, so the bubble Cetan had deflated filled right back up with hot air. Firas had initially considered inviting him to his birthday party, but he needed at least two hours to build up to his big announcement, and Cetan, sashaying through the door in a sleeveless mesh crop top, would have immediately blown the lid off what was already feeling like a Pandora's box.

The front door of Tyrese's apartment flung open.

"Hey . . . I thought you said Monday," Tyrese muttered from the kitchen. His roommate Karine had entered, hurling a suitcase that broke open the second it hit the floor.

"Goddamn it!" she shouted, her voice scratchier than usual, no doubt from another all-night row with her girlfriend.

Tyrese began picking everything up and packing it back in, gesturing for her to sit and relax. "Bad trip?"

"Don't get me started. What's that?" She pointed to the blue box by his side, tied with a luscious red ribbon.

"It's Firas's birthday today."

"Oh for fuck's sake, Tyrese!"

He shushed her, but the bedroom door was open and Firas had already heard everything. Even with the bedroom door shut, he would have heard everything, because Karine was not a soft-spoken individual and had no intention of ever becoming one. She also refused to suppress herself around Firas, whom she deemed, as the staunchest roommates often do, "not good enough." She resented the implications of Tyrese's devotion to him, witnessing over and over her friend's slow but sure progression into Stage 7 until this bothersome Stage 3 dragged him right back into place. New restaurants Tyrese never got to try, weekend getaways he never got to go on. Firas was robbing him of all the opportunities she felt he was due.

"You'll be happy to know he's doing it tonight."

"Bullshit. Guys like that are all talk."

Karine was wrong. Firas was one of the few young men out there who always did what he said he would. That was among his most notable qualities, the trait that built his network and made him feel he was part of something, even when he wasn't quite sure what that something was. He achieved goals, and he did so through thoughtful consideration of what was and wasn't realistic. No deadline ever traipsed onto Firas Dareer's path and managed to trip him up. And no disparaging bellow from a surly roommate could ever convince him that someday that might change.

When Tyrese finished packing her things back up, he scowled at her and returned to his bedroom, shutting the door.

"It's fine," Firas said, predicting an apology.

"Here. Happy birthday."

Tyrese's smile was infectious, but Firas was nervous about opening the gift. Too many potential outcomes, too few contingency plans. What if Tyrese had gotten it wrong? What if the present reflected a part of him that Tyrese wanted to create, a part that couldn't possibly exist? They'd only been together four months and had scarcely the opportunity to see the worst of each other. The only one of his flaws Firas ever let him know about was his guardedness. His sharp dodges and abrupt ducks, the sporadic vanishing acts before the morning sun hit the faux bear rug by Tyrese's bed, the constant evasion of answers that inevitably led his romantic partners to suspect his secrecy had more to do with just being closeted. Tyrese had so little to go on in getting him a present, the very reason Firas playfully needled him not to bother. This sweet, adorable, promising young man before him was doomed to fail, but that didn't bother him enough to keep from trying. It bothered Firas, however. Because Firas was the one setting him up for that failure.

He unwrapped the bow with a brave, waning smile, and opened the box slowly, keeping his eyes on Tyrese all the while as if the sight of his svelte torso and diamond belly button ring would dispel the mounting stress.

It was a badge.

"I don't get it."

It was an all-access badge to an architecture conference two and a half months away, and Firas genuinely did not get it.

"You mentioned the conference a while ago. You said you wanted to go, you just needed to save up the money."

Indeed Firas had mentioned it once, in passing. But he still couldn't wrap his head around this.

"Thanks," he eventually said. And he meant it, for it was the perfect gift: thoughtful and devoid of subtext.

An awkward silence passed between them then, forcing Firas to lament, as he'd been doing since the invitations went out, the fact that Tyrese was not among the recipients. He wanted to invite him. Truly he did. But just as a joke falls flat when spoken in the very same breath as another (what comedians refer to as a hat-on-a-hat), the revelation of being gay would only implode if coupled with the revelation of a boyfriend. Years of believing one thing had shut his parents' minds so tightly that cracking them open too wide, too fast would risk an utter breakdown. And while they weren't overtly racist, the fact that Tyrese was Black would have surely exacerbated matters, reinforcing the myth of influence, the so-called evidence that Arabs are only gay when the poison quill of the outsider is dipped into their ink. And what of poor Tyrese? So mild-mannered and humble, so understanding when it came to other people's pain, even as it manifested itself in the vilest, most irredeemable form. It would serve better to spare himself the finger-pointing, the histrionics, the slow, menacing boil of that word Arabs use to slur Blacks. Firas lamented it all so very, very much. He was, however, determined not to lament any of it out loud.

Tyrese never asked for an invitation. Never assumed one was coming. No judgment came, no pressure. Not even a passive-aggressive reference. Firas accepted this with relief and more than a little entitlement. Tyrese was an adult, after all, only two years older than he, and struggled with coming out just like most young queers. And he'd done so recently enough that the fear and anxiety tacked onto the process like an eviction notice on a broken door likely still lingered in his memory.

He did, however, ask one question Firas hoped he wouldn't. "So who's gonna be there?"

Another trait that separated Firas from his fellow twenty-somethings was the rate at which he made mistakes. Or rather, the rate at which he made the same mistake more than once. On his record (both official and self-kept), he had been negligent in the way of but one parking ticket, one unpaid bill, one failed exam, one lost book from the library, one car accident in which he and not the other driver was at fault, and one text message denouncing an asshole mistakenly sent to the asshole himself. His view of the future was cut so short that the end of everything—his family, his career, his friendships, his health, even love itself—loomed all around him, rendering every misstep a potential last step. Each time it turned out not to be, he had cheated Death. And God help the man who dares to cheat it twice. It was for this reason, then, that the mistake with which he pricked himself two weeks prior bled him especially dry: he mentioned to Tyrese the number of plates he intended to order for the party. His mother would not-so-secretly resent him if he used her good china, and the regular plates in his house seemed too bland for any party, let alone this one. And thus, that fateful order, placed on Tyrese's laptop, revealed the exact number of guests set to arrive. This may not have been a problem but for one guest in particular, their mutual acquaintance.

His choices were clear: lie or omit. Telling the truth had consequences he was neither equipped for nor in the mood to handle, mainly a series of unanswerable questions, a dot-dot-dot before plummeting off the grammatical cliff into an abyss of his own stupidity. It was not really strange to have invited his former professor/lover; most students invited Markum to their parties. He was the "cool" teacher, the one close enough in age to make them feel inspired and understood. And he often went, mostly for the confidence boost inherent in the wide eyes of the young and impressionable. In fact, suspicion would be aroused if he were *not* to attend. Besides, their relationship ended amicably, with Firas eventually deciding that an affair with an older, more experienced gay man would not grant him the shield he had initially hoped. That this man was married harbingered a scarlet letter, that he was his teacher harbingered a cloud of doubt over the merit of his grades. He broke it off, Markum so gracious it almost wounded him. He almost felt sorry for the professor now, imagining the horror across his face as Firas made his announcement and fearing their affair might be the next tidbit made public. But he was instrumental to the cause, the model gay whose professional success and personal well-being previewed the life still possible for his parents' eldest son. Tyrese was always sensitive to Firas's feelings and would thus have understood this. He would have understood it just as he understood the importance of stepping back, of not sucking out the already scarce oxygen in the small space Firas was still living in. The only reason he even inquired about the guests was to ensure Firas would have the support he needed when the time finally came. But understanding something and accepting it are two different things. The bullet would have pierced Tyrese. He would have survived it, and perhaps their relationship would have survived it, but the shrapnel would be lodged forever and the leg would always limp.

Firas began listing the expected attendees, praying all the while for an interruption—a delivered package that required signing, a shit-fit from Karine that required de-escalating. When it became clear that no such interruption would occur, his voice lumbered. Of his guests, the first one he mentioned was the first one he invited. Normally, Firas avoided discussing Mazen, because Mazen inspired far more questions than are typically asked about an adolescent sibling. And while this time was no exception, it did strike him that discussing his other guests in great detail was a necessary deterrent. Going down the list, he followed up almost every single name with a lengthy bio, and the further down his list he went, the longer the bio became, hoping that Tyrese, the dutiful boyfriend, would eventually check the time and kindly remind him that he should be hurrying off. Firas was now at guest twenty-one.

"My buddy Ted from high school and his girlfriend. They're the kind of couple that can never keep their hands off each other."

Tyrese noticed the time, but rather than hurry Firas off, he cut short the ensuing bio. "Cool, who else?"

". . . Colin, that TA I had last year."

And just as Firas was about to mention Maysa, the Dareers' housekeeper, who was technically not a guest but would nonetheless be—against his wishes—present, Tyrese interjected.

"Did you invite anyone gay?"

At that precise moment, Firas could have sworn, though viewed incredulously in hindsight, that the sun, plunging from its zenith like the head of a man dozing on a stool, streaked its rays upon Tyrese's hardwood floor and *skipped* one of the planks. Almost as though the universe were winking at him, toying with him as it did at the parade.

Aside from Markum, he had invited only one other openly gay person. One of the two *nos*. "Somebody from my old soccer team. But he isn't gonna make it." That was Buck, a roided, bearded tank whose blatant masculinity weaned teetering homophobes onto the side of tolerance. A baritone voice and the occasional grunt and suddenly queerness became a complex thing, less foreign than initially assumed. "And neither is that CrossFit girl at my gym. I guess they'll be too busy making their meal plans for the month."

He snickered, and sighed with relief when Tyrese snickered along with him. The matter was over. He didn't need to lie and he had enough plausible deniability to claim the omission wasn't deliberate.

"You should really get going. It sounds like you have a lot to prepare for tonight."

"Yeah. Wish me luck."

Tyrese gave him a peck. Firas got dressed and started for the door, before remembering his present.

"Thanks again for the badge." This time, the thank-you was insincere. Dread crept through him at the sight of it.

"Call me tomorrow, okay?"

"Tomorrow?"

"To let me know how it went."

"Oh . . . right."

Tyrese's serpentine eyes and toothy grin failed to comfort Firas the way they always had. Instead they brought to mind the envy zinnias and poppies. If Firas walked out that door, he knew, somehow, that he would never get to see this man again. This man who personified the "nice guys finish last" adage, who was doomed to sexual timidity and dire warnings from roommates he couldn't help but ignore. Even if the two of them ran into each other one day on the street, Firas wouldn't be seeing him. A completely different person would be seeing him—a completely different set of eyes absorbing the image and a completely different mind interpreting it.

"Tyrese," he said softly.

"Yeah?"

"Marry me."

CHAPTER FOUR

Maysa resented the Dareer family and would have been the first to admit that this resentment was stronger today than it had ever been before. The Dareers rented a house far from the Arab-majority city of Dearborn where she herself resided. They didn't used to, and the story behind their move was that the father got himself a well-paying under-the-table job, and the commute was more convenient from here. What was more convenient for the Dareer patriarch, however, was far less so for their housekeeper. Her trek to their house involved one bus filled with seniors who couldn't afford to spare their seats, and another bus filled with teenagers who couldn't be bothered to. Then she was saddled with a fifteen-minute trudge, arriving at a house whose mismatched bricks piled into a facade so surreally square and flat it resembled the set design of some off-off-off-off-Broadway play, and did not strike her as worthy of a move.

As she headed for the front door, she inevitably glimpsed the meditation garden Firas had designed at the side of the house, before diverting her focus to the barren front yard, the only part of the house's exterior she could tolerate. She rang the doorbell, and even before the door opened, she could smell the flowers lurking inside and knew right then and there that this single day would feel longer than the seventy-three years she'd spent on this earth combined.

Maysa Munayyer was born in Akka, Palestine, circa 1943, giving her five good years. From those five years, a trio of memories managed to latch on. The first two were scattered images of water. Both at the beach in the evening, the tide chasing her, laughter chasing her. Olive-toned skin, maybe her mother's, maybe her own. Clouded moon that bruised her for some reason. Rain. The scent of rain, the cling of rain. The unpredictability of it. *Shhhhhh*, came a voice, maybe her mother's, maybe the sea's. Little hand gives big hand coins. Big hand gives little hand ka'ak bil tamr. Dough stuck in teeth, the word *dentist* three feet above. Clouds gone, bruise subsides. Moonlight. And blackout.

Were it not for her mother's insistence to the contrary, Maysa might have spent her entire adult life believing these flickers all stemmed from the same evening. Their backdrops segued so seamlessly into one another she felt almost certain that it was her mother who had misremembered. The idea that two separate nights could share so similar a mood, the exact same bruise on the exact same part of her heart, seemed dubious.

Her third memory was much more vivid.

Caravans synced to the percussive rhythm of dragging feet and the repeated bumps of her father's shoulder blades into her backside. Bullets as toys of the schoolyard bully, laughter weaponized, the fallen clock by Teta's stove and its postmortem tick, tick, tick. Gray everywhere. Her little cough. Her giant tears.

While the first two memories melded into one, this third one felt like several. There was much more that occurred that day that she wanted to remember. So many more details constructing a mosaic of pain whose combined images overlapped, forced to trample one another to make sure they were seen, before the glass slowly began to crack. The more she tried to make anything out, the farther the fissures extended. For decades, she waited and waited for Time to show its mercy, pleaded for it to puncture a hole inside her head to let each image breathe. Every instance of salat involved proposals, bargain deals for Time to regard: promises of better use, less selfish use, complete forfeiture if necessary. Alas, Time chose to be cruel. The images detached from one another far too slowly, and old age, notorious for its stealth, crept up and marked its territory. The mosaic had corrected itself, but the eyes viewing it were now tired and weak.

What happened afterward she remembered relatively well. First it was Beirut, the Bourj el-Barajneh camp, where crowds of Palestinians choked the open desert, tents wavered in a violent breeze, and pine groves, untouchable and unknowable, observed the scene with distaste. The spirit of generosity was in the air, but there were strings. She didn't know what they were, but there had to be strings.

For a while her family made do. But a particular foe was determined to worsen their lives and alert them, through any means at its disposal, that refugees were unwelcome. Not a human foe that could be defeated, even after the war had ravaged them, but one that had been there since the dawn of time, smirking at the parade of insolent humans who trod over it carelessly only to collapse onto it, face down, in the end. This foe would then bury them, until another set of humans, thousands of years later, stuck their hands in it to retrieve the bones, an invasion that only fueled its ire. Indeed the sand was all-encompassing, studying them, stalking them, implanting in their fragile psyches the constant sense of being watched. Sand that hampered the fulfillment of their most basic human needs by inserting itself into what little they had—food, water, clothing, bedding. Maysa would don her summer dresses and find it in the pocket. She would be eating pita bread and there it was in the pocket. Every glass of water had to be checked, but on hot days her throat had neither the patience nor the will to discern clean water from tainted. It burned everyone's feet, and when they wore shoes, it sneaked inside and burned them still. Upon every walk uphill to fetch water from the communal tap, already a balancing act with the metal can atop their heads, it would hunt for them, barreling down from above like an avalanche. Eventually, some of the refugees trekked to a nearby tile factory, and with the bounty they acquired finally strangled their foe, though not to death, never to death.

In the pine groves, thieves often hid. "We've gone from one set of thieves to another," her grandfather sighed. As such, their dependence on charity intensified. The tents were never enough, sometimes sheltering four families at once. Privacy was the most elusive of luxuries, and a forced intimacy between strangers destroyed each woman's honor.

But little of this mattered, or could even be properly assessed, in the face of disorientation. The primary concern among the refugees was reunion, spinning around over and over, each time hoping a new face would appear in the whir. Maysa's family was among the more fortunate, spared from having to suffer the anguish of missing loved ones and forced only to witness it from yards away. Maysa's mother despised the crying she heard. It produced the same effect as vomit: hearing it made her do it too. She could take solace only in two things in this camp. The first was the lack of cars and streets. Maysa and the other children had safe spaces to play in, received a healthy dose of fresh air, and some of the fathers built them swings while the mothers finished the cooking. The second was the assumed transience. She knew this wasn't home, reminded herself at every opportunity, commanded her body to feel this fact as deeply as her mind had known it. But the feeling dissipated with the establishment of the UNRWA. More tents arrived, the families were spread out and given the privacy and personal space they needed. But what resulted were clusters. Clusters of what could only be perceived by everyone in the camp as villages. And with most of the families spread out, some of the more established ones, like the Munayyer family, had their village named after them. When more village clusters were created, the camp became an elaborate maze, requiring a set of directions to go from section to section. *How do I get to the beach from here?* one refugee would ask another. *Just go past Munayyer and turn left.* This horrified Maysa's mother, entrenching her deeper into land that was granted to her only upon condition.

Home is never home with conditions.

Eventually the Munayyer family, along with many others, were rounded up and shipped off to Aleppo. The al-Nayrab camp was stationed near an airport. In the mornings, Maysa would awaken to the rumbling of the engines overhead and dash outside to watch the planes fly off, energized even after a late night of doing the same. Of the camps she'd stayed in throughout her life, none made her so happy as al-Nayrab. It didn't matter where the planes were headed. What mattered was that it was they, not she, who were leaving.

Alas, that feeling her mother felt in Beirut soon resurfaced and spread to Maysa's father, her grandparents, and even her older brother. Whereas most refugees long for stability, the Munayyer family abhorred it. To them, it was nothing more than a prison, displacing them one step further from home the more time they had to adapt to it. It was better that they keep moving around, for that meant they could eventually move back. After a while, her fear had become reality: they had to leave again, but the next refugee camp would be their last. And as often happens with a fear that comes true, the actualization of it drowns the fearer in self-effacing blame. The Munayyer family was now forced into place, and all because Maysa's mother had let herself think it.

It was in the al-Wehdat refugee camp in Amman where Maysa finished her schooling. But as a concession to her mother, who had sunk into depression and vowed never again to think another bad thought, she stayed until her younger brother and sister finished their schooling as well. And she was grateful she did.

In the 1960s, al-Wehdat birthed a group of militants, becoming a hub for Palestinian nationalism in a country that did not care for it. Before the Jordanian army eventually expelled them, they founded the Lioncubs and Flowers Institutions (mu'assasat al-ashbal wa al-zahrat) to provide military training for the boys and girls of the camp. On the one hand, Maysa found this gender-neutral training oddly progressive. On the other hand, she wanted to die. Her ability to enjoy anything, already having dwindled, nearly shriveled away completely as the years passed. Even in the instances when life gifted her a rose, its thorns stretched too close to its petals to ever be able to sniff. Unlike the petals, however, the thorns never wilted, fomenting Maysa's belief that the simple act of enjoyment was unnatural.

In the mid-'70s, she was off to the Emirates, trading refugee camps for skyscrapers and destitution for possibility. She watched as the Dubai World Trade Centre soared into the sky, its concrete, steel, glass, and aluminum combining into a thirty-nine-story nod to the horizon. She listened as the influx of expatriates huddled in Kader Hotel, where plates of Pakistani cuisine fostered budding communities and life-altering decisions were born. In every corner of the city in which she stood, pastels saturated the landscapes, cumin shocked moribund hearts to life, and promises of the future nursed worries of the past. Before the days of excess—the golf resorts, the waterparks, the extravagant hotels, the desert safaris in luxury vehicles—people in Dubai gathered and talked. Modest parties centered on human interaction and shisha, pots of coffee and tea brewed over charcoal, and the occasional trip to the Plaza Cinema by Al Ghubaiba for the latest Bollywood fare or a Bedouin camp for a Merhaba dance. Before opulence erased these parties from the ethos and sneered at their audacity to exist, they made life in Dubai a most wondrous experience.

Absolutely none of it interested her.

Maysa stayed with her older brother Hassan, his wife Lina, and their twin three-year-old boys. Lina was the social butterfly to Maysa's hermit crab, and she cherished her sister-in-law's babysitting. Maysa had little else to do, her daily highlight tracking the progression of the Jumeirah Mosque. She was thirty by then, too insecure to attend university with people her younger brother's age, and she had no skills for work beyond watching other people's children. Boredom set in. The logical solution, of course, was marriage.

With her mother too depressed and her father too overwhelmed with her mother's depression, Hassan undertook the task of finding her a suitor. He and Lina chaperoned each date, often in their own apartment over a delicious dinner Lina cooked but credited to Maysa. A revolving door of one-date wonders, until finally she settled on a Yemeni engineer from Pittsburgh whom she deduced was a workaholic (he arrived an hour and a half late and ducked into the kitchen seven times to call his project manager). They moved to Abu Dhabi, where his office was located, and Maysa took his last name. The marriage led to a pregnancy, which led to an abortion, which led to a lie about a miscarriage, which led to a divorce. By the time the whole of her mu'akhar was spent, Maysa was fifty-six, both her parents were dead, and the remaining members of the Munayyer family were coming to the realization that they would not get to return to Palestine.

All that was left was West.

Unlike most Middle Eastern marriages of the time, Maysa's had seldom required her to cook and clean; her husband already had a cook and a maid, and she hesitated to get in their way or do anything that might jeopardize their livelihoods. But she observed enough of their work, and stored enough of her grandmother's wisdom (doled out during her mother's slumps), to secure a living off of it. Hearing of a diverse community of Muslims somewhere in the Midwest, with enough Arabs to mitigate the problem of her scarce English-speaking skills, Maysa immigrated to a small neighborhood in Metro Detroit where the abundance of Palestinians reminded her of the camps. Out of a combination of Palestinian pride and American pity, many of them hired her for special occasions.

At one of these special occasions, just over five months ago, the host decided, against the advice of his party planner, to hire Maysa for a New Year's Eve party at which she was to put together an elaborate feast and take care of the cleanup. This young Palestinian host, a disciple of Edward Said by the name of Kashif Hasnawi, knew little about her, having heard only a vague mention of her middling cooking skills. He didn't care to know anything more. As far as he was concerned, he owed a debt to this woman, this formidable pillar of his community still standing strong despite many violent swipes. Without her, he, like many other Palestinian youths, would be denied his history. Had he bothered to inquire about Maysa Munayyer, however, he would have learned that parties made her scowl.

It mattered not what kind of party it was, for all she ever heard among the laughter and chatter and toasting and music was a buzz that nested inside her ear like larvae. The longer the party went on, the worse her scowl became, even managing to drive away most of the guests of this New Year's Eve party well before midnight.

So when Maysa Munayyer happened upon young Kashif at the far end of the corridor of his apartment, in a space that couldn't be seen from the living room where the few remaining guests were contained, and where he thought she was still amassing empty cups and scrubbing wine spills out of his carpeted floor, he witnessed the deflating effect of her scowl while he was enjoying a private party with the party planner on his knees three feet below.

"Are you looking for something?" she now asked Firas, on his knees again, this time alone and searching the space between his desk and the wall.

Even before she spoke, he could detect her presence in his room. Her jaw clicked whenever she breathed through her mouth, which was always, and the floor she walked on creaked just an octave below her joints. When he turned to her, she was scowling at the bouquets he'd just bought (sans envy zinnias and poppies).

Indeed he was looking for something, but he was not foolish enough to tell her what it was. He'd made enough mistakes today. She wouldn't believe him if he answered *no*, but fortunately he was looking for two things, one of which he did need her help finding.

"My decorations. I had a whole bag's worth."

"Is it green bag you use again and again?"

"Yeah, that's the one."

"I throw them in garbage."

"WHAT?!!" He sprang to his feet so quickly he almost plummeted right back down.

"Problem?"

"Yes! I needed them for tonight! Why on earth would you throw out a reusable bag???"

"Oh no, I keep bag. I just throw out decorations." She retrieved a reusable green bag from her pocket and handed it to him.

Firas resolved to murder this woman as many times as he'd used that bag.

"What's all this noise?" his mother, coming in from the hallway, asked him. She was peeking at her phone, protruding from her pocket, before tucking it away and turning to her son.

"Maysa threw out the decorations for my party tonight."

"Were they expensive?"

"I crafted them myself."

"Oh good, so no."

His parents never understood the value of things. Price tags were tangible, therefore comprehensible. Art had no value and no meaning beyond whatever its audience assigned to it. It was easier for them this way, not having to invest a part of themselves in something they could never be sure would return dividends.

Firas had worked hard on those decorations. Everything from the party hats to the placemats had images of queer icons like Leonardo da Vinci and Eleanor Roosevelt and Oscar Wilde, each accompanied by either a quote or a rendering of their work. His mother admired Eleanor Roosevelt's activism, his father loved *The Picture of Dorian Gray*. And although his parents' acceptance of queer people was generally based on the conditions of wisdom, talent, and the fact of their being dead, Firas had nonetheless hoped these decorations would remind them of the greatness that often comes from queerness.

"Maybe you buy decorations. Or make again but simple."

There was a voice speaking to him, but it was the voice of a dead woman.

"Maysa, I need help in the living room, please."

Creak. Creak. Creak. He was alone in the room again.

Firas shut his door and locked it, more to keep himself in than to keep anyone else out. Despite the ticking clock, now wound half an hour forward due to the impromptu trip to the party supply store he would have to make, finding the letter he'd received that morning was a task that required all others to wait.

Part of him worried that Maysa may have found it. She was never particularly soft on him to begin with, but his humiliating encounter with her at Kashif's party changed everything. He was not much of a drinker, but every drink he'd imbibed since that night was meant purely to erase all mental trace of it. Yet he still wrestled with the incident. How could he not? In that ephemeral moment, a vortex ravaged the universe, and everything in Kashif's apartment corridor—the furled yoga mats, the hanging photos of FKA Twigs, the "All Genders Welcome" sign on the bathroom door, the flea market piano bench on which aromatherapy candles lay half melted—was sucked into a vacuum. Not Maysa, however. Maysa remained still, jaw frozen open, eyeballs dangling over the edge of her lids, a drab black frock and hair tied into an austere ponytail. Whatever power the vortex possessed paled in comparison to the absorbing power of the first gay blowjob she ever witnessed.

Kashif spent the next eight hours talking Firas down. He was terrible at talking people down. His whole essence, his whole purpose in this world, was riling people up. A third-generation Palestinian-American, Kashif Hasnawi hoped to make a living riling people up, first as a civil rights attorney specializing in anti-Palestinian racism and then eventually as a congressman.

Unlike Firas, Kashif was out and proud, having reached Stage 8 at the tender age of eighteen. His parents rejected the news when he shared it with them the spring prior, figuring gayness was like an unwanted customer in a store you could ignore until it left and found somewhere else to go. When it didn't leave on its own, Kashif was forced to leave with it. His was the exact scenario Firas dreaded. He was now older than Kashif was at the time, more mature, more self-sufficient. He had already been planning to move out of his parents' house by the end of the year, when his internship would likely turn into a job. But this resourcefulness of his unnerved him; the more fastidious his plans, the more they highlighted the tragedy he sought to avoid. It didn't matter if he lived at home or not. What he feared losing was the *option* of coming home.

With no money of his own, Kashif had no choice but to turn down his acceptance to Columbia, whose Center for Palestine Studies, created in honor of Edward Said's legacy, would have made him the man he dreamt so much of being. He resented his parents for this more than anything. They were not inherently bad people, but they were oppressively obstinate. And he was an insatiable member of that new generation that was just beginning to find its voice and make its mark, wanting to change the world as quickly as he changed his shoes, idealism pumping through his veins, seeping from his pores, spewing from his gaping mouth at whatever protest he attended. This was a young man on a collision course with history, with destiny, with Time itself. Time was his, and on the rare occasion it wasn't, when it slithered between the tightening fingers of climate change or streamed out of the eyes of Black Lives Matter, he chased after it until it was caught and round and round and round. There was no stopping Kashif Hasnawi, and there was certainly no changing him. You either accepted him or you fucked all the way off. His parents fucked all the way off.

Firas could only guess what Kashif wrote to him on this day. The letter arrived, hand-delivered, before breakfast. He was the one who always checked the family's mailbox. Kashif would have known this. He would have known it was safe from prying eyes. But he hadn't counted on Maysa's presence, conjured by his mother, who insisted, as a birthday present to her eldest, on having an extra pair of hands for the prepping and cleaning. In truth, the present was more for herself, in the event that Firas was too busy to attend to these matters and Maysa was too slow, the two of them combining to form an adequate tag team.

Firas had no legitimate reason to worry about Maysa finding the letter. She was not the snooping sort of housekeeper. In fact, she seemed to have very little interest in the personal lives of her employers. If she had any interest in outing him, she could have done it a dozen times since that night, either to his family or to her other Arab clients, whose rumors traveled far and wide. She could have blackmailed him, draining him of whatever funds he'd been saving for his move out of the house and never having to clean or cook again. Or she could have simply refused to keep working for the Dareers, spared herself the epic trip, simply distanced herself from the memory the way Firas wished he could. Instead she merely ignored him a little more than she normally did. Whenever his mother called upon Maysa's services, he greeted her, as always, with a meek *hello*, to which she used to respond by glancing at him and then turning back to the kitchen tiles she was scrubbing. Now there was no glance. Just kitchen tiles.

A corner of an envelope peeked from underneath his bed. Relief washed over him. He bent down, his dainty hands methodically sliding it out of its hiding spot. As he did, he glimpsed the caramel stain behind the velvet ottoman, its beautified state greatly dimmed since that morning. He stood, gripping the letter but careful not to dampen it with sweat, and expelled the anxiety in his chest through a slow, heavy breath. He gazed at the envelope, recognizing it as the same type in which he'd sent out his party invitations: seafoam A7 with a euro flap on printable paper. On the back, Kashif had only printed the letters *F* and *K*, separated by a pair of asterisks. Their inside joke. Kashif loved shocking people, and he laughed at how long it took Firas to finally understand the many nuances this wordplay held: the *F* always two steps behind the *K*, the *K* sitting comfortably at the end of the line, the world between them looking far less expansive than the *F* was once led to believe. And the sex. The sex at the end of the word, made pure and whole by mere virtue of its unconditional openness. Firas peeled off the flap, carefully, respecting the craft of the envelope as Kashif knew he would, and admired its liner—also akin to his invitations—patterned with lilies that flowed from the top down, a silly wink at his guests that the evening may not go in the direction they expected. But upon this admiration, designed by his subconscious to delay the inevitable reading, Firas's heart was seized.

The similarity was not a coincidence.

Kashif must have found out. Not only about the party, but about the invitations to the party. But from whom? Firas quickly scrolled through the guest list in his mind, but he couldn't identify a single person who would have known Kashif, or known him well enough to share the invitation with him. Yet he'd gotten hold of it somehow, that was certain. And now he was tormenting Firas, lashing out for not being included, when it was Kashif, more than anyone, who deserved inclusion.

They had met in high school when Firas was a senior and Kashif a freshman. From then to this day, Kashif had the resilience of a small platoon. Doffing quips about his braininess like ragged clothes, taking punches to his nose like shots of whiskey that buoyed the flame in his gut. Firas hardly noticed him for most of that year they trudged through the same building. To Firas, the freshmen were all just children. Then one Friday afternoon, as he stood before his open locker, stuffing textbooks and notebooks into his bag, mouthing to himself the assignments he had to complete over the weekend, a shadow streaked across the adjacent locker and onto his own. He shifted to the side to make room.

"You didn't forget anything," came a husky voice.

Firas whipped around and noticed what looked like a senior. Big-boned and imposing, with thick, black fur protruding from under his band collar, and precisely his height, though better-postured: poised in both stance and manner, as though he was set to deliver a commencement speech.

"Excuse me?"

"You're mouthing your thoughts like you're trying to keep track of anything you might've forgotten."

"How did you know that?"

"You do it every Friday afternoon."

Firas was unsure whether to be impressed or unnerved. But there was something in the interaction worth exploring.

"How can you be sure I didn't forget anything?"

"I trust you."

Who on earth was this boy? Firas studied his face: round and soft like a baby's, but the eyes betrayed the tempestuousness of a scorned lover.

"And why would you trust a guy you've never met?"

"We have met."

Firas's brow furrowed, prompting in the other boy a devouring grin as he went on: "In another life."

Now Firas was getting bored and impatient. The other boy sensed this and changed course.

"You're Palestinian, right?"

"Yeah."

"Me too. I figured since we don't have any classes together, I should catch you when I knew you'd be at a standstill."

"Maybe it's good we don't have any classes together. I'd hate to think of you noticing my quirks there, too."

"So you're a man of many quirks. Not a lot of guys can admit that." He laughed, an innocent chortle that reminded Firas of Mazen.

"Well you must be new to this school if we've never crossed paths before. Where were you before?"

"Miller Middle School."

It made sense now. The baby face; the childish laugh; the capricious fire in his eyes, likely spiked whenever the mind settled on the worst interpretation of an ambiguous remark; the fact that he noticed Firas, who'd never bothered to notice him back. Firas tried to hide his shock, but he couldn't help gawking. This was a *child* he was talking to.

"Kashif Hasnawi."

He held out an oversized hand, which intimidated Firas, who nonetheless shook it.

"I guess you already know my name."

"Nice to meet you, Firas."

With only two months left in Firas's senior year, he expected the friendship to fizzle soon after graduation.

It became the most significant relationship of his life.

By the end of Firas's third year in college, Kashif was nearing his own graduation. Firas had hoped, secretly, that Kashif would get rejected from the college he himself was attending. It would only be a year, but the thought of them being there together—not even together but simultaneously—disturbed him. One night, in the final portion of Kashif's closet days, the two of them were in Kashif's room, Kashif lying in bed on his stomach with his legs in the air behind him: crossed, bare, uncontrollably hairy, and meaty beyond his years. His body was aging exponentially; it intrigued Firas. On this night, Firas was helping his young friend put together college applications. Kashif's parents were both doctors, so he didn't require the scholarship Firas had earned, but the fact that he had earned it granted him a perceived wisdom from which Kashif thought he may benefit. Yet when it came time to put together the application for the college Firas was attending, he sensed in Kashif an added urgency. The boy wanted to trail him, as though he were his guide, seeing in Firas something that wasn't there. Pressure often bore down on Firas when he was with Kashif, who tasked him with leading an expedition into territory he was always wary of crossing.

"Are you sure you wanna apply there?"

With one question, a road diverged. Kashif said nothing, but he never brought it up again, and he never applied. Firas should have predicted this reaction. Four years of eclectic bullying—from classic forms like name-calling, face-punching, swirlies, and tacks on chairs, to more modern tactics like hacking into emails, embarrassing Instagram photos, and a Twitter survey about his supposed body odor—had grown the flame in his gut to the size of a bonfire and would drive him to cut the very thought out of his mind like a tumor. And he should have predicted Kashif would immediately deduce what he was insinuating. He'd been inside Firas's head since before they'd even met. That was what Firas loathed about him. His presence, at its core, was an invasion. Although he didn't regret asking the question, he understood that it changed everything. It separated them, stamping onto their relationship an expiration date. In the coming years, Firas would be forced to fuck all the way off.

He slid the letter out of the envelope. Before unfolding it, he set the envelope onto the desk, then stuffed it into his bottom drawer for fear of forgetting it and having Maysa find it later. Then he read:

Dearest Firas,

Happy birthday, habibi.
I know what this day means to you. Perhaps you can move on now.

Take care!
K

It would take Firas the whole rest of the day to sift through and classify by degree of intensity all the elements of this note that revealed to him just how much Kashif was, at heart, an absolute cunt.

Through gritted teeth, he began deconstructing it, first line by line, then word by word.

Dearest Firas. Kashif swung his hardest blow right off the bat. Too impatient even to wait one more line. Firas had gotten letters from him in the past, and they never began with the word *Dearest*. In fact, Kashif derided letters that started even with *Dear*. He ranted about them, bemoaning how they sank their readers into commonality, robbing them of their right to distinctiveness. This was no doubt his intent now. Mocking Firas as indistinct, on the very day he worried he'd be made to feel *too* distinct, and beyond the reach of acceptance.

Happy birthday, habibi. Kashif only called people *habibi* when he was preparing to condescend to them. A way to ease them for the slap of indignity before it was actually delivered. *Habibi, chili peppers are fruit. Habibi, that's not what NASA stands for. Habibi, your worldview is pedestrian.* Here he was going out of his way to be a cunt.

I know what this day means to you. This one not only angered Firas but unsettled him deeply. Kashif knew of his plan even though he had never mentioned it to anyone besides Tyrese. The line was deliberately vague, yet an unmistakable reminder of Kashif's invasion of his life, his invasion of his thoughts. He knew and he was holding that knowledge over Firas like a cloud set to rain at his command.

Perhaps you can move on now. This was also vague, but unlike the phrase preceding it, open to a number of interpretations as to what precisely he was meant to move on from. His first guess, the most directly relevant to the sender of the note, was the end of their relationship. Maysa Munayyer ended their relationship. They discovered, once Firas sprang up off his knees, that the reason she was in the hallway in the first place was simply to point out that the party was so lifeless that nobody was making a mess and could she perhaps go home now? The expiration date had been set by Firas, but Maysa trounced all over it and stamped a new one of her own. Her catching them together made him wholly aware of how reckless he became in Kashif's presence. Because Kashif was unlike his other lovers—he was so far removed from the closet he had forgotten what living there was like. He had little patience for Firas's reluctance, and not nearly enough empathy. Every day in the closet was, to Kashif, a betrayal of a larger cause. Sometimes the hand of Time felt like Kashif's hand, all over him and inside him; slinking down his pants in back seats and below dinner tables; grabbing his backside in crowded elevators; jerking him off in locker room showers where the curtains just barely reached the floor. One time they were caught on a security camera in the street. It wasn't merely the thrill of getting caught that enticed Kashif, but the principle of it. So many of his public displays of queerness were middle fingers to all the people he was sure were judging him. What began as an identity degraded into a statement. And sometimes that statement was peripherally directed at Firas.

His second interpretation was the most likely: he would be moving on from the fear of coming out, leaving it behind him in a puff of dust. Kashif once called him a pussy, and he never apologized for it. In fact, he doubled down, pointing out—nay, *flaunting!*—the fact that he himself was still in high school when he came out to everyone. Indeed, he was only months away from graduating, from crossing the finish line that would have shielded him from the increase and intensification of bullying. And he did it by posting a photo of himself on Facebook volunteering at an LGBTQ center on Burroughs. He received much love and support from some of his classmates (mostly girls scouring for a GBF) and much hate from the rest. Despite his shock at the gesture, Firas knew he was its catalyst. That night he was helping with the college applications, he stung Kashif, whose preferred method for eliminating the venom was to sever the limb it was flowing through. It was easier than sucking it all out bit by bit. It was faster.

His third interpretation of the line . . . he really hoped Kashif didn't mean it this way. It would take a special kind of cruelty, far beyond the scope of what Firas deserved for the pain he caused him. A meaning that would have involved in their malicious drama, complete with agonizing interludes of darkness and silence, a much more vulnerable person whose presence in his life made Firas more vulnerable, too. He didn't want to tell anyone about what happened with Mazen two years prior, but he once foolishly let it slip, so desperate was he to see Kashif again after their last fight, their longest interlude, that he lost control of himself and just barely managed to dodge the resulting questions. But no. No, this couldn't be it. This wouldn't do. Surely Kashif meant it as one of the first two ways. He must have.

Rather than dwell on the matter, he banished it from his mind with the next line. *Take care!* In the thousands upon thousands of languages that have existed throughout the history of the world, there has never been a punctuation mark quite so vile in its subversion as the exclamation point. With this exclamation point, Firas felt really, truly hated. He felt threatened, even, as though his ability to "take care" was bound to be impossible, any attempts effortlessly thwarted by Kashif if Firas didn't bumble them first himself.

Then finally, *K.* He never initialed his name beyond the envelope. It held in it a faux glamour, the kind one read about in dollar-store romance books, which Kashif had once bought him as a gag gift.

So much contempt packed into so short a note. What a talent Kashif had! What a star he would become in the courtroom, or on Capitol Hill, or in the White House. And there was yet more to be deciphered: the presumptuous *I know*, the disparaging *Perhaps*, the *now* drudging up his embarrassing history and—

A knock at the door.

Firas snapped out of his blinding daze and checked the time on his phone. He had no choice but to dash to the party supply store and spend no more than five minutes assembling a reusable bag's worth of replacements.

He bolted for the door, stopping as he realized the knock came from an actual living being who needed something.

"Firas," his father said. "We have a problem."

CHAPTER FIVE

"**W**hat do you mean he escaped from the nursing home? He's in a *wheelchair!*"

"Yes, but it's an electric wheelchair," his father replied. "Those are quite fast."

"And quite *loud*! How did none of the staff notice him?!"

"Apparently there was a kitchen fire they had to attend to. He used the distraction to make his getaway."

That settled it. On this, the most important day of his life, something somewhere was conspiring against him.

"We'll be back soon," his mother said.

"But why can't Suhad do it?"

"She's still at work."

This was a lie. Unbeknownst to his parents, Suhad, who claimed to be apprenticing at a hair salon downtown for the past several months, had no such apprenticeship. Firas discovered this over the course of several afternoons, catching her in random places when she was supposed to be at the salon—at the mall, at a diner, in the park, outside a dentist's office. One time he went to the salon directly and asked for her, and the furrowed brow from the scrappy purple-and-pink-haired woman behind the counter was all the confirmation he needed. It infuriated him that she should pull this stunt on his birthday, lounging around with friends she saw all the time anyway. Could she not have spared him one afternoon? He was almost compelled to blurt out the truth, but disclosing his sister's lie may somehow come back to haunt him when it came to the methodically planned reveal of his own. Besides, it wasn't quite fair to blame his sister. If she hadn't gone, questions would have arisen about the "apprenticeship." And she obviously couldn't have predicted their grandfather's madcap dash out of his nursing home. The codger. This was not his first attempt at an escape; there were two before it. The first was five years prior, when a new nurse joined the staff. She radiated cheeriness, innocence, a devotion to alleviating stress and pain. And he radiated it right back, convincing her that all the rumors she'd heard about his wiliness and his malevolence were misjudgments from people who simply didn't want to take the time to get to know the real him, the sweet old man who sometimes got cranky and difficult because he couldn't remember what made life worth living, and would surely see a new dawn if someone, anyone, would be so kind as to walk him through the park for an hour or two so he could see how beautiful the world was. And when she capitulated—much sooner than he expected—he was off. The nurse lost her job and he set to planning his second attempt. This attempt, sixteen months later, came with the help of the old man in the neighboring room, who tired of hearing him snoring and figured he would benefit from his absence as much as anyone. The plan was surprisingly elaborate, the kind of getaway one would see in screwball comedies of the 1940s, Firas's grandfather a charmless Cary Grant. When the neighbor's family arrived to pick him up for his granddaughter's wedding, they made it all the way to the parking lot of the church (seventy-eight miles out) before realizing that the old man dozing beneath a plaid flat hat, whom they'd hurriedly stuffed into the back seat of their minivan, was not the one they had come to get. Their choices were between heading all the way back, in which case they would miss the ceremony, and risking kidnapping charges.

This third time he had succeeded. Firas wouldn't have been the least bit surprised if the old man had set that kitchen on fire himself. Now he was forced to babysit another member of the family whose whereabouts had to be monitored closely. With so much preparation left for the evening—cooking the dinner, retrieving the vases, filling the vases, arranging the flowers, moving the coffee table, fetching the folding tables, setting the folding tables, fetching the folding chairs, scrounging new decorations, putting up new decorations, setting up the music station, putting out the party favors, showering, shaving, dressing, screaming—he began to sink into his mother's Neyland rug, which sucked him in like quicksand until he simply stopped struggling and his head protruded from amid the terracotta floral pattern.

As soon as his parents were out the door, he texted Suhad:
On watch duty plz can u pick up few things from party supply store on way home

Firas never abbreviated words in text messages or skipped punctuation marks. Never.

The text bubble appeared. He fidgeted; myriad possible responses swam across his mind:

Sorry, its super busy today at work
Will try but no promises
Cant mama/baba do it?
what about ordering stuff online

He would have been surprised by any of these replies. As desperate as Suhad would have been to maintain her ruse, the guilt it provoked would goad her into a redemptive act of kindness.

The text came: *what do u need*

He texted her a precise list, though he kept it short to avoid overwhelming her: strings of glittered garlands; striped and polka-dotted party hats crowned by paper balls; a set of paper pompoms and lanterns; paper fans with floral patterns that matched the plates he ordered. He had originally also intended to display a rose-tinted welcome sign by the front door, but that now seemed to him superfluous. Once the text was sent, he went upstairs to Mazen's room.

The door was open, as always. Mazen lay on his bed, reading *Pride and Prejudice*, one of the only books in the house his therapist approved of. The rest were classic horror (*The Turn of the Screw*; *We Have Always Lived in the Castle*; *Dracula*; *The Willows*), John Grisham books stacked on the back of the upstairs toilet, and Suhad's collection of celebrity memoirs.

"You good?" he asked.

"I'm okay," Mazen answered, his eyes still on the book.

"What part are you at?"

"She just got the letter from Mr. Darcy explaining his side of things."

"Are you liking the book?"

"Not really."

This answer surprised Firas. Not in its content but in its delivery. Mazen always expressed his opinions freely and honestly, but even the most negative among them were devoid of any real sense of investment in what he was opining about. To hear him sound disappointed perturbed Firas.

"Well, I'll be downstairs if you need anything."

Mazen turned away from the book to look at him. The sunlight (the day's saving grace) reflected the smoothness of his skin, the graying wonder in his eyes. "Okay."

Firas rushed back down, headed straight to the kitchen. As he did, he thought about Mr. Darcy's failed proposal to Elizabeth. Aside from the decline that instantly followed it, there was very little resemblance between it and his own proposal. Tyrese wasn't haughty; he wasn't even spirited. He was remarkably easygoing. The kind of easygoing that would bore people to death in a straight White man, but in one whose sociopolitical burdens all but precluded it, intrigued them. There was no defiance beneath it, and yet everything about it felt, to Firas, wholly rebellious. The world was a chaotic place, and Tyrese was among the few who could confront and ultimately accept this fact, floating above the spinning heads and downcast eyes of all the drifters and sprinters below, taking pity on them. In his presence, Firas often felt like he too was about to float, hoping desperately that enough days would pass that the effortless way in which Tyrese carried himself would transfer onto him. Perhaps, he now thought with restrained excitement, today might be that day.

The meal Firas had planned for this evening consisted of four courses, and he was making each one himself. For the past three months, he'd been practicing, making them separately at first, then all together to see how much time it would require. First came the soup: chicken noodle with celery, carrots, onions, thyme. Something comforting, medicinal, and miraculous, the stroll to simpler times that lowers guards. Next came the salad: cherry tomatoes, cucumber, feta, olive oil, and white wine vinegar all mingling merrily with fusilli—whole wheat to keep the guests from crashing too hard too early, but nonetheless filling them up to tame them in both body and mind. For the main course, succulent lamb brought to perfect tenderness and showing the distinct effort required for that tenderness. Next to it, roast baby leeks with bacon croutons. His parents would balk at his gall, then settle into the idea of turkey bacon—slow and steady, but taking the leap, learning to trust and relax. And finally the dessert: a cup of chocolate mousse topped with whipped cream and raspberries. Sweet to soften them up and light to unburden them, a show of mercy to be reciprocated soon after. And in each of these courses, he would include a dash of cayenne pepper for a gentle kick, to prove how easily the unfamiliar could fit into the norm.

He began with the lamb shanks, marinating them in a variety of spices he'd bought the day before (any earlier and they might have gotten used, or misused). Normally when he was on watch duty, he would check on Mazen at regular intervals of ten minutes, which even his parents thought excessive; now he could only go up whenever a moment made itself available. Once he finished with the spices and the garlic and the olive oil and the lemon wedges, he rushed up the stairs and knocked on the open door but remained in the doorway. "What part are you at now?"

"She just finished reading Mr. Darcy's letter."

Either Mazen was a slow reader or Mr. Darcy was a bigger gasbag than Firas remembered. It didn't matter. He rushed back down and, while the first dozen lamb shanks, split between three pots, braised over the stove, he set to work on the chocolate mousse. Cream, cocoa powder, sugar, vanilla extract, whip, whip, whip, whip, then back upstairs for another check-in. He was running, losing breath.

"What (inhale) part (exhale) are you at (inhale) now (exhale)?"

"Firas, your interruptions are ruining my flow."

That bluntness. That blessed bluntness. "Sorry . . ."

"I'll be fine, I promise. What are you doing down there anyway?"

"Preparing for tonight."

Mazen's neck stretched up and he gazed intently at his brother. "Can I help?"

Firas hadn't thought of this. Could Mazen actually help? Or would he get in the way and spoil everything? "Sure. If you're up for it."

Mazen set his book face down on his nightstand, open to the page he was reading, and followed his brother down to the kitchen. While Firas whipped the mousse another round, he asked Mazen to fetch the raspberries from the fridge and wash them.

"There are raspberries in the fridge?"

Firas had stashed them in the back of the crisper, beneath the vegetables for the soup and out of sight from his sweet-toothed brother.

"I love raspberries. I wish you'd told me."

Firas was already regretting his presence here.

"So what are we making?"

The *we* annoyed Firas, who was pouring his heart and soul into this meal only to now have to share the credit. He enlightened his brother; Mazen oohed and aahed.

"Once you're done washing the raspberries, I need you to wash the carrots and celery."

"Okay, sure!"

Was that enthusiasm Firas detected? There was no time to make sure—whip, whip, whip, whip, then pour into twenty-five dessert cups, then a dollop of whipped cream on top. Mazen passed him the box of raspberries and set to washing the carrots and celery. Firas was on the sixth cup of mousse before the math stopped adding up . . .

"Did you just eat half the raspberries?"

Mazen's lips were crimson, his cheeks puffy. Firas had let the fox guard the henhouse. "I figured you had enough," he said without a trace of guilt.

Firas had no time to panic. He still had the two dozen chocolate chips his brother was generous (full?) enough to give him that morning. Half the mousse would be topped by raspberries, the other half by chocolate chips. The cups went directly into the fridge.

Next, the soup and salad. He wished he didn't have to make them so far in advance, but with no decorations available until Suhad chose to come home, he had no other choice.

"Here you go," Mazen said as he handed him the carrots and celery.

"There's also an onion in the cupboard. Peel it for me." No time for pleases and thank-yous, or even the subtle politeness of phrasing his instructions in the form of a question. Mazen didn't seem to mind. He fetched the onion, peeled it, set it next to Firas's chopping board on which the carrots were being diced, and waited for further instructions. When none came . . .

"Should I chop the celery for you?"

"Yeah, do that." He handed him the celery. Mazen grabbed a knife and chopped away, trying and failing to keep up with his brother's pace.

The percussion of knives against boards evoked order and discipline, neutralizing the chaos in Firas's brain. It was only when he, currently in the lead in this imaginary chopping race, finally finished that the resounding chop coming from his left stiffened every muscle in his body below the chin.

"Stop!"

Mazen stopped chopping. "Am I doing it wrong?"

"No, it's just . . . I think the pasta is much more important right now."

"Okay." Mazen grabbed a pot, filled it with water, and heated up the stove. While he did, Firas exhaled half his tension away and his muscles began to relax. He fixated on the knife that had just been in his brother's hand, before grabbing it and tucking it out of sight.

Was he being dramatic?

There was no time to make sure. Chop, chop, chop, chop, then the peeled onion into the food processor to avoid ocular discomfort. Then all together in a large pot to fry.

When the water began to boil, Mazen emptied three boxes of whole wheat pasta into the pot, during which time Firas texted Suhad to see if she had any questions regarding the list he'd sent her. Four minutes later, she replied *Nah*. Firas's eye twitched. *Are you sure?* he replied. When another seven minutes passed and no response had come, he began to type *Don't hesi* and stopped at the sight of an ellipsis that hovered for another three minutes before eventually collapsing onto itself. He finished typing *tate* and sent it off. No reply ever came.

The pasta finished cooking. Mazen drained it and gazed down at the colander in awe. "That's a lot of pasta," he said over his shoulder.

"I'm worried it won't be enough," Firas replied as he placed the pot of chopped vegetables onto the fourth burner.

"I don't have to eat," Mazen said.

"Everyone is eating," Firas replied sternly. "Everyone."

While Mazen awaited instructions, he caught the scent of the lamb wafting from the stove and let it cuddle inside his nostrils. "I think tonight will go really well, Firas."

Firas stopped what he was doing. He knew he could not afford to stop, but he also knew he must turn around and acknowledge this sweet boy, if even for just a moment. As he did, he heard nothing, not the beating of his heart, not the frenzied stir of his thoughts, not even the hand of Time was loud enough to drown out the melody of faith sung from his brother's berry-tinted mouth. "Thank you, Mazen."

Mazen, half smiling, glanced at him to make sure he knew he'd heard him. "Do you want me to stir the soup for you while you chop the stuff for the pasta salad?"

Firas turned back to the stove, remembering he was stirring the soup and that he had but five hours left before people started to show.

"Oh. Yeah, sure." Mazen seemed a step ahead of him suddenly. He didn't like that.

"When you have a minute, can I show you my outfit for tonight?" Mazen asked as he took the wooden spoon from him and stirred.

"Okay, maybe." Firas thought about his own outfit. A dark blue blazer over a white V-neck tee tucked into black skinny jeans and a pair of white sneakers bought solely for the occasion.

"Do you need help in here?" said a voice from behind.

Firas immediately recognized it as the dead woman. Lest she ruin his dinner, too, he prepared to rebuke her as passive-aggressively as he could. "Actually—"

"That'd be great!" his brother interjected. "Firas, Maysa can chop the vegetables for the salad and we can let the soup sit for a few minutes."

Firas glowered at him, which Mazen might have noticed were he not already dragging him out of the kitchen by his hand. On the way out, Firas could have sworn he saw Maysa's infamous scowl. A picture of savagely butchered tomatoes and cucumbers flashed before his eyes.

The boys went upstairs to Firas's room. As Firas sat on the bed, Mazen stepped out and a few minutes later strutted back in like a runway model. He wore a strikingly suave tan suit over an aqua-blue dress shirt, a striped yellow-and-gray tie, and a pair of pointed-toe brown leather loafers. The price tag of the suit still dangled from its sleeve. It was expensive. More expensive than Firas's outfit.

"It's supposed to be casual," Firas told him, hiding his annoyance.

"I know. But this is an important birthday for you."

Why did he just say that?

"Why did you just say that?"

"Because it is."

As older siblings often do, Firas still saw Mazen as a child. Suhad did, too. Everyone did, even the neighbors. But children often know much more than the adults around them, untainted by years of personal hardships, aching romances, dehumanizing jobs, violent crimes, the many biases that accumulate throughout one's life. Children see things as they are and are simply unable to interpret them, carrying in their tiny hands all the pieces of life but devoid of the wisdom to know which piece goes where. This always seemed the case with Mazen, but there were times when Firas suspected that he knew exactly where each piece went and was merely waiting, as well-behaved children do, for a grown-up to give him permission to piece it all together.

He didn't say *This is an important day for you*. If he had, Firas would have dismissed it, assuming he meant because it was his birthday. He said *This is an important* birthday *for you*. Meaning there was something extra special about this special day.

For all the careful moves Firas had made (minus his sporadic public encounters with Kashif), it never occurred to him that someone may have caught him at some point. The same way he'd caught Suhad not apprenticing at the salon.

But it couldn't be. He was too careful. He was.

"So? What do you think?" Mazen asked.

"You look fantastic. I'll definitely need to up my game."

"No, no, you'll look fantastic, too. I know you will."

Firas smiled reassuringly. Then he began mouthing to himself.

"What are you mouthing?"

"Just listing all the things I still have to get done for tonight to make sure I don't forget anything."

"Oh, right. You used to do that back home, didn't you?"

Mazen hated the house they lived in. The only time he ever rebelled in his young life was just over a decade ago, in the month between their parents' announcement of their move to a new neighborhood and the move itself. Harmless rebellions, mostly: folded arms, silent treatments, unfinished dinners, and hiding the remote control, once even in a pitcher of lemonade. His parents consoled him more than punished him, adorning his room in the new house with every superhero emblem their intermediate Googling skills turned up—Batman bedsheets, Superman curtains, Spider-Man nightlight, Aquaman pajamas, Iron Man backpack—and hoping it would alleviate the pain. It didn't. He cried every night for almost a year. Until one night when he snuck into Firas's room and cuddled up next to him in bed. Firas, then thirteen, hissed him right back out. Mazen never came back, his crying finally stopped, and nothing more was said of his difficulty adjusting.

Even when, to this day, he still referred to the old apartment as "home."

"Probably," Firas answered. He headed for the door.

"I'll be right down." It hadn't occurred to Firas that he would continue helping.

When he returned to the kitchen, Firas saw that all was just as he had left it, except the scent of the braising lamb was more pungent. He relieved Maysa of kitchen duty and she was all too happy to comply.

The vegetables and feta were chopped; he mixed them into the large bowl of pasta, which had cooled, and deposited it into the fridge. Mazen came back down and took his post at the soup station. He was back in his regular clothes and looked older suddenly. Firas wanted clarification on his earlier statement, but he was too afraid to ask, in part because he might inadvertently poke a sleeping bear (checking to see if an idea existed in someone's head was the surest way of planting it). But it was partly because he simply did not want to know what Mazen knew. Because if Mazen knew what he was and accepted him, it might put him at ease for the evening when he needed very much to be on guard. No. Mazen's portent was less damaging unexamined. It was sweet of him, though. Not merely because of the struggle he was in the midst of dealing with himself, but because Mazen had every reason to take Firas's excitement about his party for granted. Mazen never needed to cancel a birthday party. He was always popular wherever he went—school, mosque, little league, neighborhood block parties. He was lit from within. His first birthday party was at the age of eight. Fearing his little brother might suffer the same misfortune he had, Firas tried to convince his parents not to overdo the arrangements. He also kept assuring Mazen that the best parties were the small ones with just family, because it is harder to get noticed in large groups. On the day of Mazen's party, all the boys from his class showed up, he was inundated with love and attention, and Firas vomited in the bathroom for two straight hours. This lucky streak, as Firas referred to it, went on until Mazen's fourteenth birthday party, when he took a page from Firas's book and canceled it a few days prior.

It was generally assumed that the party's cancellation stemmed from its inappropriate timing. Mohammed Abu Khdeir had just been murdered by Israeli settlers in East Jerusalem and Gaza was being obliterated by Israeli missiles. Any display of joy from Palestinians wouldn't do. Just as Shakespeare and Twain were required reading for every high school English class, the military aggression waged on a densely populated strip of land thousands of miles away was a required topic of conversation for every diaspora Palestinian. Most questions were about any remaining family Firas might have there, to which he said none, followed by an *Oh good* or *Thank God* before a swift relocation to safer conversational grounds. Most comments were generic condolences, which Firas accepted with a polite smile (the lateral commissures lifted three-quarters of an inch above the upper lip) accompanied by an assertive nod (angled at forty-five degrees from the axis of the neck with eyes closed for a duration of 1.2 seconds), then the swift relocation once again. Occasionally, there were references to Hamas, delivered in a variety of intonations— shocked, sardonic, devastated, terrified—soaked in the subtle relish of *This guy I know is from Gaza!* that would render the commenter slightly more relevant at their next soirée. None of these comments had much impact on Firas. But there was one that Anton had made that stuck with him: "I hear Hamas throws gays off of buildings." Firas had heard variations on this sentiment before (a terrified *Imagine if you were still there!*, a shocked *Wait, being gay is illegal?*, a sardonic *They're even worse than the people we elected*, a devastated *I pray that love wins*), but he'd never encountered a matter-of-fact *I hear Hamas throws gays off of buildings*. He suspected the remark might have had to do with Anton's inevitable return to Russia. By then, his grades had slipped so far down, the possibility was all but confirmed. Yet despite the ostensibly plain delivery of the statement, there was something in his eyes, narrow and evasive and veneered with gray, and his shoulders, slumped but tense like hilltops about to be detonated, that betrayed a deep-seated need for reassurance. Looking back, Firas wished he had given it to him, but he hadn't considered that Anton's American sexcapade would seriously come to an end. Firas liked to tell himself that, had he known, he would have said something comforting to lighten the load he sensed was there. But he didn't. Firas never said such things to people.

Kashif urged him to join in all the marches and protests to demand that the American government denounce Israel's asymmetrical warfare on besieged Palestinians. Kashif even took a week-long trip to D.C. and confronted Harry Reid and John Boehner, who offered him limp handshakes and meaningless platitudes, neither of which he accepted. Firas never considered partaking in the protests and marches. He was focused on school and work and had little time for anything else. Kashif never forgave him for it, kept chastising him for not participating in the liberation of his people when he knew firsthand what they were experiencing. This was often a source of contention between the two of them. An unspoken claim Kashif was always on the verge of blurting out: he was more Palestinian than Firas. Unlike Firas, he didn't ignore the suffering of other Palestinians or treat his schoolwork and office job (as if he ever worked one) as more worthy of his attention than bombs dropping from the sky on children. What it really came down to was the belief that Kashif was more Palestinian than Firas was by mere virtue of habit. By eating more Palestinian food and reading more Palestinian books and watching more Palestinian films. By thinking Palestinian thoughts in the shower. Kashif slid the word *Palestinian* into roughly thirty percent of his daily sentences, no doubt tracking the amount with a handheld tally counter, the Daily Pal-O-Meter no true Palestinian should be without. Firas, as far as Kashif was concerned, was barely Palestinian at all.

The front door of the Dareer house opened and from the corridor a distinct mechanical thrum pervaded the air. Firas stiffened.

No. Dear God, no.

Of all the weapons in his grandfather's arsenal—the frothing mouth projecting cuss words like bullets, the criticisms that seared one's skin like a rash, the unearthing of familial demons that could never be reburied—Firas had not been prepared for the one that would be used even before he met his Jido's eyes.

"Baba, today is a special day," his father spoke from the corridor. "It's your grandson's birthday."

His grandfather said nothing at first. Then: "The good one or the bad one?"

Firas immediately turned to Mazen, whose blank stare prevented him from gauging the appropriate response. It was inevitable, perhaps, that the two Dareer brothers, so different in every perceivable respect, would eventually be measured against each other. More inevitable was that this comparison would favor the eldest, the one who earned a full academic scholarship, who graduated with honors, who interned at a most prestigious firm, who thrived in whatever endeavor he took on, who had prospects for both his professional and personal future, while the other one was marred by a tragedy of his own doing and could barely be left alone for more than half an hour.

"Amo, they're both very good boys," his mother asserted. Then she stepped into the kitchen, eyes on her phone, and, upon looking up, completely froze. "Oh." Gauging whether her boys had just heard, and determining without a doubt that they had, she tucked away her phone and fumbled for a greeting. "It smells nice in here."

"Firas and I are making his birthday dinner."

Firas gawked at him. Did he not just hear his own grandfather malign him? Casually? Like it'd been a run-of-the-mill observation that he—and likely their own parents—had made many times before?

"Maysa helped, too."

Firas muttered under his breath. Now he had to share credit with *two* interlopers.

"Well, good," their mother said. "Come say hello to Jido."

The boys stepped into the corridor.

The old man sat in his wheelchair, head high and flaunting chiseled cheekbones, the skin along his neck much tighter than it had any right to be. His white hair was partly disheveled, likely from the rapid getaway, but for the most part it held up quite well. No signs of balding and no liver spots on his hirsute hands, which were balled up into fists. His eyes, hazel and hooded, showed no weariness in the slightest. This was not a man willing to go gently into the good night.

"Marhaba, Jido," said Firas, who took his grandfather's hand, kissed it, tapped it onto his forehead, and repeated the gesture twice more.

"Hi, Grandpa!" followed Mazen, prompting Firas and his parents to suppress a wince. He kissed his grandfather once on each cheek.

"Alhamdulillah you're safe," Firas added.

"I'm fucking hungry!" bellowed the old man.

"Firas, bring your grandfather some of the soup you made," his mother said.

"That soup is for tonight, Mama. I haven't even added the chicken yet."

"I hate chicken!" he bellowed.

"Problem solved," his father said.

Firas's body started shrinking. "I suppose I can spare a bowl for Jido." The words tasted so bitter. "I'm sure he won't want to go back to the nursing home on an empty stomach."

"Jido will be staying with us from now on," his father said, gazing at the old man, who was determined not to gaze back.

Firas expected this news the second the door had opened. But he needed to hear the words to quell the insidious hope still lingering in his heart. "So he'll be attending my party?" he asked.

"That works out well for you," Mazen said. "In case nobody shows up, like last time."

Shrinking . . . shrinking . . . shrinking.

"But first, get Jido's luggage out of the car."

As Firas fetched the luggage, he mustered up the sympathy his grandfather deserved. Fourteen years ago, the old man was torn away from his natural habitat. He'd been recently widowed, Firas's Teta shot in the Second Intifada by an occupation soldier, and not long after her burial were his son and daughter-in-law stuffing his suitcase for their escape. They knew they couldn't leave him there by himself, assured themselves of this fact over and over as guilt crept through them. One must not leave their elders behind any more than they would their children. But Jido had only two wishes: to live a long life with his beloved and to be buried next to her. Israel had robbed him of the first wish; his own kin then robbed him of the second. He couldn't decide which theft was crueler, but the latter seemed more infinite in its cruelty: Teta's graveyard had by now been bombed.

Throughout his first years in America, Jido awoke suddenly in the middle of nights, the upward jerk harsh on his bones, his wail emanating through the bedroom walls of his children and their children. He was not having nightmares. Quite the contrary. His dreams were idylls dipped in sepia, waterslides in dimpled cheeks, lush lips whispering tornadoes, and hands that quaked the earth when held together. His dreams were the resting place. His new natural habitat from which Time, not his family, now tore him away. In the waking world that drifted beside him but never through him, his only comfort was memory. The more comforting it became, the less reliable, teetering into the realm of fantasy until eventually Teta began to appear wherever he went. The old man was fully aware that she was not really there with him, but it didn't matter. Not at first. Only when the waking world subdued him into his false sense of peace did the sleep world neglect its similar duty. His dreams doubled back, capturing details he needn't see again and amplifying them without distortion, making them all the more visceral while still holding a jarring claim to truth. One night, he awoke from the nightmare and the wail came not as an expulsion of pain but as a hand reaching down his throat for a purge of everything good inside him—strength, courage, warmth, sanity. Firas's father burst into the room to check on him and Jido slapped him across the cheek yelling *DON'T YOU TOUCH HER! DON'T YOU FUCKING TOUCH HER! I'LL KILL YOU BEFORE I LET YOU HURT HER! DO YOU HEAR ME? I'LL KILL YOU!!!* The nursing home was next, followed by an abrupt move in the middle of the night to their new home, Mazen crying in the back seat the whole way there.

After bringing in Jido's luggage, Firas went to the kitchen, poured a bowl of soup, and served it to his grandfather, who was slumped over the dining room table with eyes shut and muttering *bismillah al-rahman al-rahim*. "Sahten, Jido," Firas said, knowing he'd be ignored. He returned to the kitchen and added the chicken to the pot. With his parents back, he could make a quick run to the party supply store himself while the first half of the lamb shanks continued to braise over the stove and Maysa, having earned a modicum of his trust back, attended to the soup.

He retrieved his phone from his pocket to text Suhad, when a message appeared from his employer asking him to come into work immediately. A meek apology followed, which Firas was too distracted to read, in part because of his outrage (he had specifically requested not to be called in today) and in part because of the noise emanating from the dining room.

As he began texting Suhad, Firas could hear the drill of his grandfather's slurping through the kitchen door. Between slurps the old man bellowed, "The bad one makes a great soup!"

Firas dropped his phone into the pot.

CHAPTER SIX

T he Lyft idled just outside the door. After Firas's cell phone drowned, he texted back his boss from his father's phone informing him that he was on his way. It was a Sunday, a day on which no firm ever opened, but in this case, there was a significant project for a client who kept changing her mind, often upending all the plans of the team working on it, with no regard for the deadline that was fast approaching.

The other interns would all be there, having mentioned to him earlier that they might arrive late for his party, and having informed him, in detail, about the sob story their boss had given them (the senior architect quit in the middle of the biggest project the firm has ever had because he suddenly decided he wanted to join Habitat for Humanity and boy what a spineless tool he was for not waiting another two years). Now Firas would likely run late as well, leaving him with very little time to decorate.

Just minutes before he ordered the Lyft, Suhad piled her haul onto the kitchen counter.

"Where's the rest of it?" he asked, wiping celery and broth off his phone, when he noticed that she had purchased not one item on his list. It appeared she'd gone to a store vastly inferior to the one he'd sent her to. On top of the pile, she placed the receipt for him to see how much he owed her.

"My credit card maxed out. This was all I could afford to get."

Now Firas was saddled with single-color balloons, a birthday sash, a pack of eight blowouts for a party of twenty-five, and two handfuls of confetti. With a stop at his workplace precluding a run to the party supply store, he almost considered borrowing his neighbor's Halloween decorations.

"What's wrong, Suhad?" their father asked from the living room. "Does the salon not pay enough?" The icy stare he shot at her ricocheted off her cheek and struck Firas. Their parents were still furious that Suhad forsook the college route. Breathless rants about sacrifice blared against backdrops of glazed eyes and slack jaws. She spent a year in the exploratory program at Wayne State, for which her parents paid the tuition, then dropped out when she couldn't settle on a major, thus breaking a promise to them she never knew she'd made. Afterward she spent one semester at a cosmetology school, for which she arranged a finance plan, then again dropped out when she could no longer keep up with the payments. It was unfortunate, but Firas was much less focused on the tragedy of his sister's circumstance than on its peculiarity. At home, Suhad had always done all her chores and all her homework, a dutiful daughter who obeyed her parents, transgressing only in religious obligations because there seemed to her no point in them (and even these transgressions were done in secret to prevent conflict). But outside the Dareer house, she displayed the hyperactive mannerisms of a child stuffed with candy. Everyone around her was constantly struggling to determine the best way to bring her back down to a state of calm. In school, when her parents met with her teacher, they refused to believe what she had to say: Suhad always drummed her hands against her desk, always asked to use the restroom even when she'd only just gone, always interrupted to ask irrelevant questions like what time it was or what food was being served in the cafeteria. None of this sounded like her, and the fact that her grades were always strong led her parents to suspect that her teacher, despite her sweet demeanor, held some sort of grudge against their daughter. But each year, a different teacher would repeat the same claim, questioning if perhaps Suhad had ADHD, to which her mother replied *What is ADHD?* and then balked at the answer. "If she was having trouble focusing, she would be doing very poorly on her tests and assignments." The teachers agreed, and were stumped. Her marks were not strong enough to elevate her to the next grade, as is often done with disruptive children who do well and require a more fitting challenge; but they were better than those of most other students in her class, and she never displayed any of the forgetfulness or lack of organizational skills typical of the disorder. In the end, Suhad's parents scolded her and ordered her to behave herself at school. She did, but not by eliminating her overstimulation; instead she transferred it to places like dance classes and chess tournaments, where it was not only accepted but celebrated. She grew up to live her life this way, scouring the world around her for outlets. She found them in various forms (Pilates, raves, romance, escape rooms, movie trivia nights), her life filling with countless interests and people keeping her busy at all times. But these outlets always burned out soon after she found them, and she rushed to find another one to promptly fill the void. At one point, she relied on cannabis, but subduing her energy, rather than channeling it, felt to her a crime against her own nature, a slap in the face to all the exhausted youths struggling with caffeine addictions who would have absolutely killed for it. The only place she never seemed to have this problem was at home. And yet, of the twenty-four hours that exist in each day, only ten of hers were spent there. Of those ten, seven were spent sleeping, one was spent eating, another one on chores, and the last was spent on various hygiene tasks in the bathroom. In other words, she was only at home to do what would pose too great a challenge, or one wholly impossible, elsewhere. Another outlet was always necessary for Suhad Dareer. Whether cosmetology would have lasted longer than other outlets would never be known, but she enjoyed it, and it stood as good a chance as any.

After she dropped out of college, her parents stopped speaking to her for four months, and only started up again after Mazen's attempt emphasized her necessity as a helping hand, the backup watchdog when Firas was unavailable. Sporadic mentions of her pennilessness still wormed into everyday conversations, but she and her parents resumed formalities, which is all that mattered. Looking back now, Firas regretted not coming to his sister's defense. He could've chimed in with sound arguments: *Plenty of people make a career as a stylist. It's not like she's just sitting around all day. Cosmetology is honest work. Mama goes to the salon all the time.* Yet he said nothing. One night, after traipsing home from a rendezvous with Kashif that resulted in a four-hour lecture on the sentimental merits of breastfeeding in public, he overheard them debating whether to evict Suhad from the house. Even then he kept out of the matter. What a foolish move that was. Defense of his sister would have ignited an allyship, the very kind that would serve him well on this day. The truth was, he saw value in silence. With her subversion, Suhad inadvertently galvanized a greater parental appreciation for him. He profited off the fallout. And now Suhad would profit off his.

When he got stressed in this manner, Firas often thought of jokes he could tell Tyrese. Tyrese had a distinct laugh, a guffaw cut short by a sharp gasp that instantly trickled back out in a steady giggle, wholly aware of itself, not self-consciously, not proudly, but simply aware of itself and its right to exist. Tyrese was easy to make laugh, his shoddy remembrance of punchlines beneficial for Firas, who had so few jokes to tell. Now, with his Lyft ambling along, Firas was forced to settle for the sights outside his window to calm himself. Among them was Old Main, with its ridge turrets and four-faced clock tower, originally built with conveniently located brick and limestone, and now restored and enlarged and soulless. Following that came the Grand Army of the Republic building, a triangular castle in the style of Romanesque Revival that stood boldly at the end of a lot as though headed for sea, yet failed to impress when looked at from the wrong angle, which was most. Then came Michigan Central Station, a once fertile Beaux-Arts building that was now desolate, and deserved to be desolate as penance for the sheer number of windows that riddled its face like bullet holes and the dejected American flag waving limply before a train depot more withered than Stonehenge. Firas used to worship these architectural staples of his city, but could now only sneer at them and long for the day when he could design his own building, which even on the worst day of one's life would still manage to inspire. It invigorated him, this idea of creating something from the ground up, of bringing something to life with nothing more than his imagination. More than design, he relished the idea of *re*-design, of rubble scattered across the ground, ancient and mythical and foolishly deemed unbreakable, bulldozed out of history before Firas came along and birthed a newer, better, stronger structure from its ashes.

As he gazed at these old buildings, thoughts of the old man suddenly cinched every muscle in his legs.

So. Firas was the bad one all along. And it hadn't even occurred to him. Smugness belied his assumption, giving him the confidence boost he needed to survive the evening. No wonder Mazen's face was blank upon Jido's pronouncement. There was no dim bulb behind those eyes; he saw everything clearly. And in his clarity, he effortlessly changed the subject to protect his brother, who tried—pointlessly—to do the same for him. The boy was five steps ahead of him, knowing that the grandfather he had hardly seen in a decade liked him more than Firas. Firas, who visited the old man in the nursing home every month since he'd been relegated there; Firas, who always replaced the flower arrangement in his room with a new one; Firas, who took him to the bathroom when the nurses were overwhelmed with other patients; Firas, who conversed with him, asking the old man question after question after question about his day-to-day life that sucked both of them into the boundless void of banality. The last time Mazen visited him he had the audacity to talk to Jido about "home" as though their father, still shaken from that late-night slap across his face in Jido's room, was not standing right beside them. It was decided then that Mazen had best not visit his grandfather anymore.

So what precisely did Jido have to go by to deduce his youngest grandson was the better of the two? No, not better. Good. Firas's goodness wasn't even being graded on a curve—his goodness didn't exist! Sifting through a decade's worth of memories, he struggled to pinpoint where it all went wrong. Did he do a poor job of wiping his grandfather's backside all those times? Was the old man averse to flowers? Did they remind him of some rigid nurse in the home?

Perhaps it was not merely one thing. Perhaps it was a culmination of myriad things. But what? Certainly, the conversations between them were mind-numbingly polite—he would have been the first to understand if his grandfather had asked him not to bother visiting anymore. As soon as Firas had passed his teen years, Jido made less effort to suppress his sighs, his eye rolls, his blatant turns towards the clock on the wall. But did banality really make him a bad person?

The more he thought about it, the more possible it seemed that the elderly, like dogs and children, truly did possess a sixth sense. Movies often mythologized these characters, these innocents the world forgot, who could sense upon the very first encounter that something was crooked about the handyman traipsing through the door to fix the radiator. Did he give his grandfather a bad feeling? Was his very existence a red flag in and of itself?

Firas might have preferred this possibility to the one he eventually settled on: his grandfather knew about him. There was no other plausible explanation. He wouldn't have known about his sexuality, per se, but he could easily have come upon the veil. That veil from which no amount of polite chats or backside wipes could deflect. In all the times he'd visited his grandfather and asked him his ceaseless series of questions, Firas listened to each answer with intent, and that intent was to eke out just enough detail to formulate the next question in the series. Sometimes Jido would be in the middle of answering one question when Firas began stringing together another one in his head. Because the answers themselves didn't quite matter; what mattered was the continuous procession of words from the old man's mouth into the young man's ears. Should anything occlude that procession, be it an awkward pause or a lapse in memory, then the procession could potentially be reversed. There were rare instances of this happening, with Firas fumbling to string together his answers as seamlessly as he'd done his questions.

Then there were the days when his grandfather was too tired to talk. Firas would offer to read him a story, but Jido hated fiction. He wanted to hear the tale of life as lived by those he knew. Firas indulged him with the latest news involving his parents and siblings, filtering out all the failures and tragedies. But that was never good enough. These were secondhand stories, with the beating heart that brought them to life lost in Firas's didactic translation. It had to be Firas's news, Firas's story. And it was then that a wind blew in from an unknown source and the veil was lifted high above his face. The red flag emerged and a new side to the eldest grandson revealed itself. A side of broken smiles, of ashen cheeks, of the ever-vigilant eyes that cower when humanity stares right back. Yes, there was something *dark* lurking inside this boy. He saw it. He *saw* it.

The Lyft pulled up to the curb, and the driver glared at Firas to cue his exit. Stifling a sigh, Firas went straight into the building lobby and rode the elevator to the eighteenth floor. The firm occupied the building's top five floors, all wide enough to fit twelve drawing boards and four desks. He fidgeted. Just three hours before the party was scheduled to start, four before people were expected to show. No matter how hectic everything was, Luis would never keep people past five o'clock, especially on a Sunday. With only half an hour left before then, Firas wondered what he was doing there. His job consisted primarily of research. Researching building materials, lighting fixtures, building codes and standards. The rest of his job involved assisting with design drawings, developing 3D conceptual designs, and preparing mock-ups and color boards. But thirty minutes would hardly suffice for any of that.

The elevator doors opened and the office, as always, overwhelmed him the instant he stepped in. An Escher-like succession of ash wood stairs, made more disorienting by the identical furniture and interchangeable office workers stationed on each floor. At times, he suspected the higher-ups designed it this way deliberately to instill in their workers a sense of unease, a perpetual need to glance over your shoulder to see if the boss was coming only to suddenly find yourself in the middle of a bathroom stall. Nobody would dare gossip or idle in a workplace like this.

Workers buzzed about. Their clunky steps roused the ground beneath him. Vetiver and rose oil fluttered around him like a blanket. He got on with most of his co-workers; they were dedicated, diligent, considerate, and often quite fun. His only qualm was their talent—so precise it felt as practiced as cello recitals—for butchering his name. Otherwise, he could see himself working there long-term, acquiring all the necessary knowledge, skills, and connections to eventually venture out on his own.

He walked up to Aadip, the perky receptionist. As per his custom, he handed Firas a Hershey's Kiss. "Happy Sunday, Fy-russ! I hope the day finds you well."

"So do I."

"Luis wanted you to go straight up to his office. On your way, remember to enjoy the sun before it sets!"

Firas forced a smile and dashed up the first flight of stairs. The sun gleamed through the all-encompassing windows. He ignored it.

On the second floor, he encountered Howie, the lesser of five interns. "Hey, Fear-az, what are you doing here?"

"Luis texted me. No idea why."

"On your birthday? That's weak."

"Yeah. Anyway . . ." He rushed up the stairs to the third floor.

"Well hey, happy birthday!" Howie shouted from below, drawing the attention of every worker on his floor and a few of the ones on the next.

"Look who it is!"

Firas was forced to halt and acknowledge this next person, whose voice he recognized as belonging to Raymond, his direct superior and a saccharine advocate for affirmative action whose Whiteness seldom dawned on him.

"Hey, Raymond . . ."

"Nice of you to come in today, Fur-ass. I heard the big man upstairs wants to talk to you. Be sure to fill me in later, yeah? We liberals gotta stick together."

"Are there conservatives in this office?"

"Not yet, but the times they are a-changin'!"

"Right."

And he sped right up to the fourth floor, his knee-jerk twist almost whipping Raymond off his balance.

"They did NOT call you in on your b-day!"

Firas stopped and smiled. Of all his fellow interns, Celeste was his favorite. He had known her longer, having met her in his third year at the University of Michigan. It was in his Design Fundamentals course, after which she offered him a ride home from Ann Arbor, where the Taubman College of Architecture and Urban Planning was located. Dreading the public transport to and from Detroit, and having thankfully developed an affection for her, Firas thenceforth scheduled all his courses to begin and end alongside hers. The two drew inspiration and motivation from one another, mainly through competition, but they always kept it amicable because they knew the world was cynical enough without pointless rivalries.

"I'm afraid so."

"That's so dumb! Do they really think one more intern is gonna stop this place from caving in on itself?"

"I don't know."

"Are you okay? You look a bit wrecked."

"Busy day, that's all."

She eyed his waist and began to snicker. "Nice fanny pack."

Indeed, Firas was sporting a fanny pack. After he'd dropped his phone into the soup, he rushed to spray it with an air duster before shoving it into a plastic bag of rice. According to an internet search he once conducted, this trick revives the phone after twenty-four to forty-eight hours. Well past the time of his party, but perhaps he'd get lucky.

"I better get this over with," he said.

"Good luck, buddy. And happy birthday." She hugged him, and he was off.

On the fifth floor, Luis's office door was open. He knocked quickly but quietly, so as not to startle the man whose hair was wilting at the same rate he spoke:

"Comeincomeincomein!"

Firas closed the door behind him as he entered the office, in which sketches smothered the drawing board, the desk, the chairs, the floor. Luis cleared a seat for him.

"Sitdownpleasesitdown." Large drops of sweat jitterbugged along the curve of his upper lip as he spoke. "Thanksforcoming-inFairAce."

"No problem." *Why am I here? Why the fuck did you call me in?* The words were pushing against his clenched teeth.

"SorryIcalledyouintodayIknowyouweresupposedtobeoff."

"It's okay. What's up?"

"Whatdoyouthinkofthissketch?"

He took a sketch from his drawing board and held it up for Firas to see, resembling a fourth-grader presenting his family tree for show-and-tell.

It was a design for a privately funded greenhouse conservatory that the City of Detroit hoped would foster more tourism and a pretense of environmental concern. Firas's eyes darted back and forth between the sketch and the face of the man holding it. Luis was scanning him for his reaction, bobbing his head slightly to ensure he caught it from every angle.

The design was middling. Uninventive. Luis often tried so desperately to distance himself from the zeitgeist that at times he wound up being utterly plain. Domes were in. Pyramids were in. Greek columns. Roman statues. Fountains. What he'd drawn was a greenhouse shaped like a Grimm brothers villain's lair. Not hideous, but rather awkward out of context. Cylindrical structures interspersed among pentagonal shapes that poked outward without rhyme or reason. All the chaos of abstract art with none of its mesmerism. Before it stood a pair of statues of civil rights heroes Rosa Parks and Octavia Williams Bates, whose historical significance to the city of Detroit failed to explain what either of them was doing in front of a greenhouse.

"Well?"

Firas mulled over the question. Or rather, the reason behind it. To have him come in on a Sunday—not just any Sunday, but a Sunday he very specifically requested *not* to be called in—and ask him, of all people, what he thought of a sketch for a project half the firm was already rushing to put together?

This was a test.

But what precisely was being tested? Firas's worthiness as an intern? He'd shown Raymond some of his sketches from his college courses and he loved them. But Raymond would have been impressed by an outhouse had Firas sketched one. And Luis wouldn't have seen any of those anyway, he was too high up in the company, too busy. Whatever the case, Firas readied to give his honest answer.

"Well—"

A ringing phone interrupted him. Luis swung the landline up to his ear.

"WhatdoyouwantIminameeting?" His eyes filled with an emotion Firas didn't recognize. "NOITDOESNTCOMEWITHEXTRABENEFITSWHATTHEHELLDOYOUTHINKIAMAWALMART?"

He slammed the phone down. Inhaled fast and deep. A vein was bulging from his temple and the emotion filling his eyes crystallized until Firas finally recognized it as entitlement. Now he understood what was happening. The senior architect had quit, which meant someone was being promoted to his job, which meant someone below that someone would be promoted, and so on and so forth, until a position opened up at the bottom of the food chain. Firas was getting hired six months before he predicted he would. Of all the things that had gone unexpectedly wrong throughout the day, he quivered at the thought that something—something big—was going so unexpectedly *right*.

But he didn't yet have the job. He didn't even have an offer. He had a question, and how he answered it would be the determining factor. He wasn't supposed to be honest. He realized this now. Luis was looking for a yes-man, a foot soldier to march to his beat and do as he was told and speak when he was spoken to. He was looking for someone to assure him that everything was going to be okay.

"It's subversive in a way that'll set us apart," Firas finally said.

Luis sighed, lowered the sketch, and plopped into his chair, crinkling a few of the scrapped sketches that lay on it. "How would you like to have Gabby's job?"

When Firas headed back down to the elevator, he sought to evade Raymond, as well as everyone else who may have been curious about his meeting, by pretending to check his phone. It seemed his luck was continuously improving: his phone managed to turn back on. He ordered another Lyft and sent a message to his mother instructing her to replace the first dozen lamb shanks on the stove with the second in case he arrived late and Maysa failed to keep up with her duties. With his phone now functioning as normal, a smile stretched across Firas's face. And yet he knew this smile would only last so briefly. He knew that the instant he arrived home, the day would revert to its natural course towards doom. Even now a sense of dread crept through him. He had lied. He had lied to get ahead in his career, to get ahead in life. This entire day had a singular purpose: honesty. It was meant to be a day of telling the people around him the truth, even if that truth pained them. No, lying about a sketch was not nearly the same as lying about one's identity, but it was the same brand of placation, the same self-serving goal of convenience. Yet if he were honest in every part of his life, he might have lost both job and family. Is that really what truth is for? To strip one down of everything so the world can see and hear every thought and feeling? Mustn't one conceal *some* things from humanity? The notion that unwavering honesty is a virtue does not fit in the modern world. Too many potential outcomes, too few contingency plans. So much can go wrong with unwavering honesty. So much pain would arise, and so few people know how to process their pain without transferal. It was either Firas or his family. It had to be. For the last decade or so, it had been him. It was their turn now, wasn't it? After all, there was nothing more he could do with the pain; he'd learned everything from it he possibly could, and now he must move on to the next pain, the next lesson learned. He needed this job—it would be his safety net, not only financially, but emotionally. The chaos of office work would whisk his mind away from all other troubles, and someday he would breathe again, someday he'd forget. The balance of life. The art of self-preservation. One lie for every truth. One fraction of pain kept for every fraction given.

His phone soon died again.

CHAPTER SEVEN

Firas was now at Chandler Park, having abandoned his Lyft as he neared his home for a sullen walk that he knew would delay him. Time was seizing him by the throat, but only trouble awaited at home, and in the park he found something much lighter and sweeter: Time's greatest nemesis. As he trod along the grass, verdant and piercing, almost sinful to touch, he caught the tail end of a children's soccer match. He roamed past the field, witnessed a shot taken and a shot missed, mustered a melancholy smile for the parents invested in the game and its influence over their children's self-esteem. Some yards away he watched a trio of children darting into the sky in rocket ships shaped like swings, and he wished them a safe voyage. He'd had many safe voyages in that park, and one crash landing broken by his sister's back. She cried, but he got the thrill of a lifetime.

His mother used to take him to soccer games on afternoons far more sweltering than this. Silky brown hair glazed with sweat, he ran and missed every goal he shot but one. And he was glad, for the score was all the more exhilarating for it. Fresh off the failed birthday party, his membership in the league earned him his very first friends in America. After every game, the coach and some of the parents would treat the team to ice cream, and Firas wouldn't talk until the fifth trip, because it was only then that he was able to learn Americanism, a craft far more intricate than architecture. He studied the other boys' mannerisms, their style, their lingo, their accents, their hobbies, their interests, their complete obliviousness to military occupation and national uprisings. Their indifference. He'd played soccer in Palestine and eaten ice cream many times, but it didn't transform him there. It didn't do anything for him there.

He tried to keep in touch with his teammates after the summer ended, but they lived in different neighborhoods and went to different schools. It didn't matter. They gave him what he needed, they served their purpose, and he thanked his mother for taking him to the games. It was kind of her to do so. A kindness that seldom dawns on children in this country. His father, too, often took him places. Mainly to the Detroit Institute of Arts, where he got to marvel at the work of Utagawa Hiroshige I, and where he was chastised for taking a photograph of *Cherrytime at Nippori* while pretending he had no idea that taking pictures was not permitted. The museum was wide and spacious, its space dwindling as he grew older and expanding as he grew wiser. He thanked his father, too, after each visit.

And he thanked them for the birthday presents he received until presents no longer mattered to him. They started as toys and board games, evolved into sweaters and hats and scarves, then finally a laptop and smartphone. From then on, he got the customary words and the occasional gesture that usually made little difference in his day, but it was a gesture, and it was something. The Dareers took their children to Pizza Hut once a month and Disney World once a year, and that was something, too.

As he exited the park, he strolled past the bowling alley where he had his first kiss. A girl named Rupa Bhavsar who awed him with her daring, never shy about letting him know she wanted one-on-one time together. During a game in which he scored eighty-two points and she scored seventy-nine, she congratulated him on his victory with a peck on the lips that hurtled towards him so fast it looked as though she'd tripped. He knew she let him win so she would have an excuse to kiss him, and he admired her daring yet more.

He'd heard in later years that Rupa was a lesbian, which reminded him of Anton, who had once mentioned a girl he wanted to marry back home that his parents liked for him, in no small part because of her family's relative wealth. She was closeted too, and came up with the idea of what was commonly referred to as a lavender marriage. Anton loved the idea initially, figuring it would ward off any questions about why he hadn't yet settled down without tying him to any sort of responsibility. When he was readying to fly back to Saint Petersburg, he seemed keen on going through with it, a consolation for his having to leave America just as he was finally coming into his own. He and Firas agreed to stay in touch and did so for approximately five months. They had never gotten along as well as friends who keep in touch should, but tragedy heightens the need for connection, and Firas was one of the only people to whom Anton could tether himself to his life in the West. Their emails were rather impersonal and vague—updates on the weather, work, what they were reading, the inconveniences of public transportation that vary from one neighborhood to the next; occasionally each would ask how the other was doing. With exchanges such as these, Firas was unsurprised when Anton eventually stopped responding. What did surprise him was that he really missed Anton.

Around the corner, he glimpsed the sporting goods store whence Mrs. Tullinson had bought him a pair of cleats, after bursting into tears at the register. This was the last place her son had gone before his ill-fated camping trip, which she only discovered upon the arrival of her credit card statement in the mail. But he'd stolen the card long before then. And she knew he'd stolen it and did nothing. How could she have, how could she? Myra Tullinson was not meant to impose herself onto those around her; she was meant to guide, to nudge, to sync her soul with all those that were lost. But though her gentle nature assuaged everyone in her life, it never pushed them further than a mere step from their starting point. Oftentimes she felt as though she were failing Firas as she had Bryan. With the staff gawking as tears streamed down her cheeks, she mustered a smile to assuage Firas, then at the edge of adolescence, but she saw instantly that a smile would not suffice. She took him to a bakery and bought him flan, even letting him eat it in his room while they played what would be one of their last rounds of board games before such childish fun became obsolete. The caramel stain smudged along his wall, behind the velvet ottoman on which lay his prayer rug, became the bane of nearly every morning since, made more woeful by the circumstance that led to it.

Near the end of the street, he passed by the warehouse whence his father got laid off a year earlier. A failure that penetrated his father, who expected the stench of it to emanate from every part of his body, particularly as the mounting pile of water bills nearly led to a shutoff that would have prevented him from showering. But he soon discovered that failure was not a stench. No, rather it was a sound, a buzz that only he could hear, setting him on a search for kindred spirits all around him to see if they might be hearing it too, then reluctantly relinquishing that hope before realizing the buzz was trying to tell him something, something personal, something only a man like him could understand, forcing him to overexert his ears to decipher what they heard until he failed at that too and could only beg and beg and beg for the buzzing to just STOP.

He'd been at the warehouse nine years, and within the first ten months of that tenure, he had worked his way up from a loader to a driver to a trainer to a manager. It was the sort of meteoric rise that, in America, seemed at once impossible and inevitable. As far as he was concerned, success in this country ultimately depended on the whim of Allah, amplifying his faith all the more, and all the more quickly, when he attained it. But just as meteoric rises occur, so too do their corresponding falls, and yet after his journey from loader to driver to trainer to manager eventually led to a great big nothing (including a brief stint as an aspiring screenwriter), his faith amplified still, with his fingers, withered from overuse in the warehouse, latching on to it like a plank in the middle of the ocean. His faith, after all, was the only thing in his life he knew could never be taken away from him.

This increased devoutness had mixed results, not only for Firas's father but for all of those within his orbit. His renouncement of gossip and derogatory nicknames weaponized against the people he did not like was objectively good, though it made him much duller at dinner parties. On the other hand, his abstinence from less morally objectionable practices took a toll on the Dareer house by draining much of the life that remained there. He stopped dancing and listening to music, he sold all possessions made of silk and gold, he rid the house of every figurine and portrait, including those of his own children, much to his wife's chagrin. Even Mawlid, the one religious event Firas looked forward to, its musical processions and whirling dervishes enchanting him in spite of himself, was no longer to be celebrated. Indeed, he attempted to impose his newly adopted practices onto his wife and children—attempts that were resisted just as subtly as they were made, and ultimately stopped after less than a year. It seemed as though, deep down, Firas's father knew that focusing this new phase of his relationship to Islam could not bear the weight of his family's reluctance, and so it was a journey that he took up on his own. Pleased with his self-discipline, he eventually took it a step further with no regard for whether he was taking it in the right direction: sawm at a rate his body could scarcely afford, zakat at a rate his bank account could scarcely afford, and attendance at the mosque so excessive it even managed to unnerve some of the huffadhs.

Firas remembered the day his father arrived home and announced to the family the unfortunate news. His mother solved problems with food and cooked some maqluba, which was not her best, but his father enjoyed it regardless. His mother's cooking was at its best during Ramadan, which Firas deemed an ironic feat for the one time in the Muslim calendar his parents could eat off their own fingers and be satiated. On Eid al-Fitr, the Dareers always gave their children twenty dollars each and then took them out for Thai food. Firas hardly minded Ramadan, mainly because he never actually did it. Throughout their adolescence, he and Suhad made arrangements for one of them to distract their parents while the other sneaked into the kitchen, never less than three hours before iftar, for a moderate appetite at the dinner table would have betrayed them instantly. But occasionally their mother would come upon certain bags and boxes that had been opened when she distinctly remembered them being closed or cans that had gone missing when she distinctly remembered them being very much there. The consequence was a trip to a homeless shelter to see rib cages pressed against pallid skin, followed by a bout of forced volunteer work serving meals.

The barricades along the streets as Firas approached his neighborhood recalled the pride parade. Remnants drifted about in the form of renegade balloons, miniature flags sullied by footprints, and the string of last-minute marchers still lagging behind. On the sidewalk stood a smattering of protesters with homemade signs adorned with the same glitter accentuating the nipples of speedoed men whirring by on rollerblades.

He wished somehow that he could bypass these protesters, float above them as Tyrese could and would. But even this charming fantasy was tinged with discord. Because although Tyrese was by now an expert in the art of floating above the riffraff, he seemed perpetually unable to bring Firas up with him. So Firas walked on.

This was his last day of immunity. Tomorrow he would cease to be untouched and untouchable. He would bear the brunt of those protest signs and the accompanying faces spewing spit and venom. As he crossed the street, he locked eyes with one of the protestors. She seemed to be wondering whether he was part of the parade or if he was simply a pedestrian minding his own business. Her eyes followed him until he turned a corner, but tomorrow they would follow him everywhere. He was on his way home to waive his right to disappear, to draw the outline of his body on the pavement the world would pound. The moment was imminent.

But other moments were not imminent. They were past, and when Firas relived them, he struck a blow to Time. He wouldn't defeat it, but he could hurt it just a little, before it struck right back and tenfold. The bruise would be worth it, however, for he struck it hard as he could and made his anguish known. How maddening it was. Its oscillating voice, inescapable in his head, and the chameleonic intonations that convince him it's his own. He dredged up every memory he could on his journey home, every test he passed, every film he watched, every feeling he was fortunate enough to have, and he relished the mutually assured destruction. Oh how he relished it!

On the corner of his block was the mosque his parents made him attend every Friday evening, until college and work interfered with his schedule and he promised to attend a mosque closer to campus when he was free. It was a small mosque whose exterior—red bricks, plexiglass windows, the MASJID sign missing its *J*—resembled a dental clinic shutting down its practice. The interior sported linoleum floors blanketed with large Persian rugs, gray ones interspersed with beige, and neon signs spouting holy words along emaciated columns. A few chairs, a few shelves, a few plants, and a long line of fans by the wall for the summertime. He thought about redesigning it someday, his first solo project that would surely exonerate him for his absence over the past four years. For the exterior, he envisioned something traditional: a robust body of yellow sandstone, white marbled cupolas crowning blue stained-glass domes that erupt into the night, a minaret on each corner of the roof to view the city from every angle, and no letters anywhere to write out its name, for this mosque would be so renowned that all Muslims would come to know it just by sight. Less traditional would be the interior, where purple suffused the air; in a twist on the famed haft rangi of Shah Mosque in Isfahan, a tile mosaic along the ceiling and walls would display not seven colors but seven shades of the same color—lilac, mauve, mulberry, magenta, plum, orchid, Byzantium—all melding into one another to form arabesque arches over periwinkle marble flooring and columns made of tufa so soft it tingled. People would question the choice, balk at the contrast, but gradually they would come to love it until they wondered how they could have ever gone to any mosque but this.

Would his family visit his mosque? Would they even call it a mosque?

He was steps away from his front porch when he took out his phone to try it again. If any texts had arrived bearing the latest round of bad news, he wanted to be alone so he could scream and tramp on the sidewalk with poise. It turned on, and he scanned it quickly in case it shut off again. Ten messages had come through since he left the office: a quartet of congratulations from the other interns, a fifth from Raymond, two pictures from Mazen modeling different ties to get his opinion, a reminder from Suhad about the money he owed her, and two that his mother had sent. The first one was an *Okay*, in response to his request regarding the lamb. How he wished in that moment not to have made such a request. How he wished, for once, just once!, that he had left things up to chance. But there was no way he could have foreseen the catastrophe that such an innocuous text would unleash. Even after the day's omens—the flavorless breakfast, the fragmentary bouquet, the discarded decorations, the passive-aggressive note from a former lover, the scarlet letter carved into his chest by the family oracle—even then, he could not have predicted the overestimated length of his return home and the needless ensnaring of his mother into a message chain that made her stumble. His phone had died when he needed it most, but upon its display of *I told you my husband never found out about us*, it made sure to remain alive and sear the words into his brain.

CHAPTER EIGHT

He had hardly a chance to react. When Firas stepped into the hallway, he spotted a circle of people sitting in the living room. Occupying this circle were his parents, his grandfather, Sheikh Mehdi of the corner mosque, and Amo Nasser and Khalto Noura (along with some irreverent tween), who attended the corner mosque every week. A hush swept over the room the instant they all noticed him, in the way it always does when the subject of a conversation suddenly manifests in the flesh. He surveyed the group, pausing as his eyes landed on his mother, who donned the first-class jewelry and frozen smile she always did in religious or religiously-affiliated company.

"There he is!" said Nasser, rising from his chair, which Firas now realized was one of the folding chairs reserved for his party guests. "Happy birthday!"

"Shukran, Amo," he replied. He mimicked his mother's painfully polite smile, then he glanced back at her. It was always difficult to know what she was thinking in the presence of guests. She was on her best behavior then, notably mannered.

"We hear you're throwing a birthday party?" said Noura.

"Inshallah it will be fun."

"Inshallah."

"Perhaps it can also serve as your congratulations party."

"Excuse me?"

"Your boss sent you a text to my phone," his father explained. "He wants you to come in an hour early tomorrow to settle you into the new job."

"Alf mabrouk, Firas!"

"Shukran, Amo," he replied with a grimace. He wanted to message Luis to inform him that his phone was functioning again so that his father wouldn't see more of his messages, but he also knew that the instant he unlocked his phone, his mother's text would reappear.

"How nice. Two parties in one!"

"And I'm happy to hear," began the sheikh, "that alcohol will not be served."

"Sounds like a lame-ass party to me," the tween said, not looking up from his phone.

"Astaghfirullah!" shouted Noura.

"I did initially consider serving alcohol. To accommodate guests of all faiths."

"You're a Muslim first and a host second, Firas."

"Alhamdulillah," said his father.

"I'm a gamer first and a Muslim tenth," the tween said with a snicker.

"Astaghfirullah!" shouted Noura.

Sheikh Mehdi expelled a long, despondent sigh. "Noura, Nasser, parents have a duty to show their children the path to Allah."

The tween raised an eyebrow. "Isn't that technically *your* job?"

"Astaghfirullah!"

"Mama, I get it. I'm blasphemous."

"It takes time," added Firas's mother, whom Firas now confirmed had yet to realize what she'd done.

"Not for you, it seems," replied the sheikh. "Firas is an exemplary young Muslim man. Though I was sad when he started attending a different mosque."

"His new mosque is much closer to his college," his father said apologetically.

Noura's eyebrows climbed slowly up her pimpled forehead. She seemed unsure of how the sheikh wanted her to react to this news. "What's this mosque called, Firas?"

"Masjid Al-Asghar." When Firas claimed he would be switching mosques, he Googled all the ones near his campus, visited each of them on a Friday evening, and picked whichever one was big enough and busy enough for an individual to get lost in the crowd fairly easily. Nobody there would have any recollection of him attending, but nobody would have any recollection of him *not* attending, either. The name "Masjid Al-Asghar" had been on the tip of his tongue for the last four years.

"Now that college is over, I do hope you'll consider coming back to us," the sheikh said.

"Yeah, maybe." At this point, he was ready to shift his gaze away from his mother, whose posture was so perfect he wished to see it topple somehow. But just then she retrieved her phone from her pocket. She never checked her phone in front of company, especially a sheikh. Her brow furrowed. Firas could see she was catching her mistake, and began counting the seconds, likely passing more slowly for her than they were for him, before she realized how profoundly she'd fucked up.

Her posture did topple. Slowly, like the onset of an avalanche. She would have sat all day gaping at that text message if she could have. She would have punished herself until her eyes could no longer see. Not even the reliable drill of his grandfather's slurping roused her.

"This coffee tastes like shit!" the old man bellowed.

"Baba, please!"

"I rather like the coffee," the sheikh interjected. "We appreciate your hospitality, especially on such short notice."

"It is our pleasure to have you in our home."

"It seemed a lovely idea. Especially with our new initiative," said the sheikh.

The mosque was attended mostly by South Asian Muslims, particularly Indians like the sheikh, as well as Black Muslims and a smattering of Turks, Persians, and eastern Europeans. Since few Arabs lived in their neighborhood, Nasser and Noura were the only ones who attended the mosque besides Firas's parents. In recent months, the sheikh set out to lure more Arabs into his congregation, a diversity initiative that struck Firas as very forward-thinking, a chance to show the world how broad the community truly was, how accepting. But Sheikh Mehdi seemed to have trouble bringing in new members and relied on the foursome for help. Nasser and Noura, however, made for feckless recruiters, given their constant need for validation and lingering self-doubt, which meant the burden rested mostly on the Dareers.

"Diversity is always a positive thing, Sheikh Mehdi," Noura told him.

"I wish more of my Indian congregators would agree."

"Then you're as clueless as you look!" bellowed the old man.

"Baba, you're talking to a sheikh . . ."

"Like I give a shit!"

"It's alright," the sheikh told Firas's father, flashing the warm smile of a pacifist. "Tell me, Amo, why do you think me clueless?"

"Waving your dick around like some big shot! You're not building a community. Just tearing a bunch of different ones apart and stitching together the scraps."

"Like Frankenstein's monster!" the tween cheered.

"But my members don't abandon their other communities just by stepping into my mosque."

"That's exactly what they're doing."

"I, for one, think it's a lovely idea," said Nasser.

"Who the fuck is this guy?" The old man seemed to have just noticed Nasser's presence.

"My goal, Amo, is to help Muslims of all backgrounds move past the in-fighting that pervades our community."

"My son has dragged me to your mosque enough Eids to know that that's horseshit." By this point Firas's father had given up on trying to reel the old man in. "Nobody there is learning anything about anybody else. They just end up becoming the same."

"What's wrong with that?" asked Nasser.

"Somebody please shut this guy up."

"What do you think you bring to Allah that an Indian Muslim cannot? Or a Nigerian Muslim? Or an Albanian Muslim?"

"Wait, there are White Muslims? And here I thought Islam couldn't get any lamer."

"Astaghfirullah!"

"You want to know what Palestinian Muslims bring? History. And the drops of shit it still rains on our present. Our country is still occupied. Which means we don't have the option of going back even if we wanted to!"

"What are you looking at?" Firas's father whispered, but there was just enough silence at that moment that everyone's attention diverted to Firas's mother, who was the only person in the room unaware that the question was directed at her. When the silence persisted, she finally heard it. Her head whipped up, her face flushed, her throat quivered.

"W-what?" The question echoed in her ear, and she tucked her phone away. "Would anyone like some more coffee?"

It was then that Firas remembered her entrance into the house that morning. She brushed past him in the kitchen, her eyes fixed on her phone. When she approached him and Maysa in his bedroom, she was checking her phone then, too, more surreptitiously that time. And stepping into the kitchen when he and Mazen were cooking dinner—she was transfixed by her phone again and seemed perturbed by the sight of them. He assumed it was because they'd just heard Jido's comment, but now Firas was beginning to understand.

While she poured coffee into all the near-empty cups, and a few of the near-full ones, the question hung in the air, and she realized she would not succeed in evading it.

"I was just checking the weather for tonight. I don't want rain for the party."

"It's supposed to be nice and warm out tonight," Nasser chimed in, and Firas now joined his grandfather in wanting this man to simply shut the fuck up.

"Would anyone like some more baklawa?"

"Oh no, I couldn't possibly," the sheikh said.

"I'll have one more," said Noura.

"No problem." As his mother served the baklawa with the silver tongs Firas had bought her two Mother's Days ago, he noticed her very discreetly looking in his direction, gauging the expression on his face to see if he knew what she knew.

"Firas," the sheikh asked, "do you know of any Arab Muslims who might want to join the mosque?"

Part of Firas wanted to keep his focus on his mother, but he sensed an opportunity here to test some waters. "I'm not sure, Sheikh. A lot of the Arab Muslims I know are very progressive."

"How do you mean?"

"I don't think they'd be willing to attend a mosque unless it's accepting of *all* groups."

"We are!"

"Not just racial groups."

"What other groups are there?"

Did he dare? He'd spent so much of his time, energy, and even money to prepare for this one crucial night. For him to answer the question now, just before his party was set to begin, seemed like the most spectacular display of self-sabotage he could imagine. And yet, there was something terribly liberating in the idea, like petting an exotic animal the second before it devoured you.

The tween looked up. "Do you have fags and dykes?"

"Astaghfirullah!"

Firas stopped breathing, or lost track of his breathing. His mind rushed to a night five years prior in a restaurant near Midtown, the sort of pasta place whose food could have easily been made at home, and the Dareer family was served by a high-pitched, wildly gesticulating waiter wearing foundation. Suhad, to whom queerness was a punchline, giggled from behind the hand over her mouth, while Mazen, familiar only with the word *gay* but not its real-world manifestation, stared wide-eyed as though he were learning where babies come from. Firas's parents, on the other hand, remained as cordial as they were in any other company. They smiled politely, tipped fairly, and left the evening without saying a word about it. Even as Suhad, on their way back to the car, tried to make a joke at the waiter's expense, her mother immediately shushed her. Queerness was not a thing to be joked about, yet Firas understood that this was not a sign of respect for queer people, but rather a refusal to acknowledge their existence. Queerness was not a thing to be joked about or even hated; no, instead it was a thing to be tolerated. Ambivalence crept through Firas in the face of this tolerance, this particular brand of it that was reserved for the weak-minded and strong-willed, because it made clear that his parents could endure queerness at least in the case where there remained a certain distance from it. The waiter was a random man, inconsequential to the Dareers beyond the two hours it took them to finish their meals. They needn't return to the restaurant, they could flee as far from it as they'd like; indeed that was the last time they ever went there (Firas once suggested going back and received a *no* so curt he was certain that it was not provoked by the mediocre pasta). That was the power his parents possessed. But if queerness got too close, there would be nowhere for them to flee. It would back them into a corner and press its hands against the wall on either side of them. Firas would be diminishing them of their power, narrowing their list of options. Their first choice in the event he came out was deviation. That is what queerness comes down to, in the end. Firas, by speaking and living his truth, was deviating. But while deviations like Suhad's dropping out or Mazen's attempt could prove to be just temporary, Firas's deviation was permanent. Which meant his family was permanently stuck with it and would be forced to deviate with him. The only alternative, as with any creature backed into a corner by a frightening thing, would be to fight it off until only one survives.

His eyes now shifted to his parents, neither of whom was anywhere near the present conversation. His mother had sunk into a daze, and his father was eyeing her curiously.

"We don't accept such things, no," the sheikh answered the tween.

"I'm glad to hear that," said the man who should unequivocally shut the fuck up.

"You don't think you might alienate younger Muslims with that mentality?" Firas asked this question as casually as a drink order.

"Is that why you stopped coming to our mosque?" the sheikh replied, his cup of coffee stopping halfway to his mouth to ensure he heard the answer.

"No, that's not why," Firas replied, which was technically true.

"So why do you suppose others of your generation would be deterred?"

"Why does any generation differ from the last?"

"Differences can be corrected with the right guidance."

"Everyone's the same, I tell you!" the old man bellowed. "Everyone's the same!"

"What do you two think?" Noura asked Firas's parents.

Firas's father caught the question but nothing that preceded it. Embarrassed, he nodded along and offered what seemed a safe enough response: "It's certainly interesting." He turned back to Firas's mother, still in her daze and reenacting in her mind the moment she'd sent her text in the hopes that perhaps there was a world somewhere, anywhere, in which she hadn't just destroyed her own family. She was soon rescued from both the sinking daze and an assault of analytic gazes by a ring at the front door.

Firas's father expected him to answer it, in part because he was already standing and in part because he always relieved his elders of unnecessary exertion when he could. But Firas determined to stay until his mother finally looked him in the eye.

"I'll get it." Firas's father left the room, and while his part of the ensuing conversation was loud enough for everyone to hear, the other part could only be discerned in snippets.

"Hello . . . Can I help you?" his father asked the visitor.

I'm shfkbn of fimeknj kjrsa.

"Oh I see."

Is fgerfjj imrkwl moment?

"Yes, but you're a bit early, aren't you?"

Firas flinched. It was a guest arriving hours before the start time.

Ajfnsan I'm nqez jnskejn sjn party.

"What is this regarding, then?"

Now Firas was *really* panicking. If it wasn't an early guest, it would be an even bigger problem.

Isfknsj qpokem sndjjwre aimjlem. Jkjusa sknaj qpokemw ahbscme rolmnns skjndedw.

"Oh yes, of course."

What on earth was happening?!

Firas twitched with every heavy step that neared. His first guess was an angry neighbor who resented not being invited. Perhaps Mr. Grint, the freckled Canadian who often informed on his neighbors for various infractions, whether it was parking a car on the street at night or biking on the sidewalk. He must have assumed that no one ever deduced it was him, because his smiles never waned, his waves hello never faltered, even as he watched said neighbors enjoying countless festive occasions in—and because of—his absence from them.

His second guess was the vendor who delivered the party favors—gold organza bags containing gourmet soaps with a broken heart motif (so that his pain on this day would be known and remembered, until its pieces melded back together over time)—now coming to inform him that there was some horrible defect and they needed to be recalled. Disease in the goat's milk. Aflatoxins in the coconut oil. Radioactive poisoning that required everything that came into contact with the soaps to be destroyed. Including Firas. Everyone would arrive at the party, wonder where he was, and then dive into the feast he'd made that was so delicious they instantly forgot what brought them there to begin with. *This party was pretty fun!* they'd say on the way out, and care very little that no party favors were given.

It turned out the heavy steps approaching him belonged to someone much, much worse.

"You're not mouthing anything," the husky voice said. "I guess everything is in order?"

He must have been furious to show up at Firas's doorstep and enter his family's home. He must have really wanted to hurt Firas, trip him up inches before the finish line to render the loss even more devastating.

"Who is this young man?" the sheikh asked with delight.

"I'm Kashif. Nice to meet you all."

"Please sit down, young Kashif. Perhaps you can enlighten us about an important issue we're discussing."

"Oh?" He turned to Firas, who was paralyzed from the mouth down. "Actually I came to see Firas about some—"

"I insist, young Kashif, sit!"

As Kashif searched for a seat, Firas recollected his motor skills and discreetly wiped the sweat from his brow.

"Ahmad, get up!" shouted Noura.

"Why me???"

"He's your elder, yalla!"

The tween rose from his chair and threw an over-the-top eye roll in Kashif's direction. Kashif took his seat between Nasser and the old man.

"Tell me, young Kashif, what age are you?" the sheikh began.

"I'm nineteen."

"Are you religious?"

"I'm not." Kashif had long abandoned his Protestantism, and did so rather effortlessly, particularly when he later discovered that Edward Said had done the same.

"Are your parents?"

Firas interrupted: "Kashif isn't Muslim, Sheikh. He was raised in a Christian household, so I think you'd be wasting your time asking him about any mosque-related issues."

"I don't think any discussion of faith is a waste of time."

"Nor do I," Nasser added, waiting, futilely, for a congratulatory smile from the sheikh.

"So tell me, young Kashif, what made you abandon your faith?"

"I would say, Sheikh, that my faith abandoned *me*."

"How?"

He was a Stage 8. Stage 8's never regressed, particularly when they had an ax to grind. This was it. This was how it was going to happen. All of Firas's plans obliterated at the hands of a boy he'd wronged. Perhaps he deserved this. Perhaps it was more than just breaking Kashif's heart. Firas was not as noble as he liked to believe. He suffered in silence, but he also benefited from that silence and as a result stifled the voices of those who had the most to say. And now Kashif would say it. He'd say everything.

"Science."

He glanced at Firas, whose breathing began to steady.

"Ah, you're a scientist!"

"No, but I do appreciate what science teaches us."

"As do I. Almost as much as I appreciate what it can never teach us."

"Sheikh—"

"Don't interrupt him, Firas." Firas turned to his mother, who had suddenly snapped out of her daze. Her tone was not strict, but it held in it a trace of authority. "Go check on Mazen."

Firas stiffened at the direct eye contact his mother was giving him, designed purposely to drive him out of the room. When he went upstairs, he glimpsed Mazen by his closet ironing his suit for the party. He was wearing nothing but his boxers and two ties. Firas barely registered this before heading back down the stairs and re-entering the living room, at which point the conversation between Kashif and Sheikh Mehdi continued precisely where it had left off, as though both parties wanted to ensure that Firas missed not a word of it.

"If you could imagine a scenario, young Kashif, whose details could only be felt or thought, but not studied or proven, could you imagine a God?"

"I don't follow," replied Kashif.

"Where is your family originally from?"

"Palestine."

"Ah, Falasteen! Perfect! Tell me, young Kashif, have you ever been to your homeland?"

"Not yet."

"Do you feel a connection to it?"

"Of course."

"And what is the scientific basis for that connection? As far as you're concerned, Falasteen is merely a concept, one you've seen in pictures, perhaps even in films, but not one that you've touched or smelled. Not one whose atoms graze your own."

"It comes down to simple psychology."

"No, young Kashif. Psychology is *here*," the sheikh said, pointing to his temple. "This connection of yours . . . is *here*," he said, pointing to his chest.

Firas stood in awe. Kashif knew how to get under people's skin twice as deeply as they ever got under his, with the fury of unbridled youth weaponized for a most definitive destruction. So it came as quite a shock to see him being so tamed, so seduced, even for a moment. The sheikh, too, noticed his sudden hold on him and pounced.

"These are only a few of the things I teach at my mosque. Perhaps you might be interested in joining me for a discussion sometime. You can come whenever you like. My door will always be open."

The pitch rang a bit hollow, but the hold had yet to break.

"Kashif?" Firas interrupted.

Kashif turned to him, collected his faculties, and rose from his chair with a polite smile that he dangled before the group like a new toy.

"It was nice meeting you all." He followed Firas up to his room, and as Firas closed the door behind them, it seemed to them both that a kiss might ignite. But too many feelings got in the way and they froze.

"I thought you were supposed to be at a rally today."

"It's a march, actually, and it's not until later."

Firas nodded, as though to hurry the conversation along to the main issue.

"I didn't come here to ruin your day."

"How could you, when your note already did it for you?"

"I'm sorry, okay? It was stupid."

"It was cruel and stupid."

"Cruel and stupid and a shitload of other things. All of which stemmed from love. That's not an excuse, I know—"

"And for you to drag Mazen into it!"

Kashif's head tilted slightly to the side. "What does Mazen have to do with anything?"

Thus Firas knew that the final line in the note—*Perhaps you can move on now*—was not about Mazen's attempt after all. Yet part of him, despite the illogic of it, was set on this interpretation above all others. Even less logical, part of him *wanted* it to be the right interpretation.

"Listen," Kashif continued. "I just wanted you to know that . . ."

"What?"

"I'm rooting for you."

Firas studied his face. It had the markings of sincerity, but his anxiety was now blurring most of everything he saw. "Thanks," he said finally.

"I want you to call me tomorrow."

"Why?"

"To let me know how everything went. Unless . . ." He tilted his head down and raised his eyes and eyebrows.

"You can't stay, Kashif."

"I wouldn't make a peep. I just wanna be here for you. I know exactly what this is like. You and I are in the exact same boat."

How comforting it would be to have someone so unwaveringly on his side. Behind him to watch his back, and before him to lead him through the dark.

"This is something I need to do on my own."

"I get that. I totally get that. It's just . . ."

Firas's eyes hardened. He knew where this was going. He knew the words dancing across Kashif's mind.

"I'm not gonna pussy out."

Kashif chortled, covering his mouth. "That's the first time I ever heard you use the word 'pussy.'"

"I'm trying to communicate in a language you'll understand. So you know how serious I am."

"Well, good. It's long overdue."

"My coming-out party?"

"Your happiness."

The tension in Firas's shoulders melted and he felt the weight of his body for the first time in a while. Not just the physical weight, but the sheer power it carried.

"Burn my letter."

"No," Firas said with a sly smile. "It was exactly what I needed."

Kashif beamed, then casually leaned in and gave him a kiss on the spot just between his cheek and his lips. "Good luck."

As Kashif turned to open the door, a familiar creak sounded from just outside the bedroom. Firas winced at the sight of her in the hall. Kashif, on the other hand, felt absolutely no embarrassment or shame about the incident—not even in the moment it had happened. "Marhaba, Khalto," he said to Maysa with a smile, which must have seemed to her either flippant or utterly daft. Then he sauntered out of the room and down the stairs, his herbal scent chasing after him.

Firas lingered by the foot of his bed, wondering what Maysa's relentless gaze would precede. Likely a sneer or an eye roll or her notorious scowl, something relatively vague to let her disdain nest inside him.

"Party will not help you," she said drily.

Firas recoiled. Before any words could escape his mouth, she trudged back down the hall and out of sight.

Bile snaked up his gullet and into his mouth as though ready to emit a most deafening scream. To think that this woman, this so-called pillar of the community, fancied herself an expert on what would or wouldn't help him! The audacity she possessed was so steadfast, so imperishable, he wished he could banish her from the house for the remainder of her years. She was determined, truly, not to let him release himself, not to let him enjoy the boundless air he'd only heard about in rumors. What worsened her attack was how personal it was. She wasn't seeking to destroy the hard-won confidence of all gay men. Just this one.

He sensed a rant coming on, an internal monologue of Shakespearean heft; then he remembered the lamb over the stove and rushed back down to lower the temperature before the liquid boiled over. After that, he proceeded to assess the first round of lamb shanks, tucked comfortably inside a sextet of Tupperware, by opening one of the containers. He immediately regretted the move, for there was no wall between the kitchen and the living room, so the scent that wafted out whetted everyone's appetite.

"Please, help yourselves," his father told the guests.

"Thank you!" said Nasser and sprung up from his chair.

"Nasser, no! It's for Firas's party," Noura said, restraining him by the arm.

"Oh. Right." He plopped back down.

"I think we should be going," the sheikh said. "We've taken up too much of your time."

"Not at all, Sheikh Mehdi. You're welcome anytime."

Polite smiles bounced from one set of lips to the next. But as the guests reached the door, Firas felt a distinct inclination to exploit another opportunity. "Sheikh?"

"Yes, Firas?"

"I do know of a young Arab couple having some trouble. Do you provide marriage counseling?"

Firas kept his eyes on the sheikh. He didn't need to see his mother's reaction. Nor was he certain he even should.

"Of course! I always appreciate helping young people in love!"

"As long as they're not fags or dykes," the tween added.

Now Firas had no choice but to look at his mother's reaction.

"Excuse me?" she asked, her raised brow letting everyone know that she hadn't been listening, a fact for which Nasser and Noura were very grateful.

"Ignore him," said Nasser. "He's just trying to be provocative."

"Well yeah, I'm bored."

Firas's mother winced, unable to muster even a fake smile.

"Good!" came a voice from the living room, followed by a loudening mechanical thrum. Jido rolled into the corridor and pointed to the tween, who flinched as though the old man's finger had poked him right in the chest. "This is the kind of person your mosque should have."

"What kind is that?" asked Noura, unsure whether she was supposed to feign pride or concern.

"A shit-starter."

"Fuck yeah!"

"Astaghfirullah!"

"My mosque is about communion, Amo, not divisiveness," said the sheikh.

"If it were really about communion, you wouldn't refer to it as '*my* mosque.'"

Firas credited the sheikh for retaining his sagacity around the old man. But part of him suspected he was only able to retain it because he wasn't really listening.

"Have a good night," Firas's father said, opening the door and ushering them out before anything more could come out of the old man's mouth. But before they were out the door, Sheikh Mehdi turned back to Firas.

"Feel free to refer your Arab friends to me. I will mold them just right."

"Astaghfirullah." This time, the exclamation came not from Noura but from the old man, who sank into a daze that no one registered but Firas.

"Well, when Firas gets married," Nasser added, "I hope his marriage will be filled with nothing but joy."

"Inshallah," both his parents said, cuing their son with a glance for the refrain.

"Inshallah I'll have a happy marriage."

"Inshallah I will get to officiate it!"

"Inshallah," his parents responded, another glance in Firas's direction. When the refrain did not come, they leaned forward contentiously. Alas, he was undeterred in his silence.

"Thanks for saying I was badass!" the tween shouted to the old man from the porch.

"That's not what he called you!" hissed Noura, nudging him forward.

Once the door closed behind them, Firas's parents went in separate directions, he to the bathroom, she up the stairs.

Firas stared at his grandfather and wanted so much to ask him another series of questions, only this time not with politeness to fill the time, but with meaning to fill an altogether different void. But the old man rolled himself back into the living room to gaze out the windows, their chiffon-white muntins crisscrossing oppressively along the panes. Jido had his own questions to ask, hoping for the answers to sprout from the Dareers' barren yard.

CHAPTER NINE

T he water was reaching the edge of the tub. He had originally planned for a shower, but the inevitable deconstruction would require more time. Once he ensured the water was at the temperature that always soothed him, he descended into the tub and sighed. He would take a few minutes for himself, he decided. A few minutes to enjoy his amicable divorce from chaos, the self-care that often comforted an entire generation to the chagrin of their overtired parents. The water caressed his skin, moaning to him its wisdom. *Life is rest, Firas. All else is madness.*

Before he proceeded with the deconstruction, he was forced to wonder how his mother's indiscretion began. It must have been the heart attack that prompted it. People change after skirting death. Typically they eventually change back, the fear of the other side no match for the comfortable predictability of this one. Numbness was one of Time's many jagged weapons, wielded methodically against the mind long before its victims even realized they were under attack. But surely a chosen few commit to the change, those whose glimpse of the other side goes far deeper than a flash of images. A correction is made in the lens: a higher f-stop to brighten the corners of the frame, a longer focal length to reduce converging verticals, nary a blur or chromatic aberration. Clarity in its most unadulterated form.

How long had Firas's mother had this enhanced lens?

Her stay at the hospital nearly three years ago lasted an entire week. Her job at the bank provided her and her family with terrific health coverage, and she enjoyed being waited on and pampered, despite the circumstances. In that one week, the rest of the Dareers visited as often as they could. Firas's father, every day; Firas, every other day; Suhad and Mazen on the weekend. But upon her return to the house, where she spent most of the ensuing weeks in bed or, coveting a change of scenery, the peach English roll-arm in the living room, few visits were made by any of them. Appearances were made, certainly, regular check-ins about her physical status, reminders of upcoming appointments, deliveries of meals on her glass-rimmed resin tray, which she thought too fancy for everyday use, although her recuperation was not an everyday situation. But no one in the family sat with her as they had in the hospital. Firas's father was working long hours, Firas and Suhad were buried by their course loads, and Mazen was a helpless child.

Firas proceeded with the deconstruction of his mother's text, beginning with the last segment: *about us*. To whom did *us* refer? As far as Firas had ever known, the word *us* never emerged from his mother's mouth but to describe herself and her husband, or herself and her children, or herself and society. There was no *us* that did not include another Dareer. Yet someone had infiltrated *us*. Stained the word with strangeness, poisoned it with anonymity. He tried to remember how many months it had been before his mother was back to her normal physical state. It must have been three at most, or she would have surely lost her job. Three months without visitors, aside from the sheikh and a handful of congregators who seldom made an impression on her. He remembered one time hurtling past the living room towards the front door and glimpsing Maysa sitting there with her. He heard no dialogue as he tucked his feet into his shoes, no noise beyond a hoarse *Do you need anything?* Could it have been then that she'd had the idea to do it? Could Firas really have been one of the seeds to sprout an extramarital affair?

Then the second segment: *my husband never found out.* The word *never* implied a long time, and was the main reason Firas suspected the idea came during her recuperation. For the most part, his mother appeared as tired as someone in recovery would. She lay there, waiting for the strength to return and wondering what to do in the meantime. Reading the Sunnah to strengthen her mind, strolling across the bedroom to strengthen her body. But what of her soul? That, too, needed recuperation; that, too, was weakened by the scuff of Death. Maysa was certainly not the answer, which meant someone else needed to be.

Firas thought of his cuckolded father and winced. Less out of pity than out of sheer disgust. The man truly had no clue.

Even as his mother kept checking her phone in front of their sheikh(!), his father seemed genuinely bewildered and willing to believe she was merely checking *the weather report*. Perhaps that obliviousness was the problem. That a man could be so ignorant about his own wife seemed, in a way, an even bigger marital tort than the adultery. It was exemplary of a need some spouses had to see only the best in one another, an expectation that no misdeeds be committed, a right they felt they'd earned simply by saying *I do*; eventually the complexity of their partner, taken for granted after one too many passionless nights, bubbles to the surface and explodes. This obliviousness reminded Firas of Tyrese. He had never cheated on Tyrese, but it was remarkable how easily he could have. How easily he could have withheld from him, how easily he was *already* withholding from him. Tyrese never could see through the veil, no matter how thinly Firas wore it. One time after making love in Tyrese's bed, Firas received a barrage of text messages from Kashif asking him to meet. They hadn't seen each other since the New Year's party, every pixel of Firas's memory still in painfully sharp focus. The texts displayed the spelling and grammatical errors of unsteady fingers, and their content was bold even for Kashif; he was drunk-texting him at three o'clock in the morning—a booty call. When Tyrese, awoken by the repeated dings, asked who was texting, Firas told him it was his mother, whom he'd forgotten to lie to about spending the night at a study partner's house given that he had a final exam the next morning. When the dings continued, Tyrese asked what his mother wanted now, to which Firas replied she was just wishing him luck on the exam. There were seven dings between the first lie and the second. Firas added that his mother was also texting him a list of things to purchase from the halal butcher shop because they had guests coming over the next night. In a panic, he turned off his phone without texting back. The following morning, Tyrese said that Firas had made him crave halal food all night, then he kissed him and jokingly wished him luck on his "exam." And that was it. An overbearing mother needing him to purchase halal meat was a believable spin on fourteen successive texts at three o'clock in the morning. No, Firas had never cheated on Tyrese, but this blithe naïveté almost made him want to. In fact, it almost made him hate Tyrese. The way he laughed off his marriage proposal that morning, so sure it was some sort of gag. Firas absolutely despised that laugh. A piercing cachinnation, a mutation of something pure and hearty shamelessly overstaying its welcome each time it made an entrance. Had Tyrese really known him, known him in the way that only love could make one know somebody, he would have recognized the proposal as the rare moment in which the veil was lifted. The even rarer moment that the face behind it was just as it was in childhood: gentle, chaste, eager for whatever came next. Firas was giving himself to another person wholly and bravely. And he was laughed at. No words preceded the laughter, no words followed it. Tyrese simply checked his phone, made his bed, went about his business. The message was clear, the blow cataclysmic. Tyrese rejected not merely Firas's marriage proposal; he rejected Firas. The *real* Firas, not whatever he'd been pretending to be all this time. The Firas that nobody had ever been graced with.

Firas had left his apartment without saying anything, the architecture conference badge grasped loosely in his hand. He should have known Tyrese was not the right man for him.

The fact that he never even *asked* if he could come to his birthday party was itself a troubling sign. If he had really loved Firas, he would have wanted to be there to support him, to nurse him back to health, for surely his mind and heart would ail. Tyrese was always sensitive to Firas's feelings, but without any nerve to help resolve those feelings through actions, what precisely was the point of him? What was the point of their relationship? A star and his spectator, the latter chiming in with critiques about the show but always leaving out the part of how well the role was played. This was not a relationship. This was, Firas now suspected, what his mother and father had.

He moved on to the first segment: *I told you*. This referenced their past; more specifically, it referenced a past conversation between the familiar half of *us* and the unfamiliar half of *us*. The words denoted a hint of frustration—*I ALREADY FUCKING TOLD YOU!*—for she now had to *remind* this other half of something she didn't want to have to *keep* reminding him of. This other half was a terrible listener, never hearing his mother's words, her assurances of which, in her fragile physical state, she already had so few left to spare. Or if he was listening, he refused to believe her, insinuating that her assurances were falsehoods, calling her a dirty rotten liar, accusing her of revealing their affair to the one person in the world she promised never to reveal it to. He gaslit her into thinking she really *had* revealed the affair to her husband, forcing her fragile mind to trace back every single step for the past three years to see if it was true and she simply forgot. Surely this other half knew what she'd done better than she herself had known it, surely he was the more trustworthy of the two, the smart, sensible buck to the feeble, helpless doe. This other half was a gaslighting, misogynistic, sociopathic CREEP!

But it may have been concern. This other half might have been terrified that word had circulated somehow and was now desperate to control the damage. Terrified that his wife would discover his infidelity and desperate to remain good and true in the eyes of his children, who, in the late-night hour at which their mother dragged them into her minivan and towards a distant motel, would cry out weak and weary for their Baba.

Baba.

Firas assumed this other half was Arab. He had no reason to assume he was; he simply had trouble picturing his mother with a man of a different race. Then again, she had no Arab friends, aside from Noura and Nasser. Only Noura, really, for Arab couples of that generation could only ever be friends with the partner of their own gender, mere awkward acquaintances with the other. And Noura wasn't even a close friend, for they had little in common beyond their regular attendance at the mosque and matching hairstyles—wavy, medium-length, with wispy bangs—which his mother suspected Noura had deliberately copied just to outshine her. He recalled when the Dareers first moved to Dearborn. In their old apartment, they were surrounded by Arabs, Palestinians in particular. All of them flashing warm smiles, extending warm invitations, baking warm knafeh whose tranquilizing smell hovered in the crisp night air of their neighborhood. The sense of community thrived there, each neighbor sharing with one another what they could not share with others: language, mannerisms, tastes, ideals, beliefs, goals, history, identity. Whatever differences existed in the crevices of these similarities were negligible as far as they were all concerned. The Palestinian cause in particular held meaning for everyone, the glue that bound together this elaborate support system. His parents initially accepted all these shared traits. Then they didn't. Then they moved.

The Dareers didn't hate that they were Palestinian, nor did they ever hide it. It was simply irrelevant. The equivalent of what color their eyes were or which shoes they wore to the grocery store. When Firas first met Kashif, the latter regularly asked him about his time in Gaza, what it was like living under occupation, what did he do on a day-to-day basis, did he ever feel angry or scared. And Firas disappointed him each time by claiming he didn't remember much. He did remember certain things, of course—groves whose lemons hung just out of his reach, congested alleyways he used as shortcuts, his family friend's irrigation tank that doubled as a swimming pool in the summer, the handcrafted ceramic plates in the cragged hands of potters who knew how to haggle, and the swirling rumors of an "*Indian pendant* state" that eventually fell silent. But none of these memories would have satisfied Kashif, who was looking for something more significant, something along the lines of Firas witnessing his grandmother's murder at the hands of an Israeli soldier. Something that would further validate his anger and his hunger for righteousness. When he realized that Firas would not be the one to satisfy these needs, he finally stopped asking.

As for the Second Intifada, Kashif figured if Firas could hardly remember the happy or even ordinary moments of his life in Gaza, then he would likely not remember the more traumatic events a child was bound to suppress. Firas did not, however, suppress anything. He remembered the Intifada quite well, at least the part he was there for. But each memory was muddled by the fog of childhood. Friends of his parents showed up at the house, never to be seen again. "They went to Japan to preach the word of Allah," his father told him with a brave smile. Regular trips to Jerusalem were canceled. "We have already seen it, we must let others have a turn," his mother explained with frightening zeal. Airplanes no longer shimmered among the stars over their house. "The airport is being renovated," his father whispered as he wiped the sweat from his brow. The rest was cacophony—wailing car horns, raspy plane engines, thunderous shakes of the ground, the twang of bullets, and squeals cut short before they could echo—all buried beneath the nasheed his parents sang to their children, usually a cappella and sometimes with an oud.

He also remembered much of what preceded the Intifada. The stationing of Israeli soldiers in venerable neighborhoods; Gazans stumbling home under a bleak sky to meet curfew; weddings and funerals interrupted by arrests; bulldozers demolishing homes older than the state that sent them; the Hebrew language stretching its shadow across new settlements; raucous protests he only caught in peeks through his bedroom window; friends who were in school one day and became urban legends the next. But the Dareers endured all this—at least until the day Firas's Teta was shot. The first Dareer to succumb to Israeli terror since the Nakba; before then, the family had lived under a cloud of dread that was waiting for the right moment to rain its storm onto their lives. They knew they were not lucky or special; they knew that if Fate were singling them out from the brutality of occupation and colonialism, it was for a more severe punishment than any other Gazan in their camp had ever suffered. Firas couldn't remember any of the details surrounding his Teta's murder, nor could he remember how exactly his family had managed to flee after the Israel-Gaza barrier was rebuilt with an added buffer zone and new high-tech observation posts. But he could not legitimately claim to be traumatized. All of that was irrelevant to him now, as much so as the nasty English teacher who once called him an imbecile in front of the entire class after Firas noted his teacher's confusion of *its* with *it's*. Now he didn't even live near Palestinian-*Americans*. Like his mother, he had no real Arab friends, besides Kashif, and even that seemed destined to evolve into something more.

He was never quite sure what kept drawing him to Kashif, given how often he unnerved him. Firas would convince himself it was the sex—Kashif was the greatest lover he'd ever had. The fact that he could make Firas feel so good at such a young age foreshadowed a sex life of icons. Kashif would grow up to become everyone's greatest. His secret was in his utter lack of technique. There were lovers with technique who were good, some who were great, and some who were awful; but those who had no technique at all were almost always the worst. They made such a mess of things: hands that squeezed the chest too tightly, teeth that grazed the shaft too sharply, thrusts that were either felt too hard or not at all, and an assault of pecks forgotten just as quickly as they were delivered. When these lovers bottomed in reverse-cowboy position, Firas had the added responsibility of making sure they didn't lose their balance and tumble off the bed. At times he was forced to intervene, offer instructions as a teacher to a student he knew would never pass the course. But with Kashif, technique simply would not do. He made love with abandon, the sweat blasting off his hair, cascading down his chest, igniting a bright light directly below it that you soon discovered was your own body, his sweat pooling around your navel and glistening onto his reddened face, accentuating his velvet skin, his head jittering down, down, down until his lips brushed against yours so faintly it tickled. His movements were chaotic; he never thought about what he had to do, relying solely on instinct, an instinct that was never wrong because of how much faith he always put in it. And he was never passive in bed; even when he bottomed in missionary, his hands developed minds of their own and they stroked, pinched, squeezed, rubbed, scratched, gauging the resulting moan or gasp to know just how much further he could push without falling over the edge. Why couldn't Tyrese make love in that manner? Why didn't Tyrese ever urge him to come out of the closet? For a long while, Firas thought this a good thing, a relief. But now he saw it as a way of enabling the fundamental lie of his life. Was Tyrese so indifferent as to whether Firas lived a life of honesty? Sometimes it seemed as though he only cared so he could get his roommate Karine to stop lecturing him. He didn't love Firas. People in love don't give conference badges as birthday presents. Even though Tyrese had said to him the words, he could no longer believe them. Yet even though Kashif had never said the words, Firas knew the love was there. It was there when he called Firas a *pussy*. It was there in all the times they fucked in not-so-private places. It was there when he visited the Dareer house to apologize for his vicious letter, for such a reckless act could have only come out of a misguided sense of honor. The fire that burned so hot had by then dwindled, and its ashes bore the bitter taste of regret. All Kashif really needed was someone to tame the fire before it burned anyone else. How perfect he would be with the right partner.

Firas returned to the last segment of the text. Scanning his memory for all the suspects who might fit the bill of his mother's right partner. Outside of mosque, he'd only ever known eleven men in America who factored regularly into her life. The first four were her husband, her father-in-law, and her sons. The fifth was the manager at her bank, who was in his mid-sixties and looked in his late seventies. The sixth was an Islamophobic teller. The seventh and eighth were Mazen's teachers, whose hygiene she always wrestled with. The ninth was her former cardiologist, whom she stopped seeing when she discovered he was gay. The tenth was Mr. Grint, the whiny neighbor whose personality disorder his mother might have forgiven were it not for her intense dislike of freckles.

That left the only person Firas was really hoping it wouldn't be.

He could hardly blame Mazen, who didn't conjure a meeting between them out of will but had it forced upon him by circumstance. Yes, he conjured the circumstance, but even so, he had no say in whom he got his treatment from. In fact, it was his mother who had chosen. Mazen had little interest in choosing for himself, nor any interest in the process by which the choice was made (it was mentioned in passing one day that his mother had found stellar reviews on "a website, I forget the name"). But even then, he couldn't blame Mazen for the indifference that enabled his mother to meet this accomplished psychiatrist with three prestigious degrees from three prestigious colleges. And he couldn't blame Mazen for his father's obliviousness, particularly given that his father was in the room with the familiar half of *us* and the unfamiliar half of *us* throughout almost every single session of the last two years. Nor could he be blamed that a twenty-two-year psychiatric veteran ("Smallah! Twenty-two years!" his father would say with only a hint of jealousy) would violate the professional ethics that earned him those stellar reviews to begin with. There was plenty of blame to go around, but certainly none could be placed on poor Mazen.

Firas had never met Dr. Al-Khatib. He closed his eyes and tried to imagine his face. He pictured something long and thin, glasses with round, oversized lenses, thin lips that accentuated the length of his grin, which he no doubt flashed at his mother whenever his father's back was turned. A sense of his demeanor was even more vague. Was he soft-spoken? Or did he ever raise his voice? Did he dress formally or casually? Did he shake his patients' hands goodbye or merely wave on their way out the door? And how often did he name-drop those prestigious colleges he attended? Firas had no way of knowing, but he was certain that Dr. Al-Khatib was significantly different from his father. The affair would have made no sense otherwise. Why cheat with a slight variation on what you already had? What could his mother possibly benefit from such an affair that would compensate for the damage inflicted upon her family?

There was one trait he was quite certain of. As far as Firas's little brother was concerned, Dr. Al-Khatib was fairly ineffectual. In the two years since Mazen's sessions began, he had not gotten any better. Just more numb. The Zoloft came in smaller doses at first, in combination with hour-long talks twice a week (again, thanks to his mother's terrific health coverage). Throughout these talks, Dr. Al-Khatib learned a great deal about Mazen, half from Mazen himself and half from his parents, boasting about their son to stave off any fingers Dr. Al-Khatib may have pointed in their direction. He discovered that Mazen was, at the time of his attempt, what most adolescents strived to be: handsome and popular, as he'd been since preschool. He played on the basketball team, he was part of a video game club, and he was so gregarious that a third of the student body knew him well enough to come over to the house on occasion simply to hang out. He also performed fairly well academically, obtaining mostly B's and ripe for a promising college education. Most significantly, he often had a girlfriend, a fact Dr. Al-Khatib only learned when he eventually insisted on speaking to Mazen without his parents in the room. He learned, also, that Mazen had lost his virginity five months prior to the attempt. It was a feat that garnered him the greasy high-fives of his peers and the curious envy of his older brother who heard the entire event (and all the repeat occurrences) from the upstairs corridor on the occasions their parents were out for the day. All that considered, Mazen truly had it made.

The sessions, perhaps inevitably, turned to Palestine. Mazen was still only two years old when they fled. And having birthed him mere weeks before the Second Intifada, a mistake for which she often cursed herself, his mother guarded him with the ferocity of a bear, taking him out no farther than their own front yard, and even then, just briefly. On any trip to the grocery store, she left him with her mother-in-law. Their next-door neighbor was a pediatrician, and thus the majority of his medical checks were conducted at home, at least until the neighbor was detained and tortured by the IDF for his distant relation to a militant. So the possibility that Mazen was harboring some sort of deep-seated trauma seemed unlikely, and was officially ruled out in a session of hypnotherapy. His parents had reluctantly agreed to the tactic, growing increasingly wary of a second attempt. When all Mazen revealed in his state of entrancement was that he wanted to go back home because that is where his family was, Dr. Al-Khatib suggested that Mazen be homeschooled. Both his parents were working full-time then, which left no one but their recent college dropout daughter, whom neither parent entrusted with the task. The only other solution was increasing the dosage. From then on, Mazen drifted. His suicidal ideation vanished, but so had every other part of him: he stopped having friends over, stopped playing basketball, stopped getting B's, stopped having sex. He had become a shell with a Band-Aid over the crack where Death had struck its blow. Firas suggested to his parents that they take him to a different psychiatrist, but they dismissed the idea, figuring a shell was better than a corpse.

But in fact, they hadn't dismissed the idea. His mother had, and his father simply went along. And now it became clear to Firas exactly why that was. His mother initially opposed the idea of a psychiatrist altogether; his father did, too, albeit less fervently. Psychiatry was such a foreign concept to them. A Western solution to an Eastern problem, a square peg in a star-and-crescent hole. But Mazen was not like Firas or Suhad; he was wholly American. So they agreed to it, and ultimately got what they wanted all along, even if their guilt stopped them from admitting it: drugs that held the problem at bay and rendered their lives more convenient.

It rendered Firas's life more convenient, too. Granted, he occasionally suffered pounding headaches for which he was denied the cure (Mazen's attempt involved the bottle of ibuprofen in their shared bathroom, and no bottles had been allowed in the house since), but aside from that, and the sporadic watch duty, he hardly ever thought about Mazen's problem at all. The ever-elusive answer to the ultimate question: *why?* There were many *whys* that plagued Firas, that burrowed under his skin and hatched the dread that sometimes drove him mad. Why was he born gay in a conservative Muslim family? Why were all his past employers so painfully unqualified? Why did his condom break with the one lover who had chlamydia? If he spent any time trying to answer these questions, he would hardly get anything done. But on this day, the question was not so easy to dismiss. For the longest time, Mazen's attempt struck him as completely nonsensical. There were no problems in Mazen's life as far as his family and school were concerned. Certainly not compared to anyone else his age. In fact, apart from the birthday party he'd canceled the month before his attempt, Mazen seemed as fine as he'd been throughout his entire life. And it was this, the utter lack of logic, that warded Firas off the question for so long.

But now he was forced to think about it. He didn't want to be thinking about it; he wanted to focus on all the unfinished tasks for his party. *Parties.* Two of them for certain, a third one pending. The celebration of his entry into the world and the celebration of his ascent up the ladder; ideally, a third celebration would arise after his announcement. Yet his familial troubles clung to mind. His mother's affair especially, not merely clinging to his mind but captivating it. And it captivated him today more than ever, because he, too, was considering having one.

Firas thought about something Tyrese had mentioned that morning: the concept of looking at the wrong map. Now he compared his mother's map to his own, determining whether he could or should go the same route she had. There must have been some appeal in an affair; she must have gained something from it that she'd been missing all those years, something driving her to return to Dr. Al-Khatib, even seeing him that very morning. And she hadn't been caught in the years since it happened, so no consequences emerged to substantially alter her life.

There were quite a few differences, however. For instance, Firas and Tyrese had been together only a few months, and despite the depth of his affection for Tyrese at the moment of his proposal, the brevity of their relationship made Tyrese's decisive rejection cut much less deeply. Moreover, Firas actually knew the man he would have his affair with, knew him even better than the man he was dating. He was also known by him better than by the man he was dating. He wasn't a stranger found on some website who had known nothing about him beyond what a suicidal family member told him in private. And his relationship with Tyrese, while important to him, had thus far been lived mostly in the shadows, which meant, for better or for worse, he could end things relatively easily. His mother, on the other hand, had everything to lose. She and his father had built a life together, and she risked destroying it simply because of a few blemishes.

To be fair, there may have been more than a few blemishes. None of the Dareers could deny that the family had grown apart since arriving in America. They were forced to navigate the country's intricacies only to find the space too narrow to pass through all together. Of course they were always there for one another: they never failed to show up for important occasions; they came to one another's rescue in moments of emergency; they even ate dinner together at the kitchen table almost every night. When mentioning these facts to Davida, the high-functioning stoner who interned at his firm, and citing specific examples (the entire family attending Firas's graduation; Suhad doing all the house chores when Firas and her parents were too tired; Firas taking an overcrowded bus to Mazen's school to deliver the lunch he forgot), Davida responded with a fervent nod: "That's dope. Sounds like you have the perfect family."

That was precisely it. It *sounded* like the Dareer family was perfect. Most people who met them were very impressed by what they saw. But this ostensible perfection was not deliberate; in no way were they attempting to deceive anyone. The Dareers understood full well that all the things they did for one another were important. They knew it was important to ensure the children did their homework, ate their vegetables, and occasionally had fun. They knew it was important to spoil them a little, but also to enforce discipline. They knew it was important to sacrifice much of their time, energy, and money for their children's well-being and growth. And the children knew their share, too. They knew they had to respect their elders. They knew they had to work hard to succeed. They knew they had much in this world to be grateful for.

But they all knew these things in the same way a lab technician knows to store compressed gas cylinders in the upright position. It was one long family checklist monitored regularly to ensure no boxes were left blank.

Throughout their dinners, Firas's parents always asked the appropriate questions: *How was school today? Is your stomach feeling better? Have you heard back from Wayne State?* And the children answered with the appropriate responses: *Fine. Yes. Not yet.* Once the essentials were covered, dinner was eaten in silence broken only by intervals of *Can you pass the labneh/ zaatar/zeit zaytoon?* For years, Firas's father drove him to the museum, but he never went inside with him to see the exhibits; instead he dropped him off and picked him up an hour and a half later. Firas's mother brought him to his soccer games, but she never actually watched the games; instead she sat on the sidelines, perusing furniture catalogues. They were always there, but they were never quite *there*. Something was amiss in the way the Dareers interacted with one another, and until today it had never occurred to Firas to wonder what.

As he compared his mother's map to his own, he began to question whether she loved Dr. Al-Khatib. He questioned whether the only reason she had ended the affair (he assumed it was over based on the verb tense of her text: *never found out*) was merely because she was supposed to. Because nowhere on that lengthy checklist did it say *Fuck my suicidal son's shrink.* She hadn't been acting immorally; she had been acting discourteously. But if she was once in love with Dr. Al-Khatib, if she was *still* in love with him, then perhaps her map didn't differ from Firas's in any way that mattered. Perhaps as long as the affair was driven by love, then it was right, it was purer and truer than anything a certificate or ring could mean. Firas loved Kashif. Kashif was his first great love, and he stood a chance at being his last. Dr. Al-Khatib was not his mother's first love, he knew this. Throughout his childhood, he had caught enough furtive glances and gentle strokes of pinky fingers to know his parents once harbored deep affection for each other. But amidst the impersonal yet incrementally expensive anniversary presents and the kisses doled out, even in private, chastely on the cheek, their affection had faded, and seemed unlikely to ever be rekindled. Yet if at least one of his parents could find a way to rekindle that feeling with someone who might become their last love, he could understand it, he could champion it. Suddenly Firas found himself actually rooting for his mother's affair, praying that at the end of her map lay a marriage bed in which she smiled and blushed, and often.

Somehow, though, he could see no smile at the end of his own map. Studying all the roads available to him, Firas noticed that at the end of each one stood something strange. No, not something. *Someone.* Someone distinct despite the blur over their face. He could deduce who it was from the bag of chocolate chips in his hand and the suave tan suit on his back. What he couldn't deduce was what on earth he was doing there. Of all the people who had made a seminal impact on Firas Dareer's life, his little brother didn't even factor into the top ten. He loved him, no doubt, just as he loved Suhad and his parents, who all, in turn, loved him. But the love, like any other aspect of their relationship, was born out of a sense of duty. How long was it now, since any of them had actually spoken the words? How long since it ceased to matter to them? He'd been saying it to Tyrese for the past several weeks, and almost all of his friends had been on the receiving end of the phrase, even after instances in which they were too embarrassed to say it back. The only reason he had never said it to Kashif was because he knew it might further complicate matters between them; but were that not the case he would not have hesitated. He would not have been able even to stifle it had he wanted to. But with his family, it was different. His love was mechanical, pieced together with scraps and churning automatically without him being able to stop it or willing to change it, for the mechanism was functioning well enough and why fix something that isn't broken?

It would not have surprised him, then, if his mother's affair wasn't sexual. It was likely that she cheated emotionally, mentally, spiritually, but never with her body, which she deemed too priceless to share, too human to venerate. Her type of cheating was worse, in Firas's view. She cheated in the way it counted most: her feelings were Dr. Al-Khatib's feelings, her thoughts were his thoughts, her soul was his soul. She revealed herself to him in the way his patients did; but in this case, he revealed himself right back. And they liked what they saw. They liked it enough to understand how fragile it was, how delicately it needed to be held to prevent the inherent crack from forking and spreading across this precious thing she was sure she'd lost forever. Firas needed to know this man, he needed to *see* this man. He had to, or he'd be left in the same dark shrouding as his father, and he couldn't bear the dark any longer, he just couldn't!

He reached for his phone, which he'd laid on the aquamarine bathmat for fear of dropping it into the water. Scrolling through, he found several new text messages, realizing now that the soup had damaged the speakers on his phone, so he could not hear the ding. But first things first. He Googled *dr. al-khatib*, finding over a dozen listings. He narrowed the search: *dr. al-khatib detroit*. Now just under ten. Another search: *dr. al-khatib detroit psychiatrist*.

And there he was. The first and only relevant image that appeared in the results was the portrait on his website. In it he had a gray suit and an effortless smile, both granting him an air of eminence they likely wouldn't on most men. Dr. Al-Khatib's face attracted Firas, more in what it promised than in what it offered. Bulbous cheeks against an aquiline nose, long lashes and unkempt eyebrows obscuring the asymmetry of his eyes, and a single tooth on the left side of his mouth protruding ever so slightly from an otherwise perfect set. A face with contradictions and character, it invited you to explore the brilliant mind behind it and taking no offense if you declined. His father was much more handsome, but so were a lot of men whose faces invited one to a cup of coffee and a tepid kiss goodnight. The more Firas stared at Dr. Al-Khatib's face, the less his father seemed entitled to his mother's love.

Not long after Firas's father lost his job, his mother seemed to question things in ways she never had before. His father spent all his time searching for another management position, refusing to climb back down the ladder, but when it seemed as though he wouldn't find one that offered the hours and salary he required, he spent most of his time in the den, working on a screenplay based on a science-fiction concept he concocted with a friend who gave him his blessing to write it alone. When they were by themselves, Firas's mother would ask his father for news about the job search, but he always found a way to slip out of the room before she could get a satisfactory answer. At dinner, his parents reserved all the standard check-ins for the children, but when his mother became desperate, she asked his father about the job search right then and there, figuring he would have a tougher time avoiding the question if his children served as an audience. But he didn't answer even then. He simply sat there, seething. His mother regretted the move, but the damage had been done; he'd even stopped working on his screenplay, instead only applying for management positions whose hours and salary fit his criteria but then always finding some caveat that made it unfeasible (location too far, boss too arrogant, building too noisy). Firas's mother saw an opportunity to follow through with Dr. Al-Khatib's idea of homeschooling Mazen, given that his father was now at home nearly all the time, hardly even going out to buy groceries. But his father refused, insisting that Mazen was doing just fine, in order to hide the fact that he was too impotent to offer anything to anybody. More than that, he hated the idea of this man, with his impressive degrees and his prestigious job, devising a plan to help his son that he should have been able to devise on his own. Firas's mother, too, must have noticed this contrast between them.

This contrast, however, grew more alienating upon his father's increased devoutness. Part of his purification involved a change in appearance. He grew out his beard, long, dark, and thick, and donned modest attire in the form of a red checkered ghutra upon his head and a white thawb upon his body kept always above the ankles. He wore this whenever he went out and often when he was at home. Everyone thought the look suited him, physically as much as spiritually. Everyone, except his wife. Although his new look certainly made him more attractive, even as his regular bouts of fasting caused several of his thawbs to fit loosely, she found herself barely able to look at him. She, too, was a devout Muslim, but could relate only to his practice and not to the extent of it. Somehow seeing him outpace her in their journey towards the divine felt unnatural to her, unreasonable even, for she had always felt that men were inherently less virtuous than women. Yet here was one who was becoming closer to Allah just as she herself was drifting towards a devil with beetling brows. She convinced herself that there was something sinister in this change, an air of ostentatiousness, a desperate need to impress the world at a time when he had nothing else to impress with. If she looked more closely at her husband, however, she may have realized that she was only partly right, for there was indeed a newfound godliness in him. But there was also panic. So panicked was he that the resulting distance between them benefited him just as much as it did her: her religious inferiority would not drag him down to even lower depths, and his religious superiority would not worsen her guilt.

There was a silver lining to this whole situation. Firas hated himself for thinking of it, for spotting it so quickly and so easily. But he couldn't deny that this revelation gave him a tactical advantage. His mother no longer had the option of chastising him. She could no longer preach to him the word of Allah (her interpretation of it, at any rate), nor could she claim to be any sort of moral authority. She had no grounds to expel him from the house, denounce him as a pervert, disown him as her son. Firas shuddered at the possibility that perhaps now his mother might even *empathize* with his struggle. She might see a bit of herself in him as he now began to see himself in her. And when his father raged at his news, she could tame him, or try to, and all would eventually be well.

He checked the texts he'd received. One was from Bethany, the single mother from the cooking class he took last winter, which she'd joined to escape her children: *How much food you serving? This girl can eat! See you soon :)*. One from his former co-worker Adaku, a Nigerian expatriate who could find the good in every tribulation: *Long day at work. Your party will be oxygen!* One from Mr. Lindstrom, the neighbor who replaced Mrs. Tullinson next door and sported a dad bod despite having no children: *Should I bring something? I feel like I should bring something.* Firas's heart should have burst at these covert expressions of love and support, these titanic reminders that he was not alone, and perhaps never would be. It was more than many other queer people got. But it was also much less than Mazen had once gotten, back in his golden days.

Mazen. Firas couldn't help thinking about Mazen.

Mr. Popular, Mr. Perfect, Mr. Nice Guy, Mr. Right.

Why did all roads lead to Mazen? What could even be said about him at this point besides the fact that he existed? Or used to exist, now hovering like some ghost haunting a household whose members can't seem to accept that he died long, long ago. Surely there was more to his existence for him to appear at the end of so many roads on his brother's map and obstruct each one without sway.

Firas remembered finding Mazen in his room upstairs, the last room on the left, which he never entered except to call on his brother for dinner, typically stepping in no farther than an inch or two beyond the threshold. His skin was pale but not white, his body lifeless but not dead. Firas didn't dare ask him why he did it. Theories spattered across his mind, until eventually he settled comfortably on the one involving statistical data on suicide rates, which, according to the Centers for Disease Control and Prevention, had risen among males aged ten to fourteen a staggering thirty-seven percent in just fifteen years. Suicide was in the air, even for fourteen-year-old boys. Nothing particularly unusual about it, nothing worth the risk of triggering another attempt by asking questions. Firas was perfectly satisfied with the bow with which he'd tied up the matter.

Perfectly satisfied . . .

Nothing unusual . . .

In the air . . .

Firas closed his eyes. Bathwater that rippled upon his entry began to slither briskly over his skin, then through it, peeling layers of his being with the fervor of rapacious claws of unfed critters, siphoning his air, numbing his senses, and it occurred to him suddenly that pain, the pain that existed only and ubiquitously above the water, would waver along the cracked rim of the tub and up the grimy walls until it reached the skylight and evaporated as a drop of rain before it crashes into the merciless cement of a July afternoon. If not, the pain would disappear in the waking moment from which the boulder of airlessness whirs off his shoulders, a feather in the face of a bright new dawn of tangerine that cradles his eyes open for a view of a world only he could know, for he created it, and conquered it, and banished pain from it before its cruel, inevitable return to its home. And he arose at the sound of gargled, heavenly sirens.

"Are you gonna be much longer in there?" shouted his sister through the door.

"The guests will arrive soon," added his mother.

He propped himself up, the whoosh of water dizzying him, then dried himself off and stepped out of the tub. As he began to respond to his texts, a slew of new ones emerged. All of them asking for the start time, the address, the dress code, all the information he had already disclosed in those beautiful handcrafted invitations that took hours to assemble and mere seconds to read. Why oh why couldn't people acknowledge and respect the meticulous effort he had put into his party? Why did everyone have to treat this day like it was any other? Was everybody in his life really so unbelievably DENSE?!!

"Firaaaaaaaaas?" His sister again, this time adding four consecutive raps on the door.

"Almost done," he told her. He responded to each text, suppressing anything that could be interpreted as passive-aggression. Then he breathed. So immersed in his breathing he was mouthing the words *In . . . Out . . . In . . . Out*. That was the only way he could do it. That was the only way he could keep himself going.

CHAPTER TEN

The bacon had burned. He'd left it on the stove three minutes too long, and now a pan full of flat ebony squares lay before him. He hadn't yet added the bread, but though regular croutons would have gone well enough with the baby leeks, they did not serve the goal the turkey bacon was meant to.

In those three minutes that slipped away from him, Firas had been attending to his grandfather.

"Jido, I need to get you back into your wheelchair," he pled, his hand gloved with latex.

"Don't bother! I want to die on this toilet."

"But I have *guests* coming over."

"There's another fucking bathroom, isn't there?"

There was, but Firas's mother never allowed guests to use the upstairs bathroom. Even Sheikh Mehdi, bladder full from two cups of Turkish coffee, was once required to wait ten minutes.

"I promise I will put you right back here after my party's over. Sound good?"

"No!"

"How about I carry you to the upstairs bathroom instead and you can sit there? It's much more comfortable and it smells like lavender."

"Lavender is for dickheads!"

Before the negotiation could proceed any further, the blare of the smoke alarm in the kitchen snapped Firas's hunched back upright and he dashed straight over to it. Alas, the damage had been done. Also, the shit-stained latex glove was still on his hand.

"Please tell me that's not the glove you've been prepping the food with."

He glared at Suhad, who, to her credit, dazzled in her glam-rock outfit: vinyl leggings and a silver-sequined blazer over a Runaways tee cut just high enough to provoke little more than an eye roll from their parents. He tossed the glove in the garbage can, and as he grabbed the frying pan to empty the grease into the sink, he heard his mother moan.

"Is that bacon in my house?"

"Yes, but—"

"Tistahal! That is what you get when you dishonor your faith."

"It's just turkey bacon, Mama," he said through gritted teeth.

"Where is your grandfather?"

"Still on the toilet."

"Well I can't lift him myself, and your father is showering, so when Jido finishes—"

"I know, Mama, I know." He tossed the burnt bacon squares into the garbage and carried the garbage bag into the bin in the garage. When he returned to the kitchen, smoke still billowed in the air. He washed the soot out of the pan and set to making the baconless croutons.

"So I know you said I couldn't bring anyone," his sister began, and Firas immediately tuned her out.

"Sorry but no," he said once her lips stopped moving, knowing that whatever she just requested would be to his detriment.

"Maysa, can you make sure there's no more bacon in this house?" his mother shouted down the corridor.

"Mama, that was turkey bacon and—"

"Well maybe you grabbed the wrong kind by mistake. It doesn't hurt to double-check."

"Right, but it all burned so—"

"I begin search now," Maysa said sternly, and rummaged through the fridge, bumping her sharp elbows against the mousse cups.

"Be careful not to spill anything!"

"I must search good."

"Can we at least play one of his songs?" Suhad asked.

"What? Whose songs?"

"DJ Shiv. Since you don't wanna play the livestream."

He had no idea what she was on about, but under no circumstances was he willing to change the playlist, particularly given how many other elements of his party had by now been tarnished.

"I already have a playlist, thanks." That list consisted entirely of classical pieces, the first half of scores including Mendelssohn's Allegro vivace, Schubert's Allegro giusto, Denza's "Funiculì, Funiculà," and more recognizable pieces like "Hoedown" and "Flight of the Bumblebee," all of which would bolster people's spirits, inserting positive vibes into their brains like coins into a pinball machine. The second half, set to begin playing throughout the main course of his elaborate meal, consisted of pieces like Massenet's *Méditation*, Bill Evans's "Peace Piece," and of course, the "Moonlight" Sonata. Calmer, yet no less life-affirming, both halves combining to remind his guests of the simpler, subtler pleasures in life that make everything else, from one's sexual orientation to a bygone extramarital affair, seem sublimely trivial.

Suhad just stood there, in a kitchen that now began to suffocate him, and wavered between backing down and pushing forth. She wasn't trying to guilt him or weary him, so he had no legitimate right to be annoyed with her. Besides, he figured he would do away with her more quickly if he provided her some hope.

"I'll consider one song."

"How 'bout two songs?"

He figured wrong.

"Firas, you never told me which tie you liked better," Mazen said, wearing his suit and two ties, one macaroon and one eggnog, hanging loosely around his neck.

"Uh . . ."

"You still like my outfit, right?"

"I find bacon in cabinet."

"Maysa, those are Twizzlers."

Upon hearing the word, Mazen wondered if they were for his brother's party. It didn't matter. He was already eating them.

"Firas, is that bread whole wheat?"

"Firas, are there any Sour Patch Kids?"

"Firas, check on Jido."

"Yes it's whole wheat, no there aren't Sour Patch Kids, and I'll give Jido another minute to finish."

"I'll never finish!" the old man bellowed from the bathroom.

"What is he talking about?"

"I don't know, Mama, I'll deal with it in a minute." The croutons were starting to burn.

"What about my outfit? You still haven't told me which—"

"The one on the left."

"Your left or mine?"

"Mine."

"Firas, you're not even look—"

Glass exploded against the kitchen tiles. Two dearly departed mousse cups.

"Yah Allah!" Firas shouted.

"My search over now. This house halal again."

"It was always halal!"

"Thank you, Maysa."

"I told you to be careful, Maysa."

"Firas, she is just doing her job."

"Ouch!" Maysa cut herself on a shard she was recovering from the floor. Firas pretended to feel sorry.

"Suhad, take her to the bathroom and bandage her hand."

"I'll die before I let anyone into this bathroom!" bellowed the old man.

"Just take her to the upstairs bathroom. Your father should be finished his shower by now."

"Can my guests use the upstairs bathroom, too?"

"Don't be silly. And sweep up the glass. I'll go check on Jido."

Halfway through the sweeping, the smoke alarm blared again. Firas winced.

"Sour Patch Kids might make up for the food you're burning."

"Mazen, I'm not going to get Sour Patch Kids. I have two hours before people start showing up. I don't have time to get Sour Patch Kids, or to tell you which tie looks better, or to do anything that isn't on my docket. Okay?"

Mazen nodded solemnly. "That was stupid of me. I'm sorry."

Firas ignored him, flailing his arms about until the smoke dispersed and the alarm stopped blaring. Then he set to sweeping and disposed of the shards he collected into the garbage can, realizing that he'd forgotten to replace the bag he just removed. He reached for the box of garbage bags only to realize it was empty. He had planned to purchase more that morning after the flower shop and never did. Now his guests would have nowhere to toss their trash. Trash would smother the house.

He texted Mr. Lindstrom, letting him know that he could in fact bring something after all.

I meant something along the lines of coffee cake, but no problem! came the speedy reply.

"Why do you keep burning things?" Suhad asked on her way back from the upstairs bathroom. Maysa stood behind her, but only for a moment so she could display her wounded hand to Firas as if somehow it were his fault. "By the way, I'm still waiting for that money you owe me."

"I don't have cash on hand."

"How long before you get some?"

"Once I'm free."

"How long before you're—"

"Suhad, why do you need the money right now anyway?"

"I was thinking I'd get a slice before your party."

"I'm serving food!"

"I also need some new sunglasses."

"The party's indoors!"

"Well maybe I can run to the store, pick up some more turkey bacon for—"

"Suhad. Please, please just stay."

She sighed. "Okay."

Firas's father came into the kitchen, hair still wet from his shower. "It's good you got us some soap," he told Firas. "We were all out."

"What are you talking about?" The scent of sand, water, and summer air wafted past Firas's nose. "You used the gourmet soaps I got for my party guests???"

"Those were party favors? But they had broken hearts on them."

If only he could explain to his father. If only he could just get it all over with.

"Well it's possible one of your guests will end up not coming."

"Don't say that!" Firas's slightly raised voice startled Mazen into dropping the bag of Twizzlers, its contents scattering across the kitchen tiles for Firas to inevitably sweep up.

Firas's father smiled awkwardly, poured himself a glass of water, and went back upstairs.

Firas reached for the broom, but it was snatched away.

"I can clean up my own mess," his brother told him. Firas smiled, but under his furrowed brow it only made him look deeply uncomfortable. "Unless you don't want me to."

"That'd be fine, thanks." Having all the food as ready as it could be at this point, Firas began decorating the living room with Suhad's pitiful haul. He blew air into the balloons, all blue, then tied them to various fixtures—the curtain rod, the coffee table legs, the corner lamp—and let a few huddle loosely in the corner. Then, as he examined the eight blowouts and wondered how he would distribute them, who would be among the lucky few granted the joy of blowing, he noticed one of the folding tables was missing.

"Maysa?" he shouted.

Maysa shuffled into the living room, scowling at the sight of the balloons. "Are you looking for something?"

"I had five folding tables this morning. Now I only have four. Where is the other one?"

"I don't know."

She was lying. She was lying and he was ready to strangle her. Sensing from the twitching of his eyelids that he very well might, she dropped her scowl and sighed. "I go look for table now."

She left. He looked back at the blowouts and began figuring. Five folding tables each seating four, plus the dining room table, which seats six, so the most adequate distribution would be one per folding table and two for the dining table, but his parents and Jido who would be at the dining table would surely not partake in the blowout so it would be a waste to put a second one there and the quartet consisting of his cousins from Sterling Heights who would be seated together at a folding table would all delight in having a blowout so it might be wiser to put four there and none at the dining room table but then Suhad would be at the dining room table and she might grow bored without a blowout and some of the other guests like his high school friend Ted and Ted's girlfriend Rochelle would likely not mind sharing a blowout given all the things Ted boasted the two of them did with their tongues and yet Firas's parents would appreciate not being near such noise and so it became a catch-22 over the blowouts and Firas was quite certain he should just spare himself the trouble and throw all the blowouts in the garbage as soon as Mr. Lindstrom brought over new bags.

He was getting a migraine. There was no cure for migraines in the Dareer house. One simply had to suffer through it until it went away on its own. But Mazen couldn't be blamed, Mazen must never be blamed.

He sprinkled some confetti onto each folding table, and just as he was heading for his mother's peach English roll-arm—

"Don't even think about putting that stuff on my roll-arm."

"I'll clean it afterwards, Mama."

"Confetti never goes away. And don't throw any on the rug, either."

For the first time since he'd read her text, Firas stared at his mother—really stared at her—and in her face he saw a determination not to neglect her household duties. Despite the awkwardness of his discovery, he felt more comfortable in her presence than he ever had before, so much so that he indulged her finicky demands. He tossed the remaining confetti into the garbage can, just as he remembered there was still no bag inside. He groaned.

He proceeded to the flowers, which were up in his room. Part of him dreaded that Maysa may have plucked their petals off; fortunately, they were intact. But he faltered as he surveyed the arrangement: without the envy zinnias and poppies, it fell flat. When placed together, the remaining flowers—butterfly weeds, Carolina jessamines, forget-me-nots, irises—seemed random. Not even an exciting sort of random, which might have sparked conversations about aesthetic innovations in this underappreciated art form or philosophical debates about what is and isn't beauty; rather, it was an awkward random, an assemblage of things that didn't belong together even as Firas tried desperately to make them fit.

He brought them downstairs one at a time, placed them at the center of the folding tables.

"Maysa! The fifth table!"

She came into the living room empty-handed. "It downstairs in den."

"Well can you bring it in?"

"It too heavy for me."

It wasn't too heavy for her to carry *out*. But rather than arguing with a woman with a penchant for sabotage, he headed down to the den himself, holding his palm up to his nose to shield it from the smell of mold, even though his palm now held myriad other smells—raw bacon, leeks, gluten-free bread, latex, even the confetti still stuck to his hands—that made him cringe. He carried the folding table up the stairs, and on the way back to the living room he passed Jido sleeping on the toilet, snoring unabashedly, pants still around his ankles, the door wide open. He walked up to him and gently shook him. When his grandfather did not wake, Firas shook him a bit harder. Again he did not stir.

"Jido!"

Now the old man awoke.

"Did you go again?"

"Yes! And there's plenty more where that came from!"

Firas tried to peek into the bowl, but his grandfather snapped his legs shut to stop him from seeing. Given that Jido was never shy about such things, Firas suspected he was lying. When he sniffed, no stench arose. His patience had already worn thin, so he seized Jido by his underarms, lifted him up, and pulled up his pants. But as he shifted him towards his wheelchair, a savage cry exploded into his ear.

"DON'T YOU TOUCH ME!"

Firas flinched, dropping his grandfather back onto the toilet seat and causing a resounding clang.

"DON'T YOU TAKE ME OUT OF HERE! DO YOU HEAR ME? DON'T YOU FUCKING DARE!"

Firas shivered, then poked his head out into the corridor to see if anyone else was nearby to help. When he looked back at his grandfather, he, too, was shivering. The obvious guess was the onset of dementia. But Jido's eyes hadn't relinquished their lucidity even for a moment, which meant those bitter words and cry of desperation were in fact meant for Firas.

But why?

The doorbell rang.

"Firas, can you get that?" his mother shouted from the top of the stairs.

He answered the door, his mind still adrift but whipping back to the present when he saw Mr. Lindstrom on the porch. "What are you doing here???"

"Uh . . . you invited me. And look, I brought garbage bags! And coffee cake." Firas stiffened. "Problem?"

"You're early." He was, and not merely early because people were not supposed to arrive at the official start time, but because he arrived even *before* the official start time.

"Oh, I guess I am," Mr. Lindstrom said, checking his watch. "Should I come back later?"

"Firas, what is this mess on my kitchen floor?"

Firas stewed, not because of Mazen's inept cleanup, but because he should have known to follow up.

"Do you need help?" Mr. Lindstrom asked.

Firas smiled and thought this might be another bout of good fortune. "Yes!" He pulled Mr. Lindstrom in by the arm and led him to the kitchen.

"Hey, Mrs. Dareer!" he said to Firas's mother.

"Hello, Mr. Lindstrom." As Firas handed him the broom, his mother gasped. "Firas, you can't make your guests clean up your mess! Eib aleik!"

"Mama, he's a friend, that's what friends do."

"Come," she said to Mr. Lindstrom, relieving him of the broom, the garbage bags, and the coffee cake, and dumping them all into Firas's arms. "Try my roll-arm. It's very comfortable." Mr. Lindstrom's entire purpose at this party—to help with the preparations—was thus thwarted. What's worse was that not only did Mr. Lindstrom serve no other purpose, but whenever his eagerness to please went unfulfilled, it made Firas feel awkward. He was a middlebrow middle-management worker who volunteered to be the designated driver at every after-work happy hour he attended. Although his co-workers initially appreciated this about him, they soon found it to be his most insufferable trait. Mr. Lindstrom seemed to have no idea how to have fun. The gravity of Firas's party became all the more glaring in his presence.

Firas glowered at nobody in particular, then turned to sweep up the Twizzlers on the kitchen floor. His glowering eyes were forced to soften, however, when he suddenly noticed that the mess on the floor that had been improperly swept up did not consist of Twizzlers after all. It was the shards whose cleanup was his own responsibility.

"Firas," his father hollered, even though they were only three feet apart in the kitchen. "A birthday is not an excuse to neglect your responsibilities."

"I'm cleaning up the glass now, Baba."

"What are you talking about, glass? Your grandfather is still on the toilet!"

"I don't think I can help with that."

"Since when?"

"Since he grew weirdly attached to it."

"I can help Jido into his wheelchair," said Mazen.

"No, no," said his father. "You just enjoy your snack. I'll take care of it." He headed for the bathroom.

"Are those Sour Patch Kids?"

"Yeah, I picked some up from the corner store after I finished sweeping."

"How come Mazen gets to pick up food but I don't," Suhad said, eyes half closed as though she'd just awoken from a nap.

"I didn't know he was getting candy! Here," he said to her as he handed her the garbage bags. "Put one in this trash bin."

"We have coffee cake?" Mazen asked, spotting it in Firas's arms.

"I'm serving food! Stop eating!"

Mazen frowned. "I thought I was making things easier for you." He set down the candy and lumbered into the living room, like a scolded child sent to bed early, to sit with his mother and Mr. Lindstrom on the peach English roll-arm.

Firas went into the living room to set up the last folding table. He crouched, staring at it.

"What are you doing?" his mother asked.

His eyes narrowed. "This table is uneven." He flipped it upside down, studying with his eyes and hands all four of its legs. "She did something to it!"

"Who?"

"Maysa!" he called out.

"Firas, what are you talking about?"

Maysa lurched into the room. "Do you need help with—"

"What did you do to this table?!"

"Firas, calm down."

"Mama, she busted my folding table!"

"It looks fine."

"It's slanted!"

"Are you sure?" asked Maysa.

Firas pursed his lips, dying to expose this woman's malevolence once and for all. He flipped the table back upright and lo and behold he was right. It was indeed slanted.

"See what I mean?" He was addressing everyone in the room—his mother, his brother, Mr. Lindstrom.

"What's all this noise?" his father asked upon entering.
"Maysa messed with this table and now it's uneven."
"I did nothing to table."
"She's right," said Firas's mother.
"No she's not!"
"Firas, you've got it all wrong," added Mr. Lindstrom.
"No I don't!"
"Firas, look." Mazen pointed to one of the legs, which, unlike the other three, stood just off the living room rug.

Firas winced, measuring the weight of what would inevitably come next.

"I think you owe Maysa an apology," his father told him, switching between a glare in Firas's direction and an embarrassed smile in Maysa's.

"I'm sorry, Maysa . . ."
"I go get last flowers for you." She went up the stairs.
"Eib aleik, Firas!"
"What has gotten into you?" his father asked.

What *had* gotten into him? Firas understood and predicted that today he might be anxious, terrified, perhaps even cynical. But now he was losing his mind, believing with unfathomable conviction that a septuagenarian housekeeper possessed the ability to somehow shorten a metal table leg without anybody catching her. Everyone in the room could spot his mistake. How is it that he didn't? How is it that he even made it to begin with? He'd miscalculated the measurements of the folding tables within the floorspace of the living room. Now no matter how he arranged them, one would either stand unevenly or have to be placed so close to another that some of the guests would barely be able to back out of their chairs.

"I know what has gotten into him," his mother said. Firas looked at her, knowing she would be wrong but curious about her theory nonetheless. "He has been so busy preparing for his party he has forgotten to pray. Without Allah, he has begun to lose his mind."

This was not the guess he hoped for, but one he should have predicted. He assumed she would have at least jumped first to a more logical conclusion, a bout of overexertion or malnourishment, perhaps. He was all but ready to dismiss his mother's theory as that of a typical religious conservative, but he couldn't. Because what followed this theory shook him to his core.

"As a result of his sinfulness, he has ideas in his head of things that did not happen and would never happen."

He didn't recognize the iciness in her eyes, pointed directly at his jugular.

There was no empathy coming his way, as he had earlier posited. Instead here was his own mother, the woman who had birthed him, leveraging his small mistake in order to gaslight him. Laying the groundwork for her defense in case he ever tried to expose her to his father. People would behold her superior devotion to Allah, her exact right place on the moral spectrum, and never dare to question her righteousness against his. How long would she continue on this route? To what extent could she turn her own son into an adversary? How many points was she bound to win in the round that would follow his announcement?

"LET'S GET DIRTYYYYYYYY!!!"

Into the house burst the quartet of cousins from Sterling Heights with the Bluetooth speaker Firas had requested they bring, blasting the latest single from DJ Shiv.

"That's what I'm talking about!" shouted Suhad, strutting down the staircase with a fist pump.

"What the fuck is that noise?" bellowed Jido, who, to Firas's shock, was at last out of the bathroom and back in his wheelchair. Behind that wheelchair stood Mazen, who had left the living room without Firas even noticing.

"Thank you for helping with Jido, Mazen." A phrase his mother was very much saying to Firas, before she rose from the roll-arm to greet the cousins. "Keefkom, habaybi?"

They turned the music down at her request, then exchanged kisses with Firas's father and grandfather, with his sister and brother, and with Mr. Lindstrom, who was not accustomed to three kisses on each cheek (or any number of kisses) but appreciated it nonetheless. Then their eyes landed on Firas, still crouching to devise a solution to the folding table dilemma.

"Hey, cuz!" said Abdullah, the eldest. "Ah, you're already in position. Perfect!" He sat on the roll-arm and extended his legs so that his shoes were on Firas's lap. "I wanna see my reflection in these bad boys!"

Cackles erupted. Firas's parents loved this sort of humor: sappy, but with a touch of irreverence that often appealed to the older generation.

Normally, Firas would have joined in on the laughter, knowing that the cousins were not malicious people and genuinely wanted to make everyone laugh. These cousins—in fact, second cousins, as Firas's maternal grandmother died giving birth to his mother, and his paternal grandparents did not wish to bring another child into an occupied Palestine—were raised not too poor and not too rich, with a relatively well-adjusted familial environment (their parents were only mildly religious, also known as "religious when convenient") and little to no racial discrimination due to their pale complexion, leaving them to contend with the existential crises inserted into their heads by an overabundance of Time, with humor the only available raw material with which to fill the hole. Normally, Firas had no problem laughing along with them, even when it was at his own expense. But on this day, this unequivocally anything-but-normal day, when someone, some higher power, was already having an abundance of laughs at his expense, he was in absolutely no mood.

However, before he could scream or cuss or do any of the unseemly things the human mouth was occasionally prone to do, that higher power, as though suddenly, finally, taking pity on him, cut its laughter short and graced him with relief.

The left frontal leg of the peach English roll-arm on which Abdullah was sitting cracked under the weight of his and Mr. Lindstrom's bodies, launching them both onto the floor. And although Firas felt bad for Mr. Lindstrom, who had always been kind and gracious to him, and who had been the only one in the room not laughing at him, he was, Firas felt, acceptable collateral damage.

"Yah Allah!" Firas's mother shouted.

"Are you okay?" his father asked.

"Nothing bruised but my ego," Abdullah answered, to another eruption of cackles.

"I'm okay, too," added Mr. Lindstrom, who would inevitably bruise elsewhere.

"Firas, is your mind still crazy or can you fix the sofa for our guests?"

Holding up a fragment of the shattered sofa leg, he returned her icy stare. "What exactly do you think can be done about this, Mama?"

"I'm sure you will figure it out. In the meantime, I'm going upstairs to pray the maghrib."

"I'll join you," said his father.

"Maybe you should ask her if she minds," Firas said.

The entire room came to a standstill. "Why would she mind?" his father asked, taken aback. All eyes turned to Firas's mother, who scoffed without even a hint of anger or surprise.

"See?" she said. "Crazy." She turned to Firas. "Get upstairs and do some praying yourself." Then she walked away, her husband right behind her, and Firas pondered the expression on her face, hidden from his father's view, as she climbed up the stairs to their room.

Ibtisam, the painfully sweet second-oldest cousin, turned to Jido and flashed a set of bleached teeth that pierced his eyes. "And what are you wearing tonight, Haj?"

"A diaper, what the fuck is it to you?"

Without even flinching, she replied: "Well that makes two of us, Haj! Twinsies!" More laughter, though now with fluctuating levels of sincerity. Jido rolled his eyes and departed down the corridor.

"You know," Suhad said, addressing the cousins, "you guys are unfashionably early. Maybe we should grab a slice of pizza before the party?" Just as she saw Firas's mouth twitching: "And don't worry, Firas, I'm sure the cousins can spot me a few bucks for now."

"Definitely! Pizza's on us for everyone who wants to join!" said Samira, the quartet's least oblivious member.

Before Firas could object with another firm yet increasingly ineffectual *I'm serving food!*, Suhad, the cousins, and even Mr. Lindstrom, were already out the door.

Still crouched in the corner of the room, the bile rising once again, Firas muttered under his breath: "I should just cancel this party."

A shrill gasp startled him, knocking him off his balance and tipping him over for a light fall. He realized then that Mazen was still in the room. His eyes wide, his mouth agape, he stared at his older brother as though he'd just said the most hurtful thing imaginable. Firas waited for some sort of verbal response, some explanation that could enlighten him as to why his brother appeared so perturbed, and what, if anything, he was meant to do about it. But Mazen said nothing. He simply fled the room and scurried up the stairs, shutting his bedroom door loudly enough to startle Firas once more.

Firas fetched some superglue from his room and set to work, as best he could, on the broken sofa leg. While he did, he thought about Mrs. Tullinson. He wished so much that they'd met before his failed twelfth birthday party. Perhaps she could have dissuaded him from having it, insisted instead on making him the banana chocolate pancakes he grew up to love. If only she were still around, she could even have dissuaded him from throwing *this* party. She could have spared him all the trouble it took to plan and execute it only to watch it crumble to dust, bit by aching bit.

But she wouldn't have dissuaded him. She would have gently nudged him to face his fears. She cherished the time they spent together all those nights playing board games by her fireplace, but her enjoyment was always tinged with sorrow, for a young man like Firas had so much more to offer the world beyond the wholesome fun splayed across her living room floor. The possibility that he might go the way of her son, killed not by the twitchy swallow of a nearby lake but by the sharp claws of misery, never ceased to loom over her. If Firas had come out, at least reached Stage 4, he could have shared with her a joy whose bounty grew from honesty. How many more honest moments would elude him throughout his life? And this was unlike his twelfth birthday party; people were going to come. People were *already* coming. They came *early* because they couldn't wait to celebrate with him. Now, finally, after all these years, he was going to get the celebration, the joy, the freedom he deserved.

And yet . . . he still sensed something was missing. It was the worst sense of something missing, because that sense was not coming from his mind, it was not based on anything rational, anything that could be explained or analyzed for the purposes of finding a solution. This sense emanated from somewhere deeper. He had forgotten something, some detail, small enough not to be noticed yet capable of crashing the entire mechanism of his life. But what could it be?

He suddenly began to regret not inviting Kashif. Firas would have used him as a crutch—but so what? Crutches are inherently temporary, and he would have eventually stood all on his own. There was no shame in it. And yet still he couldn't bring himself to make the call.

He turned the couch right side up to see if the newly glued leg would hold. It did, but that could easily change the second someone sat on it again. He figured it might make for a good laugh, ease his tension. So he abandoned it and headed towards the stairs to go up and get dressed. But he stopped, abruptly, when he heard fighting in the hall.

"Baba, why are you making my life harder?"

Firas watched the interaction between his father and grandfather, the former's hair still a mess from his shower. It had been a long time since he'd seen his father look so dejected. But nothing could have worsened matters than Jido's response to what was essentially a rhetorical question:

"Because it needs to be harder."

Firas's father had no words, and would not have been able to voice them even if he had, for the old man kept on going:

"You're making a mistake raising your children. There is no family in this house. There's a man and a woman and three youths. You're all spare parts, so corroded by Time you'll never manage to fit back together!"

For a split second, Firas's father appeared ready to say something, but he knew the old man wouldn't let him say it; he knew it would immediately be rendered obsolete by the vitriol to come.

"These children are not yours. You let go of them. You surrendered them. You're a failure as a father." Jido's head sank. "So am I." As Firas's father debated whether to defend himself, Jido's eyes arose and landed on Firas idling by the banister. Firas wanted his grandfather to look away, to look anywhere else, at anyone and anything but him. "And so your son will be."

And that was it. That was the last thing his grandfather would ever say to him. "Take me back to the nursing home," he told Firas's father, the words spoken at the lowest volume he'd ever shown.

Within fifteen minutes, his parents were getting the old man into the car and driving away. Firas still needed to get dressed, set the tables, and complete a hundred other tasks. He had also scheduled a ten-minute break to cry. He had resolved not to cry on this day, but the break could perhaps still serve another purpose. It never hurts to prepare oneself just in case, even as Firas remained undeterred. And he was undeterred. Time would never grant him another chance. It hadn't even granted him this one; it had simply let just enough moments slip from its grasp for him to catch like snowflakes on his tongue, no two the same, neither in their formation nor in where they land, similar only in the way they vanish from consciousness, only in the fact that they could never be reclaimed and never be recreated.

CHAPTER ELEVEN

His outfit for the evening fit perfectly. Firas was concerned he may have lost weight over the course of the past week due to the stress leading up to the party. But he looked elegant in his simplicity of style. He smiled at his reflection. A small victory he was needing more and more as the deadline approached.

He sat on his bed, and although he had no intention of crying, he felt he should use this time to enjoy the quiet that now permeated the house. His parents were not yet back from the nursing home, nor were Suhad, Mr. Lindstrom, and the cousins from the pizza parlor. Even Maysa was gone, Firas having informed her that he would not be requiring her services until the cleanup and sending her home for a few hours. Rarely did silence occur inside the Dareer house, even when, as was often the case, each member of the family was in a different room. Regardless whether his bedroom door was closed, Firas could hear Suhad traipsing up and down the stairs in thick-heeled boots; he could hear his mother clanging silverware as she set the table; he could hear his father watching television in his bedroom and leaving it on after falling asleep.

He didn't want to be thinking about anything. He wanted to enjoy some peace of mind, enjoy it as though it were his last chance, because it very well may be. Yet he couldn't help himself. He still had so much left to consider. He had far more to contend with now than when he awoke this morning, which seemed like a million mornings ago. In the wake of discovering his mother's affair, suffering Jido's scorn, maneuvering around Maysa's sabotage, and lingering in the profound tenderness of Kashif's lips against his cheek, his announcement seemed to portend something even worse, much worse, than everything that preceded it. And what would happen then? What was to come in its immediate aftermath? Even Firas could hardly plan for that.

A week earlier, he had booked himself a four-night stay at a hotel in Corktown. He knew without question that his parents would not want to see or speak to him for some time, and he couldn't bear to be around his friends until after he managed to firmly regain his footing. The hotel offered free breakfast and Wi-Fi, though he hardly imagined himself eating or going online. He would even leave behind his phone, cut himself off from his world until all its pieces reassembled into a quasi-recognizable image. After the fourth day, if his parents were still angry or disappointed or, in a worse case, vindictive, or, in an even worse case, indifferent, he had planned to stay with Tyrese until he could find his own place. But the newly ambiguous status of his relationship cast doubt on this portion of the agenda. He hadn't planned for a problem with Tyrese. Tyrese seemed the only constant in his life, the only factor that would never vary. And he didn't. It was Firas who varied, it was Firas who turned their relationship into something it was not. He set the rules and then he broke them, figuring Tyrese would go along but ultimately losing everything. But he also hadn't expected a promotion, which came with a salary, albeit an unimpressive one. He could now afford a few more nights at the hotel if need be, a few more moments of quiet to no longer have to think about anything at all.

But while that settled the matter of his thoughts, what of his feelings? What was the plan for those intrusions on the human heart? Firas was not worried about *all* feelings. He wasn't worried about anger or sorrow or fear. These were manageable emotions, ones wholly dependent on internal factors and thereby capable of being subdued and eventually expelled. One can choose to be angry at/sad about/fearful of the outside world and one can choose not to be. Nor was he particularly worried about feeling lonely. He had enough friends to whom he could turn, and who would likely offer him support after witnessing firsthand his family's disdain. And even if he had no friends to support him, one can just as easily feel lonely when not alone and be alone without feeling lonely. As far as he was concerned, none of these potential feelings posed any real threat to him and his path forward. What did pose a threat was despair. Despair comes as much from the external world as it does from the internal, and the choice to subdue it or expel it is not entirely in one's control. One cannot maintain hope solitarily; it's too expansive a feeling, too fragile and spontaneous to count as anything less than a sheer miracle. Hope never stems from anything rational. Nothing drives it, yet almost everything is driven by it. It is the ultimate motivation for human progress, yet it brushes over humanity so fleetingly. There is a shortage of hope in the world, and were Firas to retain a piece of it, he would need to wrest it from the hands of another lost soul. But could he? Would he be strong enough for such a fight in his vulnerable state? While their feelings are still raw, people often do things they later come to regret: they quit jobs they need, start fights they can't finish, disown children they raised and loved. Could Firas, for all his meticulous planning, make such a grave mistake?

He also considered that his parents might try to contact him with some inane plan to "fix" the problem, some trek to a conversion therapy center in the middle of a Mormon town. He'd heard rumors of an organization in Utah where the counselors theorized that homosexuality arose in men because they'd not gotten enough male affection throughout their youth, leading the older male counselors to wrap their arms tightly around the young converts' bodies for hours on end until this affection they were receiving finally satiated their thirst for cock.

On the other hand, his parents might try to convert him in another, less scientific way, or rather a different kind of science, trading psychological tools for anatomical ones. They once arranged a dinner party for their friends, a cheerful Turkish couple who brought with them their daughter. This daughter, a pre-med student, was pleasant and charming throughout the entire evening, cracking jokes about her red hair and alabaster skin and the shock on White people's faces when she explained to them that no, in fact, red hair did not originate in Ireland or Scandinavia but in Central Asia, which meant she had, by geographical proximity, more claim to it than Patrick O'Shaughnessy or Astrid Eriksson, and the Dareers and their guests laughed merrily at that and at every other thing that was said during the evening until the parents went into the living room and simultaneously chatted and eavesdropped to see if the chemistry between their offspring was there and lo and behold it wasn't. Firas had long sensed that they might try again, and now he was almost certain of it. As soon as he refused the offer—or the command, as it was likely to be—his parents would either find a more effective strategy or opt for a clean break, an abrupt stop to all forms of communication and the slow erasure of their firstborn child from their memories.

Had Anton gone through with his lavender marriage in the end? Firas took out his phone and typed Anton's name into the search engine, thinking that a wedding photo might appear in the results.

He was floored.

There was Anton draped in a rainbow flag on the streets of Moscow. He was alone (though a boot headed in his direction protruded from the edge of the frame) and dressed in a full-length sable fur coat, underneath which Firas could see he was shirtless and suspected he was pants-less.

Anton had actually done it. He had leapt from Stage 3 to Stage 8 in one of the most notoriously homophobic regions of the world. Were there a feeling to describe the all-too-common mixture of pride and envy, Firas would have unleashed its width and length and depth across the landscape of his humble Detroit neighborhood, and continued to unleash it until it shot all the way up into the stratosphere where doctrines wilt like petals then burn like embers.

He kept staring at the photo, letting its vibrancy—the rainbow flag blending into the backdrop of Saint Basil's Cathedral, Anton's pale face framed by shoulder-length ebony hair—nourish him until his own moment came.

But the more he stared at the photo, the more its light began to dim. Because now, inching towards his fateful party, he realized that Anton's eventual disregard of his messages was not the result of the increasing mundanity of their conversations.

They arrested him.

They must have. There were no reports anywhere in the search results, but what was the likelihood that such reports would be made public? Anton's courage may have gotten him not only arrested but also tortured and killed.

Arrested. Tortured. Killed.

Firas pictured these words in his head: stooped and sickening gargoyles, as stiff in their composition as in their composure, dusty pearls for circles in their wide, haunting eyes, their bodies now rumbling to life through air ripped from human lungs and light snatched from murky skies. How lanky they were. How towering. These were quiet words, words that dripped, streaking black, slimy ink across the surface of his mind to imprint the chiaroscuro portrait of his bruised and bloodied friend. No, Firas was not in Russia; yes, his map differed from

Anton's, and Tyrese's, and Cetan's, and Professor Markum's. But the starting point, for each of them, was the same.

Firas gazed back at his reflection. Despite the disturbing nature of his thoughts, he took solace in how clear they were, clearer than they had been all day. He wished for his thoughts to always be so clear, for the noise to always fade. He needed to return to the preparations, but if the silence remained, he told himself he would allow his break to go on just a little while longer, for it was far too precious to squander.

Unfortunately, he started to hear something.

A buzz. He remembered hearing a buzz in the flower shop that morning, thinking, momentarily, that he was losing his sanity, that it was all in his head. He gave himself the benefit of the doubt and assumed it was real. A real buzz. But from what precisely? It was too persistent to be a doorbell, too melodic to be a fridge. He waited a minute, listening intently until his ear whittled down the noise like an archeologist scraping the surface of a buried fossil and a discernible sound emerged.

It was music.

His music.

Someone was playing "Flight of the Bumblebee." He had connected his laptop to the Bluetooth speaker in the living room, and someone had then gone into his playlist and started it. But that didn't make sense. No one was home; he would've heard them. Now he considered the other alternative, that it was indeed just in his head. The evening's suspense was building in his mind, the terror, the excitement, all of it. Firas was fortifying his nerve, letting the tubas, the trombones, the trumpets, the horns, the bassoons, the contrabassoons, the clarinets, the oboes, the flutes, the English horn, the piccolo, all shoot across each corner of his mind and rebound again and again until every part of him absorbed every instrument and all the notes with which they graced the score.

Except now the buzz was getting louder. Not only that, it became less familiar to him, less the old friend it had been since the first time he heard it, more like a prowler invading his home.

It was not, in fact, "Flight of the Bumblebee." Upon closer examination, he identified it as Niccolò Paganini's *24 Caprices*, and when Firas stepped into the hall to locate the source, he noticed, oddly, that it was coming from the last room on the left.

All roads lead to Mazen.

He stood there, gawking at the closed door, hesitant to move towards it because for a moment he couldn't remember which room it was. The music was blaring from the other side. A door that until now had not been closed since the last time Firas entered the room, finding his little brother lying on the bed with eyes that wouldn't open.

He had foolishly assumed that someone else would be on watch duty. No—that was a lie. He hadn't thought about watch duty at all, hadn't even fallen prey to the diffusion of responsibility that too many are comfortable relying on in such cases. Whatever he found on the other side of that door would become the stain on his hands that would never wash clean.

He paced towards it. His sweaty palm denied him his grip on the doorknob. He wiped both it and the knob with the sleeve of his dark blue blazer and tried again. He pushed the door open with his pinky finger, the weakest—a desperate attempt to slow down the door's trajectory. Once the door was fully open, the music accosted him. He winced. But he didn't enter.

The bed was just out of view. One more step and he would see it. One more step and a world would implode. An implosion so great that even its most distant neighbors would feel the vibration and inevitably implode in turn, one after another after another after another, until nothing but the void was left.

The bed was made. Made unevenly—the tops of pillows poking out from under the flat sheet, the flat sheet almost entirely covered by the duvet, the comforter hanging farther down one side than the other—but it was made, and his brother wasn't in it.

Mazen, still in his tan suit and, having finally made the decision himself, the macaroon tie, was sitting on his window board gazing at the street. His room faced the neighbor's house, the one on the left whose resident was seldom home and which was now mostly obscured by his body. Firas, almost instinctively, checked his brother's hand for a bag of chocolate chips, before remembering he'd used the rest of them on the mousse cups.

Was he supposed to say something now? Or could he simply take comfort in the fact that he hadn't failed the chore he had temporarily neglected?

"I didn't know you were a classical music fan," he finally said.

Without looking at him, Mazen replied: "I knew you were."

How had he known that? Firas never played music at home. He'd once switched to the classical radio station while driving a ten-year-old Mazen in his parents' car. But surely that wasn't how. It couldn't be.

"Why was the door closed?" he asked.

"That was the only way I could get you to come in here."

Throughout the day, Firas had thought constantly about his party. Even when wrestling with the myriad problems that had nothing to do with it, he could only view those problems through the prism of what this day meant to him. Yet now, thoughts of his party completely abandoned him. Now all he could think was how much smarter his little brother was than he himself had ever been.

"Jido left," Mazen said. "I saw Mama and Baba drive away with him."

"He wanted to go back."

"Why?"

"I'm not really sure. Who knows with people that age."

"He isn't senile, Firas."

"I know . . . I just meant that he has a different way of thinking, that's all."

"Different from who?"

Firas teetered backward, one step closer to the doorway. "You picked the right tie."

"It doesn't matter now. You said you were canceling your party."

Firas had forgotten that Mazen heard him utter the words. He had also forgotten that Mazen was not inside his head and therefore never learned that he still had every intention of going through with the party. Before he could assure his brother of this fact, Mazen spoke:

"I really thought it would fix everything. If you had gone through with it."

What do you mean, 'fix everything'? Firas thought, forgetting, again, that his brother could not read his mind.

"Why were you crying that night?" Mazen asked him.

"What night?"

Mazen sighed. For the first time since Firas entered his room, he tore his eyes away from the street outside his window and looked at him. "You know what night."

Of course he knew. Since the age of nine, Firas had cried only a smattering of times, and only once in front of his brother.

"I was sad that my birthday party got canceled."

Mazen hung his head. "No, Firas. That isn't why."

He was right. But Firas couldn't fathom how his little brother, then just five years old, could have deduced that his tears had little to do with a canceled party; how he not only remembered the incident to this day, but understood something that was neither told nor shown. Looking at him now, melancholy dripping down his chin like honey, it seemed as though Mazen understood those tears even better than Firas did. Because while Firas expelled from his mind as much of the incident as he could, Mazen held on to every inch of it, dreamt about it night after night and thought of it day after day, framing it within the various genres of the human story (drama, horror, fantasy, mystery), its meaning constantly evolving as his understanding of the world expanded, until eventually it became just as much Mazen's tragedy as it was his own.

That night was the first moment Firas realized that the new life his parents were trying to build for him would fail. They had moved to America for a better future, to acquire for themselves and their children an abundance of things both tangible and not. Yet upon arriving here, he was robbed just the same. But what had Mazen, so young and unmarred, been robbed of?

Firas half expected his memories of his twelfth birthday to resurface just then, not only of the details of the party he had planned but of how he felt when he delivered the invitations, when every single boy he invited said he would come, when he stayed up all night imagining what presents he would receive, when he discovered he wouldn't be receiving any presents at all because the other boys were lying to humiliate him, and when ultimately his parents took him to a sushi restaurant in Dearborn as if everything was just fine.

Mazen turned his head to look back at the street, at which point Firas noticed the window was wide open.

"He was my age when they killed him."

Firas flinched. ". . . Who?"

"Mohammed."

As all Muslims do, Firas knew many Mohammeds. But none who had died, and certainly none who'd been killed.

"Mazen—"

"I couldn't go through with it. You understand that I couldn't go through with it, right? You understand that?"

Firas did not understand. He witnessed firsthand that his brother *had* gone through with the suicide attempt.

"I just wanted to go back home, Firas."

"What?"

"If anyone asks. That's what you'll tell them."

Mazen Dareer loved to play basketball. He loved playing video games and hanging out with friends. He had had four girlfriends by the age of fourteen, and with one of them, it had been love. He possessed an insatiable appetite for sweets, particularly chocolate chips. He listened to the works of Niccolò Paganini, Nikolai Rimsky-Korsakov, Richard Wagner, and others. He was born in Gaza City, Palestine, and raised in Detroit, Michigan. He made his Jido incomparably proud and put his brother's smarts to shame.

When he was done falling into the abyss, and the window facing the neighbor's house was no longer obscured by his tan-suited body, this is what Firas would tell everyone, if and when they asked.

CHAPTER TWELVE

Time stopped. Not out of mercy, of course, for Time knows no such thing, no such benevolence, no, rather it stopped out of necessity. One might argue, in fact, that it did not stop at all, but was brought to a stop by the magnitude of its own weight, its own self-seriousness, the sweeping fog it created suddenly turned against its master and parked comfortably and cruelly across its back like siblings roughhousing on the front lawn of their childhood home that Time had ripped away from them. It was all happening now, as it must have happened long ago, as though now even existed, as though long ago ever existed. Time stopped, and everything stopped with it, everything but the feeling of rising above one's body and studying the scene below, scattered and fleeting and fogged, always fogged. Pieces here and there coming together, maybe, maybe!, but likely not, and likely never. Time stopped, and he pictured its emblem, its last-known fingerprint inside his world, brown and viscous and rancid with sweetness, smudged across the wall mere yards from his brother's room, behind the velvet ottoman on which lay his prayer rug. How he had tried and tried to wash it away, tried harder at this than at any other thing in his life. Yet it refused to disappear, always taunting him from the corner of his room, out of the corner of his eye, it was there and would be there forever.

Forever.

It would never leave, frozen in place by the certainty of its own worth. He would leave this house before it did. It would outlive him and outlive everyone around him. Dear God, how it outlived so much already. Even Mrs. Tullinson, who was there when the caramel was spilled, and who pushed him gently, so gently, to clean after himself, only to be met with promises Firas never thought to keep until it was too late. Now the stain was etched into his wall, into his life, into his most excruciatingly private moments, undressing, manscaping, masturbating, thinking thoughts he'd been told all his life were wrong. Time stopped, but it did not disappear, it was lurking about, ready to strike and keep him fixed in place. All he could think was how to get rid of it, how to float through space without its pull dragging him in directions he did not wish to go. It would require something grand—a fire, an earthquake, a hurricane. Alas, such disasters would not come, he knew. He was stuck with it, clung to the wall next to it, an imprint beside an imprint, growing fainter and fainter yet never fully disappearing. This was it. This was his fate, revealed to him as Time stopped, the glimpse one receives upon the brush of Death, it was right there in front of him, so close he would not see or hear or touch anything again; instead he would be seen and heard and touched, but not in his current form, not as Firas Dareer the enemy of Time but as something else, something he was just beginning to decipher, requiring just a little more effort, just a slight stretch of the arm already bursting out of its socket and he might reach it, he might reach it!

And then Time resumed.

CHAPTER THIRTEEN

The manager of the flower shop had once suggested to Firas an interesting idea: landscape architecture. He understood and appreciated architecture, and he loved being around flowers and, she assumed, other elements of nature. Were he to combine what he knew with what he loved, he could make the sort of living people spent their entire lives dreaming of. He thought it a wonderful idea, both financially practical—he could save enough money for a truck, acquire a few clients here and there, and then expand through positive word of mouth—and personally fulfilling. He pursued the idea for a while, starting, naturally, with the Dareer house. When he put forth the idea at dinner one night, his mother grimaced.

"Do you have to start with *our* house?" she asked him, his father equally keen to hear the answer.

"I wouldn't do anything drastic."

They agreed, so long as he didn't do any work on the front yard where people could see. He found that condition unfortunate, but he understood, and he assured them that he would work only on the backyard. But they didn't care for that idea either, as they possessed no fence and the neighbors behind them would also be able to see the disaster. (His parents did not use the word *disaster* but they certainly thought it.) They suggested he do something on the left side of the house, because the neighbor who resided there, a full-time teacher and part-time bartender, was seldom home. This was not an ideal bargain, but one he felt comfortable accepting.

A few weeks into a course at school, and after a few days of unclogging his mind to let the ideas flow, Firas decided to put in place a little garden where people could meditate. He planted a small wisteria tree and some pink lotus flowers that dotted 120 pounds' worth of round banded gneiss. He also installed a globe-shaped light in case anyone wished to meditate at night. His work impressed his parents, who then permitted him to do the same thing on the side of the house facing Mr. Lindstrom. Firas was eager to proceed with the plan, though with the intention of changing the second garden somewhat, perhaps replacing the wisteria tree with a Japanese dogwood and the lotus flowers with some gerbera daisies. But before he set out on this endeavor, he wanted first to see if any members of his family actually used the meditation garden. For a while, nobody did, so an addition seemed pointless. He debated whether to go through with it anyway, if only to expand his portfolio; but the idea of building something never to be used, of creating something never to be experienced, was no less stifling than screaming at the top of one's lungs with a closed mouth.

Then one day, as Firas arrived home from class, he witnessed, to his surprise, Mazen sitting cross-legged beneath the wisteria tree, on the largest, smoothest rock he could pick out, with his eyes shut. He watched him for approximately ten minutes, before heading inside the house with a self-satisfied smirk. He still saw no point in replicating the little garden on the other side of the house, given that none of the other Dareers took to it; but it did make him realize the potential of this career move. To see that very same rock on which his brother once sat, now coated in blood from the skull it cracked open, somehow vindicated his choice to forgo the landscape architecture business in favor of his internship at the firm.

He had failed watch duty. It was possible, likely even, that Mazen might have found a way to do the deed regardless of how closely Firas monitored him. But that would hardly matter to his sister and parents. There was no A for effort in the field of keeping one's brother alive. There was success and there was failure; anything in between was as meaningless as the reason behind the plummet.

Certainly Mazen couldn't be blamed. Certainly this was entirely the fault of Firas, who had nothing else on his mind, nothing of importance that could justify his shameful neglect of duty. And even if Firas *had* been preoccupied with something important, it didn't matter, because Mazen was the priority at all times.

What harrowed him more than the sight of his brother's bleeding head was Firas's vision of himself beating that head against the rock over and over and over again. Even beating it against some of the other rocks in case the blood pooling over the first rock softened the blow.

This was my day. This was my day.

Indeed the celebration was not meant to end, or rather start, in this manner—abruptly, as only tragedy could end it. As only the whims of Fate could dictate. With questions, so many questions, that would take two, three, five, ten lifetimes to answer.

Where the hell did Mazen get off killing himself?

Mazen was not a closeted gay man in a homophobic family. Mazen hadn't lived under a military occupation, at least not one he could remember. Mazen was not the one who grew up friendless, plain-looking, and burdened by the inherent responsibilities of a firstborn. He had, and he was, everything he needed for a happy, well-adjusted life.

"You fucking idiot," Firas said to his brother's corpse.

He liked saying the words. He liked hearing them. He enjoyed their harshness of sound, their acidic taste. Mazen had thrown it all away, thrown it right out of his own window. And in doing so, he took Firas's plans right out with him. There was no chance he would get to make his announcement now, no chance he would get to come into his own and survive the lie that had been slowly poisoning him all these years. What's worse was that the weight of Mazen's death on his family might deny him another chance to tell them for who knew how long. He may *never* get another chance to tell them!

Opportunities are brittle as clay, as fickle as the friendships of children. Firas could feel the bile rising again, in monstrous form. Such rage had never arisen in him before. Anger, yes—soft anger, loud anger, passive anger—but never rage, which became so palatable he wanted more, more, more! And it would surely come, because this brother, this *chore*, was the bane of his existence. And after all the coddling, the check-ins, the therapy sessions that went nowhere but the land of adultery, it became extremely, completely, painfully clear that it was about fucking time somebody fucking blamed Mazen. Blamed him for making his problems everyone else's, and for taking Firas's life just as he took his own.

Unless . . .

Did he dare?

No, that wouldn't be right.

But it wouldn't be especially wrong, either . . .

Between the street and Mazen's corpse stood the wisteria tree. The neighbor on the left always arrived from work well into the night, he could unscrew the globe-shaped light—

No, no, stop it! he told himself. *Stop it!* He was being silly, insane. Worse, he was being impractical. Too many potential outcomes, too few contingency plans. Someone was bound to find the body, pedestrians were passing by, all it would take is for just one of them to see it. When they did, they would balk at the little, the nothing, that Firas did in response.

But he could write it off as shock. *Don't do this.* People always respond to tragedy in odd ways. *I'm begging you.* Firas was no less impervious, no less human than anybody else. *Go. Inside. The. Fucking. House.* It would be believable. He could get away with it. *You've lost it. You've completely fucking lost it.* Yes, he was going to get away with it!

Just then, he glimpsed Mr. Grint across the street, watering his grass. He and Firas locked eyes. Knowing a party was scheduled to take place, Mr. Grint would inevitably wonder what Firas was doing by the side of the house and tread over to find out. There was also the question of what he would tell his parents when they noticed Mazen was not in his room, a question to which any response would lead to countless more questions and an exponentially smaller number of cogent answers.

He staggered back into the house and dialed.

"9-1-1, where's your emergency?"

"It's not an emergency. I need to report a death." He provided her with the address.

"Have you checked this person's pulse?"

"He's dead."

"Sometimes a person can seem—"

"He's dead." Firas was ready to repeat the phrase as many times as it would take to end the conversation, and in precisely the same catatonic voice.

"Can you describe what happened?"

"He killed himself." This, too, he said catatonically. "The rest I can fill in when you get here." He hung up, then plopped down on what he at first failed to realize was the peach English roll-arm; surprisingly, its leg held up. He sat there stiffly, determined not to slouch, determined not to relent. His hands gripped the edge of his seat, but he soon relinquished it; if he was going to sit stiffly, it was his responsibility, not that of the roll-arm, to keep himself from wavering. His reddened cheeks were beginning to whiten; he willed them to a faint pink, because it conveyed the appropriate amount of agitation for the scene. If he was sweating, he didn't feel it. He had chosen a breathable outfit for the occasion, anticipating sweat from all the movement required of a host and from all the bodies of his guests as they pressed up against one another in a small room. His breathing, like his posture, never wavered, with short, steady breaths requiring little movement. He could not hear or feel those breaths. He gave his body the benefit of the doubt and assumed that they were happening.

He thought of how he would deliver the news to Suhad and his parents. There were several ways to deliver good news, but never more than one to deliver bad. He needed to get it right. On any other day, he likely would have. But not today. Today was a day of wrong. He didn't know why, and he didn't know why he should care. Understanding something does not in itself mean it could be prevented or corrected. Sometimes tragedies occur because a void needs to be filled.

The catatonic voice he'd used with the operator seemed most appropriate for the occasion. But it wouldn't work. Firas needed to be strong, to cradle them all into the news, to thrust his shoulder forward for their tears and pry his ears open for the inescapable pleas to say that he was wrong, that it was all a misunderstanding, the youngest Dareer had survived the fall.

After the initial delivery there had to come the defense. The fault was his, after all. He was the hero of his own story, and the villain in Mazen's. The villain won, but the story was not over. The other Dareers would avenge the lost son, and would do so via an endless and righteous stream of passive-aggressive remarks and silent treatments, and the occasional exclusion from family-related events like their monthly dinner outings. Likely they would devote themselves more closely to Allah, not the merciful one who loves all beings but the wrathful one who smites them. Then Firas would alter his voice and mannerisms to fit the lifelong apology to which he was sentenced. In his attempt to break free from one confinement filled with shame, he wound up getting transferred to another, filled also with guilt and regret. Even now he could see this confinement shrinking.

He scanned the living room and cringed. Nearly everything had been set. The party blowers rested comfortably on the folding tables alongside the flowers at their center. He could have waited until later; he could have let Maysa take care of everything as she was hired to do. But too vividly he could hear the noise that was to be. Not only the party blowers, whose ill-timed wheezes bounced from guest to guest, but all of it. He heard the chatter among the guests, the introductory *So how do you know Firas?* and the compliments they may have shared of what a wonderful person he is. He heard the rustle of wrapping paper from the gifts he instructed everyone not to bring but were brought anyway because *don't be silly!* He heard ceramic clinking in toasts to his honor, the beastly chewing of his lamb and the clicking of tongues prying pieces of it out of teeth. He heard the music as an undertone, then as something greater, a more all-encompassing thing that refused to settle for underscoring the mood of the moment and insisted instead on dictating it, guiding everyone to the state they were supposed to be in, which was anything but mourning. He heard the slow sizzle of his tension dissolving and the deceleration of his heartbeat against the rib cage of the warm body enveloping him.

And then he tore it all to shreds.

Crashes of cups and plates, volcanic thrusts of food, the violent jerking of flowers that so resembled strangulation. One by one, he popped the balloons with his feet and fists until their flaccid remains littered the terracotta rug. He upturned the folding tables with a scream that blunted the resulting thump, and then smashed the Bluetooth speaker against the windowsill before wondering if he'd forgotten anything, if any element of his party had survived the massacre so he could make sure to kill it too. The monster in him had fully emerged, and while he had satiated most of its appetite, Firas suspected some of its remaining hunger would set it loose again soon.

As he surveyed the mess, he remembered the final strap before pulling the switch to complete the execution. He couldn't believe it had come to this, after all these years, that he would be forced to do it again. He thought of how precisely to go about it. Calling them was out of the question, for the monotony of his voice would be instantly detected and its root unearthed. To text them made sense, but not for Firas, not for the man who crafted invitations by hand. It would require an email, no less cordial and professional than a cover letter. Its content would need to produce a sense of regret over any inconvenience combined with a sense of urgency, of legitimacy, regarding the reason behind it. But it also had to convey the need for privacy. He began typing:

My dearest guests,
Unfortunate circumstances prevent me from hosting my birthday party on this day. I appreciate you all for making space for me in your busy lives, and I hope you can understand that I would not be canceling this event, to which I was so looking forward, without valid cause.
Sincerely,
Firas Dareer

He read and reread it, then diverted his eyes away from it for precisely five minutes before reading it once more with fresher eyes. But before he could assure himself of its adequacy and send it off, a rush of footsteps barreled into the house.

"We got a call about a suicide?" A pair of officers arrived, one hunchbacked and withered, the other plump and boyish. Firas led them to the side of the house, whence he glimpsed a prying Mr. Grint across the street and flashed him a vicious scowl. He also noticed there was no ambulance in the driveway. He understood why, but somehow he thought he would be exempt from the process, from being questioned in the way the man who found the body always is.

"Is this your brother?" asked the hunchbacked one, while his partner took notes.

"Yes."

"He jumped?"

"No. He let go."

"Is anyone else home?"

Firas shook his head, wondering if he was displaying sufficient sadness, and whether it would look more or less suspicious if he amplified its audiovisual cues.

The officers assessed the scene, peering up at least three times at Mazen's window, and so many times at the meditation garden that Firas lost count. They instructed him to wait for them inside and he did. Eventually, the hunchbacked one came into the living room and took note of the mess.

"What happened here?"

Firas stared at him for a second, praying the scene would speak for itself and then knowing it would not. "I'm not in a partying mood anymore."

The officer noticed the birthday sash on one of the folding chairs. He had no reaction to it, because reactions were not part of his job. "Has he ever tried to—"

"Yes. Once, two years ago, with a bottle of ibuprofen." Firas had seen enough films to know most of the questions coming his way, hoping to use his flimsy grasp of the process to hurry it along before his parents returned from the nursing home.

While waiting for the medical examiner to arrive, most of the questions were cleared: background information on Mazen's mental health, the medication he took, the contact information for his psychiatrist.

Then the officer questioned him about his final interaction. Firas lied, claiming to have witnessed the fall before words could be exchanged. The officer nodded, then asked: "Can I use your bathroom?"

Firas initially suspected that the officer was merely pretending to need the bathroom to verify the bit about the ibuprofen, to deduce from its absence whether Mazen truly did try to kill himself before. An absurd notion (there were much easier and more substantive ways of confirming it), quickly dispelled and quickly replaced. Firas's thoughts turned to his grandfather's nursing home—specifically its distance from the Dareer house. He estimated a thirty-five-minute drive given the detours caused by the pride parade. As for how long it would take his parents to get Jido resettled, which may have come with a fervent fight from the management (it was his third escape, after all), he calculated approximately an hour before they would arrive back home. Likewise for Suhad, who was likely enjoying her time with the cousins and would be in no hurry to return.

The hunchbacked officer returned from the bathroom.

"How much longer is this going to take?" Firas asked him.

"The M.E. should be here in a few minutes."

Firas's panic swelled. All he could hear now was the hand of Time, drumming its fingers along the parts of his back he couldn't reach, combined with the sputter of an engine crawling up the driveway and the jarring screech of brakes and frightened parents. Police tape stretched across the front of the house, barricading the neighbors who now wandered over with the elongated necks of ostriches risen from their hole in the sand. The plump, boyish officer blocked their view of his brother's corpse, but at some point he would have to move. At some point Firas's failure would have to be witnessed and judged.

The medical examiner arrived, dressed in protective gear: gloves, booties, goggles, face mask, hair covering, and a white jumpsuit, all of which struck Firas as embarrassingly excessive for the occasion. She evaluated the scene and the body and took pictures of both. Then she mumbled something to the officers that Firas couldn't hear, or didn't wish to hear. Before long, she was done evaluating and photographing, and the officers approached him.

"We're gonna be taking the body now," said the hunchbacked one, and he informed Firas of whom he needed to contact to retrieve it.

Eventually the tape came down and they were gone. What Firas hadn't expected was that they would take some of Mazen's possessions with them. He knew they had to take the body, of course, but the inanimate objects that composed his brother's life seemed to him off-limits. As though the loss were not great enough on its own, it had to include the removal of the things he owned and used and now, in his absence, had no real sense of themselves.

Firas stood in the doorway, watching his brother being carted away, the blood seeping through the white sheet over his head, when the sound of mouth-breathing and bone-creaking pierced the air.

"Bismillah . . ."

Struggling to tear his gaze away from the body, Firas turned to her. "What are you doing back so soon?"

Maysa stood there, gawking at him. At his unflinching eyes. At how dry they were. "I come to clean our mess."

CHAPTER FOURTEEN

Mazen looked peaceful lying there, his leg dangling off the side of the bed. Firas was always quick to approach his brother when it was time to alert him to dinner. But when he saw that Mazen's eyes were closed, he could not help but take a moment before waking him. Such peace did not deserve so quick a disturbance. It was much too elegant, the dangling leg punctuating its serenity. A serenity that softened the contours of his face. Brushed aside his hair. Massaged his shoulders. Pried open his mouth. Whitened his skin. Stopped his breathing. Erased his heartbeat.

It was the not knowing that unsettled Firas, really. He was unaware of the protocol, as no school he attended ever taught it. They taught racial tolerance and sexual consent and never getting into cars with strangers; but no instructions were ever given for handling the discovery of a self-harmed sibling. Despite the initial shock, Firas remained calm. He alerted all the appropriate people, drove everyone to the hospital, brought his parents and sister water and food as they sat in the waiting room. Then, after Mazen's return from the hospital, Firas set about petitioning local schools to educate the masses on how to handle themselves in such a situation. Of the thirty-three high schools that exist in the city of Detroit, all but five went ahead with a lesson plan they deemed "long overdue," with many even giving an additional one at night for the general public. This lesson, as Firas envisioned, would educate people about the steps required when one finds an unconscious body: checking the breathing and pulse, calling emergency medical services, performing CPR, stopping blood flows, and a long list of things *not* to do when administering first aid. Having already gone through the experience once and, for the most part, succeeding, Firas never felt the need to take the lesson himself. Instead he basked in a sliver of pride, rigid and bland as his bouts of pride often were, and continued to live his life.

It never occurred to him, somehow, that such a lesson would include the warning signs that come before, and the many steps thereafter.

There was no cleanup required in Mazen's bedroom now. Even the first time, Firas had little to do beyond washing the glass of water his brother had used to swallow the pills. Then, upon seeing the bottle of ibuprofen on the nightstand, he noticed that its cap was missing and determined to find it. Finding it was crucial to Firas, and the more time he spent searching for it, the more crucial it became, leading him to every crevice in the room, and a few just outside the door, until he eventually discovered it in a vent that blended into the walnut-brown carpeted floor. After that, he was done. The bed didn't even need to be made, just unwrinkled.

He gazed out the window and saw Maysa kneeling by the meditation garden. Without any instruction from Firas, she had retrieved the stiff-bristle brush his mother kept under the kitchen sink and set to scrubbing the blood off the rock with a solution of water and washing soda. She was being helpful and it unnerved him. He'd spent years seeing this woman as his enemy, and did so more on this day than any before it. He had by now *conditioned* himself to view her this way, and in less than an hour she completely upended this view. He wondered, then, what she did for the other families she worked for. What kind of messes did she clean for them? Generally, her work at these other houses was quite standard. She dusted and mopped and occasionally cooked, or, in cases where the woman of the house was of a domineering sort, merely assisted in these tasks. But there were moments, as this one, when she came upon the anomalous. Moments that took place at crowded gatherings—backyard weddings, memorial services, baby showers, and so on. More often than not, however, they occurred in the background during commonplace chores. The foreground, really, for Maysa herself was the background. Maysa and her brush, setting the stage for spouses quarreling, spouses making up, children sneaking out, medical emergencies, basements flooding, kitchen fires, and so many incidents that would prove scandalous upon public reveal. She never spoke a word about them, even when Firas's mother, desperate for interaction during her recuperation, prodded her. Nonetheless, Maysa remembered every bit of every scene, her peripheral vision honed to ensure that she never missed a detail, never dropped her guard against the joy that still existed around her even as it ceased to exist within her. She could remember the exact number of volumes in the Hadith collection the Najjars always flaunted to their guests; she could recognize how much thyme had sprouted from the Abu Hassans' garden since the week before; she could recall what time the smoky scent of arabica would float out of the Asghars' kitchen; she could recite by heart the Bible verses etched into the gold-plated plaques above Yara and Michael Shehadeh's bed, and every vulgar word they shouted when they fucked. She knew every color of every slate tile, every length of every curtain, every barbecue in which the kebabs were grilled to sheer perfection.

But this was rarely the case with the Dareer house. Throughout most of her tenure, Maysa remembered its details only upon stepping through the front door and forgot them the instant she stepped back out. Her peripheral vision became obsolete in this house. It was only after New Year's Eve that this began to change. Suddenly Maysa took notice of things, her peripheral vision heightening exponentially with each visit, seeing more and more no matter how little of it she wished to. At times she even found herself inserting her presence into their lives, reading text messages and hiding folding tables, in ways that inevitably placed her in *their* peripheral vision. And now, as she scrubbed Mazen's blood off the rock, she found her peripheral vision going from obsolete to completely nonexistent, rendering her unable to see anything *but* the blood. In spite of herself, and despite several decades of training, Maysa had become a part of this foreground as much as anybody else.

She could not even see that Firas was watching her from Mazen's room, looking terribly uneasy. This uneasiness, however, had more to do with her than it did with the blood. In Maysa, Firas now saw an alliance forming, a secret slithered into their everyday interactions, and he wanted nothing more than to break it. He hated growing close to her. It reminded him of the irksome connection he felt whenever he caught her praying. Somehow the fact that she never saw him watching her made the connection even stronger. He simply stood there from behind, wondering, just as he wondered about her now, what precisely she prayed for. He grew curious about her family, her apartment, her finances, her hobbies, her passions, her *stories*, always balking at this curiosity yet never managing to rid himself of it. The truth was, Maysa prayed for very little, engaging in salat much less out of faith than she did throughout her youth. Nowadays, she did it simply because she had nothing else to do.

Firas marched back out of Mazen's room and into his own. He opened his laptop and searched for the necessary address. He doffed his party outfit, threw on a mismatched tee and sweatpants (his laundry day outfit), and by the time he was ready to head over, Maysa was already sweeping up deflated balloons and ceramic shards from the living room floor.

"Where are you going?" she asked. "To police station?"

When a lie presents itself, it is one's duty to welcome it. ". . . Yes."

"What I tell your Mama and Baba?"

"Tell them we went to get candy."

She gawked at him, but nodded as though it were any other instruction given from an employer to a maid.

As he stepped out of the house, he noticed Mr. Grint stepping out of his own house, rushing while trying hard not to look as though he were rushing. He hoped that Firas would inform him of what had happened—not out of concern, but out of a need to ingratiate himself into a conversation no one was having to begin with. When it became clear that Firas, barreling towards the Lyft parked directly before Mr. Grint's house, would not initiate any such interaction, Mr. Grint took the liberty himself.

"Is everything okay, Firas?"

"Have a good evening, Mr. Grint." He opened the back door of the Lyft.

"Are the police shutting down your party? I swear I'm not the one who call—"

Firas slammed the car door, and he could see that Mr. Grint finished the sentence anyway. As the Lyft drove off, Firas noticed Mr. Grint's beagle idling in his doorway. Firas pitied the dog. He was adorable and friendly enough to merit an abundance of attention, yet none of the neighbors ever bothered to pet him in the presence of his owner—except one. Mazen had always wanted a dog. It was haram, of course, so there was no chance his parents would ever get him one, and eventually he stopped asking. Firas, however, once thought of asking on his behalf. It was shortly after Mazen's first attempt. He wondered if a dog might elevate his brother's mood, but no studies had confirmed a direct link between pet ownership and suicide; for this reason, he abandoned the idea. Or so he claimed this was the reason he abandoned the idea. The truth was, he didn't dare ask his parents to procure Mazen a dog, because what if they had said no? The mere possibility that their faith might supersede their son's very life absolutely horrified Firas. Horrified him not only because of how it would affect Mazen, but also because it guaranteed the demise of his own relationship with them.

As the Lyft proceeded down the block, Firas saw what appeared to be his parents' Ford Focus. He worried that Mr. Grint might still be outside and raise the issue of the police. But upon glancing back, Firas noticed that the license plate didn't match. It wasn't even a Ford Focus. The threads of his sanity, having already begun to unspool, were now reuniting in the shape of what he slowly recognized as a noose. He labored to keep his attention on something, anything, other than Mazen. He would never lift the burden of his brother's death from his mind, but he could plow it all the way to the back and bury it beneath another. Should space become scarce, he would create more by eliminating some of the more expendable items: memories, fantasies, opinions, beliefs, and even, if necessary, facts.

He quickly steered his mind towards more positive thoughts, particularly of his promotion, the saving grace of the day. How he enjoyed his time at the firm. It was the one place he had ever worked where everyone was pleasant. His superiors (which was nearly everyone) never made him fetch coffee or refill the soap dispensers, never gaslit him that these tasks were a necessary path to success in the field and not simply a convenient way of exploiting the young. They always assigned him work that would mold him, championing his contributions without stealing credit, and thus inspiring him to contribute more and buoying his hope for the future. Even his mistakes were often met with a shrug, a zealous *You'll get 'em next time, champ!* that assuaged his self-flagellating tendencies. And the other interns were such fun to work with. A rare group that supported rather than undermined one another, especially Howie, who fumbled more than any of them and still never got scolded, even when he accidentally sat on a model of a chalet twenty minutes before Luis was set to pitch it. It was wonderful to know they were sincerely happy for his promotion. Although he did sense that at least part of their joy stemmed from pity. They all had trust funds to get them through months, even years, of unpaid labor, and knew full well that he didn't. He hated that they pitied him. Or rather, he hated that they pitied him for being poor, for something he didn't quite mind. It was as though they were painting a portrait of him that didn't match his image of himself. And yet he knew that they were more intuitive than he gave them credit for. Throughout their lunches together, none of them ever remarked on how he ordered the least expensive item on the menu or drank nothing but water, but it was unlikely that they never noticed. It was unlikely that they found it perfectly normal that he always paid his bill ten minutes before theirs arrived so as to avoid having to split it. For a time he sent them terrible reviews of the high-end restaurants they chose in order to deter them from going, before one too many refrains of *My treat!* sunk him into his ergonomic mesh chair and he stopped.

But if he minded being poor, it was only because it was among the first things people noticed about him. Not that he was bright or hardworking, not his potential for success or his occasional bouts of courage. But something over which he had little control, and adversely affected the way he connected to the world around him.

Of course, despite the affection they all had for one another, things were now bound to change, the dynamic would be different. He would be their superior, and the possibility of resentment loomed all around him. Not only that, but he had a growing suspicion that the mistakes that were often shrugged off would now be weaponized against him at every moment to deny him the pleasantness he had previously taken for granted. Luis was mayhem personified, and he never made the contingency plans that encompassed so much of Firas's life. He threw himself into the fire and did his best not to get burned, sometimes succeeding, sometimes not. He would never tolerate mistakes from a paid employee. Even Raymond, who strived so desperately to appease the firm's minorities, would likely develop microaggressions, some form of condescension that tied Firas's mistakes to his ethnicity. Everything in the office would be different: the toothy smiles exchanged for crushing glares, the sighs of relief replaced with groans of menace, the leisurely pace at which he accomplished his tasks now pushed to improbable speeds. And this new phase of his career would begin tomorrow.

Tomorrow.

Was there even such a thing?

It occurred to him now that there was, and he had no plan for it. He was set to begin his new job early. How could he possibly go into the office now, how could he possibly explain this to Luis? He supposed the other interns, particularly Celeste, would provide him with moral support, as they were supposed to on this night. He questioned their helpfulness, however. Not only for tomorrow but for the party and what would have been. Lovely as they were, he sometimes doubted, throughout the preparations, whether his guest list added up to a sum greater than its parts. His guests were, after all, facing off against his parents, and by extension God. His mother had already turned against him earlier that evening; a roomful of strangers would hardly deter or deflect her ire. Publicly, perhaps, but not privately.

Unless it wasn't ire. Unless she hadn't, in fact, turned against him. There was something that rang false in the display, wasn't there? Typically, her anger showed in wizened lips, the upper sliding over the lower as if attempting to swallow it, and her arms stiff by her sides, knowing that if she moved them she would knock whatever they touched halfway across the room. But he had seen no such traits this time around. Her eyes were cold and her voice was taut, but both betrayed something beneath: a sort of desperation.

It made sense that she reacted to his knowledge of her affair the way she had. As far as she knew, he was Firas the Pious. He had lied to her about his relationship to Islam so much and so expertly that she couldn't possibly know he was actually on her side. The claws she brandished were not to attack but to defend herself against her husband's son. Surely he would take his father's side; surely he would help him tie her to the stake and burn her in front of all her neighbors, all her fellow Muslims. Even if her husband decided not to divorce her, this would be a scandal she could never live down. Every meal she cooked would be penance, every word of kindness an apology. On top of her own destruction, her own immortal soul, Firas would destroy that of the man she loved. Not only his, but his wife's as well, as she too would be punished and burned at the stake for her failure to satisfy her husband, the prestigious doctor who gave her everything a wife should want. Firas's father would hardly go unscathed himself. There was always so much talk at the mosque about his unemployment; how much more there would be were his marriage to end as his career did, how much more demoralized he would feel. If any hope remained for his parents to rekindle their love, it would surely evaporate. Firas's mother would lose more than she even had to begin with. Her entire life was in the hands of this young man who looked and sounded vaguely like her son.

Firas gazed out his window and thought about his parents arriving home. Doing the math would occupy his mind, so he began his calculations. The most probable scenario was that his parents left the nursing home just as he left the Dareer house, which meant they were a mere thirty minutes away from pulling into the driveway, minus five minutes if the traffic lights were in their favor, plus another ten before they would begin to wonder why neither of their sons was home. Yet no matter the myriad scenarios he envisioned for their ride home, no matter how much comfort he drew from the numbers, every calculation Firas did amounted to bloodshed. Thirty minus five plus ten totaled thirty-five droplets that Maysa forgot to scrub off the rock in the meditation garden. If Maysa scrubbed seventy more times than she normally did when cleaning, then she was twice as likely to have gotten all of them. But seventy more scrubs across the rock meant seventy fewer across the side of the house on which the blood splattered, which would mean there was approximately a fourteen hundred percent chance that she missed several droplets and the moonlight shining twice as brightly as it did the night before meant a two hundred percent increase in the likelihood that the blood would glisten enough to catch his parents' attention as they pulled into the driveway in thirty minus five minutes. As he sought to calculate the exact number of droplets that remained on the rock in the meditation garden that his parents never once bothered to use, and determine the exact angle at which the moon would bear down its glow across the surface of the earth, and figure out the amount of patience Mr. Grint would have as he waited in front of his living room window for the opportunity to once again pry, Firas noticed that he had arrived at his destination.

CHAPTER FIFTEEN

He knew he'd found him when he saw the sign, which only Kashif would have been both clever enough to conceive and bold enough to display. Firas staggered along the march's bank, on which a flurry of marchers flowed before ebbing back onto the street with their brethren, a repeated occurrence that bothered nobody but the pedestrians trying to get past. Occasionally Kashif's sign would be sucked into the hurricane of so many others, all pulsing up and then dipping back down like a game of Whac-A-Mole. Fortunately, and just as Firas would have expected, Kashif's sign ultimately soared above the rest:

WITH 3 BILLION DOLLARS A YEAR ISRAEL CAN AFFORD TO BUY US DINNER FIRST

"I can't believe you're here," Kashif said with endearing zeal. "What happened to your party?"

"I canceled it."

Kashif slowed, causing fellow marchers to bump into them and propel them forward at an accelerated pace. He turned cold, and Firas instantly guessed what he was about to say. "You pussied out."

"No. I'm still gonna do it. Just not with a party."

"Oh. Okay. Well, good. But why are you here?"

Firas tried to think of an answer, but his thoughts were mostly strangled by the rousing chants around him. And he was grateful; even if the cacophony was not pleasant, it was also not the sound of his brother's skull cracking against a rock. Kashif ignored his own question and resumed his chanting along with the others.

The brigade took a smooth turn to the right, just as the steel barricades from the pride parade were being shifted off to the curb.

"Mercutio's is closing," Kashif said, gesturing to the establishment around the corner.

"Why?"

"I guess business is bad. I haven't been there in a while myself."

Mercutio's was the restaurant he and Kashif frequented during the summer after Firas's high school graduation. It had been open since the late 1940s, barn-red lighting draping black button-tufted double booths that made it an ideal place for closeted queers to nestle into each other before the sunlight faded and the town was engulfed in waves of anonymity. Throughout the 1970s, the red beat on, but the booths extended to half circles and shriveled so the tops of heads soon poked above them and faces could be discerned. By the time Firas and Kashif were regulars, the lighting had brightened drastically, and among the things that could be discerned about Mercutio's was the fact that its food wasn't very good at all.

"Do you think we should go back, before they officially shut their doors?" Kashif asked.

"If you want. I don't really see the point though."

Kashif did, for he had had many of his best moments there with Firas, the only man with whom he'd ever gone. Firas's indifference wounded him, but his presence at the march compensated.

"This is my second march of the day," Kashif said, raising his sign to offset the pause in his chanting.

"Mine too."

Kashif gaped at him and the arm holding his sign sank. "You didn't tell me you were at the parade." Firas detected his disappointment, the sting of his exclusion from one momentous occasion in Firas's life now replaced by the sting of his exclusion from another.

"I wasn't planning on going, it just sort of happened."

Kashif's disappointment morphed into modest glee: Firas's attendance at the parade confirmed to him how serious he was about coming out.

"Well next year you'll join me at the alternative march we set up. No cops or corporations. And we can march in it together." He sped through his enunciation of the word *together* with the confidence of someone who owned all subsidiary rights to it.

The conversation lulled, and Kashif resumed his chanting. The cacophony of the scene was loudening, bearing down on

Firas to unholy depths. But if he didn't submit himself to it, thoughts of the bloody rock would consume him.

"Where does this march end?" he asked.

"Brightmoor." Kashif scanned the area to see where exactly they were. "We should get there in the next half hour."

Firas dreaded marches, or at least dreaded being part of them. People who marched were simultaneously loud and peaceful, chaotic and organized, singular and inextricably bound. Such dissonance made him vulnerable, because even when the march came to its stop at Brightmoor, it seemed to him as though it, and by extension he, was going absolutely nowhere.

"I ran into my parents on the way here," said Kashif.

". . . Did they say anything to you?"

"Nope. They were heading towards the rally, saw the sign I was holding, and then turned the other way."

"Oh."

"Apparently they're only interested in a *gay*-free Palestine."

"Well, doesn't it make more sense to free it step by step?"

"Is that a joke?" Kashif gawked long enough for Firas to understand the question was not rhetorical. "Firas, we need collective liberation. Nobody gets left behind."

Every phrase Kashif uttered made him think of Mazen. *Ran into my parents. Turned the other way. Left behind.* The burden he pushed to the back of his mind was fighting so fiercely that a discussion of the most innocuous and incongruous topics—credit scores, the *Mona Lisa*, honeybees communicating through dance—would have led him to think of his brother.

"I agree," he told Kashif, desperate to change the direction of the conversation.

"I'm glad to see you taking an interest." There was the underlying censure that Kashif was notorious for embedding into his remarks. It wasn't quite sarcasm; it was something more pernicious, something oblique designed to force onto you a different view of yourself, like a funhouse mirror exaggerating your worst flaws in ways that only you could truly see. But whereas he normally would have stopped after just one remark, his trademark eloquence infused with throat-slashing precision, this time he went further. "Maybe you could continue taking an interest."

This deeper jab betrayed a hint of anxiety and foreshadowed a favor asked; Firas wondered what it could possibly be, knowing that any hesitation from Kashif, the boldest person he'd ever known, stemmed not from any doubt in his own righteousness but from an understanding that his boldness sometimes scared Firas away. Whatever he was about to ask, human rights issues were merely the prelude.

"I've been thinking about what that sheikh said," Kashif told him. Firas could hardly grasp the notion of Kashif paying heed to a religious figure, particularly one of a different religion from his own. This sort of thing has been known to happen, but Kashif was not a lion that could ever be tamed nor a horse that could ever be led.

"What are you getting at?" Firas asked, nervous he may have just lost the only person he could turn to in this moment.

"I'm going to Palestine."

"For what?"

"What do you mean, 'for what?' I need to see where I come from. I need to contribute to the land, to make my mark on it."

Firas struggled to understand the reasoning, wishing he could be in Kashif's head as much as Kashif was in his.

"I'll be volunteering in the Aida refugee camp during the summer."

"Who are you gonna be staying with?"

"I have plenty of friends who live there."

"Really?"

"Of course."

"Where did you get the money for the flight?"

"I'm putting most of the cost on a credit card."

"And how are you gonna pay it off?"

"It doesn't matter, Firas."

"It doesn't matter?"

"Yeah. My credit card isn't what I'm worried about right now. Look around you. Look at what's happening to us."

Firas surveyed the march. The sea of righteous indignation emanating the rattle of impending change.

"Do you know what this march is about?"

Firas opened his mouth to answer *Palestine*, but Kashif mercifully interrupted him. "Obama is negotiating a deal to give Israel billions of more dollars every year. That money means more occupation, more colonization, more apartheid. More bombs and bullets and blood. And it's being funded with *our* tax dollars! How many more of us have to be killed for something to be done?"

Firas winced, partly at Kashif, who often sounded as though he were already on the campaign trail, but also partly at himself, for his inability to feel roused in the middle of what was unequivocally a rousing scene.

"We cannot fight for our rights and our history as well as our future until we are armed with weapons of criticism and dedicated consciousness," Kashif added.

This time Firas did feel roused, not by the words, which he knew must be Edward Said's, but by how effortlessly Kashif could transform them into something entirely his own.

"When I get back to the States, I'm moving to D.C.," Kashif continued.

Firas stopped abruptly, and he stopped Kashif along with him by tugging back the arm holding the sign, resulting in another bump from the people behind them, only this time it didn't propel them forward. They simply stood there, the other marchers bypassing them. Firas pulled Kashif over to the sidewalk. "What are you talking about?"

"I'm leaving, Firas."

"What are you gonna do in D.C.?"

"I got accepted into Georgetown. I start in the fall."

"Georgetown?"

"I wanna be close to the action. Go where my voice matters most and learn all I can to make it sing."

"When did you decide this?"

"A little after I left your house."

"So everything you said to me—"

"Still applies. I'm rooting for you, Firas. I'll always root for you." Here he inhaled deeply, paused deliberately. "I want you to come with me."

What surprised Firas about this proposition was the fact that it didn't immediately make him scoff at its ostensible absurdity. Because right beneath it lay a floor of perfect sense.

After all, what did he really have to stay for? Surely his family would never accept his sexuality now. Years of overt homophobia cruelly interspersed with more subtle forms: pursed lips to stifle disdain, furtive glances to gauge proximity, accelerated walks to avoid proximity, even the changing of a news channel to ignore reports of hate crimes. And now, he had killed one of the straight Dareers, the most vulnerable, whose death was tethered to his sexuality no matter how much ground he cultivated between them or what joyous crops he harvested from it. *He did it because you're gay*, they would think to themselves. They would never say the phrase aloud, for doing so would highlight its sheer madness and retrieve the common sense that expels rage and leaves in its wake a gaping hole. Rage was a horrible thing, but it was Heaven to emptiness's Hell.

It was not only consequence he thought of as he considered Kashif's proposition. The futility of his life in Detroit hinged not merely on the disapproval of his family, but also on the possibility that their disapproval might not even affect him. The Dareers were not close, a bond incrementally diluted by things unspoken, so why bother preserving this familial bond when the risk of staying proved so much greater than the reward? Did he believe on some level that his announcement would bring them closer? Did he believe it was the missing link, the key to a treasure whose immeasurable cost—the life of his own brother—was justifiable? No. He had fought hard to maintain his relationship with them merely because it was fundamental. Identity starts with family, and every other part of oneself is built upon it. One can tear down the showy penthouse suite, but the ground floor is another matter entirely.

For Firas to lose this bedrock would be to restart the very core of his being. The sheer energy required for such an endeavor, the sheer energy required just to *imagine* it, was too much even for him. But with Kashif's help, he could perhaps succeed. If he left them, he would give no explanation, barely a goodbye. They would welcome his departure from their family, from their house, even from their town, for Detroit no longer belonged to him any more than Palestine did.

Kashif fidgeted. His eyes darted back and forth between Firas and the march, which was now trailing ahead and ready to jettison them. This raised the other question Firas needed to ask himself: Was Kashif the right man for him? Was he truly the one with whom Firas needed to take this next step in his journey?

"Yes, I am," Kashif said.

Firas recoiled, despite a great effort not to. But unlike all the times before, he now found comfort in Kashif reading his mind and unloading, in the process, some of its contents.

"I know we've had our moments, Firas, but I love you more than anything. And you love me. We wouldn't keep coming back to each other like this if we didn't." Firas ran a couple of his fingers across his mouth, as though wiping from them the stain of his lingering thoughts. "But that's not the only reason I think we're destined to be together." For all his brilliance and wisdom and fearlessness, Kashif could not help sometimes sounding like a lovelorn teen.

"What else is there?" Firas asked.

"Again, look around you. Palestinians are disappearing." Firas suddenly noticed that the marchers had turned another corner and were out of sight. Kashif seemed not to mind anymore. "We need to stick together, now more than ever. Especially queer Palestinians. We're being erased on both ends. Think of how much inspiration we could bring to our movement as a gay Palestinian couple. We could make a huge difference together!"

Firas had little knowledge of social and political activism, but Kashif knew enough for both of them. And it was true that Firas loved him. Not just loved him, but felt his presence at all times, even throughout the most chaotic day of his life. And when he did, when Kashif Hasnawi pricked his mind or his heart, he threw Time over its own head and dangled it by its ankles above the void with which it threatened humanity. Time was no match for this young man he loved so dearly. Yes, Firas had little knowledge of social and political activism, but he knew with absolute certainty that Kashif was right about one thing: the two of them could make a huge difference together. Something ethereal was born out of their encounters. The minutes skipped past the hours, the days, the weeks, the months, the years, snapping at the heels of eternity, which was not a vast ocean as Firas had always pictured it, but a lone cloud mousing overhead across sterile skies invisible from the dunes of errand life. Kashif was a missing piece finally found, their love forever frozen at the precise moment of its discovery.

"But I have one condition," he continued. And in the moment before he stated it, Firas, so eager to say yes to anything Kashif asked of him, grew nervous, because the one condition he could not accept and the one condition about to be forced upon him would inevitably turn out to be the same.

"You have to tell your family *tonight*. Not tomorrow, not next week. Tonight. That's the only way I can be sure you're really in this with me."

Myriad scenarios flashed through Firas's mind, and he tried not to sweat. He would lose his family no matter when he told them, but to tell them now would cost him something else: the moral high ground. Were he to wait years into the future, he could convince everyone he was the victim of an intolerant, ignorant family; but were he to do it on the night he let his younger brother die because he was too preoccupied selecting music and burning croutons, he would never claim the sympathy he was owed. He would never convince the world their relationship died on the sword of his sexuality, but instead because of the selfish timing of its reveal. Nor would anyone believe that the reveal had been planned long before Mazen's death, or care even if they did, for the plan should have been rescheduled to a tragedy-free night. And no one would forgive him for subjecting his grieving family to more grief simply to hold on to the man he loved. Not even Kashif would forgive him for it. Kashif would want Firas to do the right thing and wait for grief to wilt.

"Okay," Firas answered.

Kashif beamed, the smile still stretched across his face throughout the kiss he was imprinting on Firas's lips, which pursed shut to restrain the giveaways of his guilt: the giggle, the trembling voice, even the damning secret itself, which was biding its time, slowly and calculatedly as though unwilling to settle for any moment in which it couldn't wield its deepest, sharpest cut.

"Come over after you tell them. We'll celebrate."

Firas nodded, his still-pursed lips convincing Kashif he wanted another kiss.

"Bye," said Kashif, who scurried to catch up to the march. Firas watched his body melt into the stygian backdrop of the city. A bus headed directly to his block rumbled up to a nearby stop and Firas rushed to board it. On the way, he saw the marchers once more, the vantage point of an elevated seat granting him a view of a sign that jutted up higher than the others. It featured the picture of a teenaged Palestinian boy above the question *HOW MANY MORE MOHAMMEDS?* and Firas saw in its undulant trajectory the pieces of his life slowly coming together, the drainage of all that matters little, until he turned away from the window and peered instead at the smattering of passengers who may have been harboring their own Sunday tragedies. In the morning he would reunite with Kashif after pretending to have told his family, and he would rejoice in the fact that the march in which he had just ingratiated himself would lead him somewhere after all: away.

CHAPTER SIXTEEN

A s a child, Firas had a stalker. This stalker was big and wide, flashed amber eyes, prowled the streets in green skin, and purred like a curious cougar. Occasionally, the purr snapped into a roar—a brief one that shocked and shook him long after it subsided. This roar came without warning; in fact, it *was* a warning. One designed to ensure that Firas never forgot his stalker was there.

More than the roar, what disturbed him was the languid roll of his stalker's feet. The way in which all four of them trampled the gravel along their path, crunching it like bones. The sound of it was threatening in its consistency, violent in its ubiquity. Unlike the roar, however, this noise was not designed to scare him, nor even to make its presence known. Quite the contrary. It was designed to make its presence *felt*—to train the ears to accept it as part of everyday life, so that the mind may never question its place.

The stalking began three days after his seventh birthday, as though the Israeli state were vigilantly tracking the ages of Palestinian children and rushed to sic its soldiers on them just as the candles were blown. Seven was the most appropriate age at which to monitor them: it was the transitional period in which Palestinian boys exchange their stuffed toys and Lego blocks for action figures with guns. By age eight, they throw stones that scratch the occupation soldiers' helmets or, more tragically, their chins.

The Second Intifada had not yet erupted, but it was boiling, and the more sensitive Palestinians could smell it in the air and taste it in the dust the soldiers' boots kicked up off the ground. Firas's parents debated whether to let him go off on his own. His mother was very pregnant, on her way to becoming extremely pregnant, and her maternal instinct pounced at any thought of her children being harassed or harmed. His father, too, was made anxious by the idea, though his mother voiced it loudly enough for both of them. But a third voice, one buoyed by the wisdom and insouciance of old age, arose in the boy's defense.

"It's just down the street," his Teta said to them. His mother and father never dared to argue with her. The mere sight of her, with her lily-flecked hijab accentuating her leathery skin and elevated cheekbones, often dwarfed whatever words she spoke. In the end, however, it was more than Teta's intervention that persuaded them. His mother and father did not want Firas growing up scared of the world around him. Yes, it was frightening for a child to see occupation soldiers with guns and faces that oppressed in equal measure. But the most insidious facet of fear is its capacity to devour hope. Because while safety may have kept Firas alive, it would not keep him living.

His destination was a friend's house. And while he could not now remember much of what transpired on those exhilarating adventures along the corridors of boyhood imagination, he did remember the walk over there. He never saw his stalker, never met its eyes—not even its third eye, a smaller red one dotting a black square on the left side of the hood as though to cement the vehicle's distinctiveness—but he knew exactly what his stalker looked like. He knew the width and length of its windows, he knew the crisscross pattern of its grille, he knew the color and shape of the twin lights that stood watch atop its roof like vizslas sniffing for bombs. He also had a fairly accurate idea of how many seven-year-olds could fit into the back. He knew these details, and many others, because his stalker had siblings, dozens that multiplied in the mind of a child to millions, and he eventually came to a point where he recognized the jeep's features more than those of the Palestinian boys they stalked. He even knew and long remembered his stalker's name—AIL Storm M-240 Mark II—a familiarity he could not, in subsequent years, afford to the friend at the end of the street on which the stalking began.

Essential to the stalking of all these boys was the deliberate mimicry of their movements. When they sped, so sped the jeep. When they turned, so turned the jeep. When they stopped, so stopped the jeep. The boys worried so much about being seen and heard and *known* by these strange monstrous entities that they wondered if they should even go where they were planning to go, and the result was a cat-and-mouse dynamic in which the cat was not tracking the mouse but directing it.

But of all the things Firas knew about his stalker, one mystery always remained: the driver. He never had any idea of their age or their gender or what they may have looked like. They might have been short or tall, rugged or baby-faced, porcelain or olive-toned; the combinations of facial features were endless, and he spent most of his steps—extended beyond the customs of childhood to ensure a speedier arrival, yet never too much as to arouse further suspicion—mixing and matching them into the least frightening configuration. He pictured a slender, soft-skinned soldier with a perfect set of teeth that showed in frequent smiles; but once this kindly image settled in his mind, it was swiftly overcome by one of this slender, soft-skinned soldier squeezing through a sliver between buildings, yanking a hidden Firas by the arm, and tossing him into the back of the jeep. He pictured a soldier with upturned eyes and a cleft chin who liked to tell funny anecdotes. Then that image was quashed by one of the soldier turning Firas's arrest into a funny anecdote. *There was this one kid who actually thought I was there to* protect *people!* When he realized that no combination of features would assuage him, Firas focused on counting the number of steps it took to reach his destination. Something quantifiable and unvarying to infuse his journey with the safety of predictability. He couldn't pretend to be incurious about his stalker's master. But no matter how closely it crept up behind him, he was never curious enough to turn and look back.

As he sensed a new stalker on his way home from the bus stop after the march, Firas debated whether to look back. He considered first the possibilities by order of least to most unwanted: the police coming back to interrogate him further; a local reporter on a slow news day starved for a story; a hearse returning his brother's corpse as a sort of punishment; his parents, who would surely have gotten back from the nursing home and now wondered where their sons were. As the debate raged inside his head, he eventually came to a compromise whereby he glanced as far back as the hood of the car; it was more polished and expensive than the jeeps of his youth, but no less alarming. When the car jerked up right beside him, its passenger-side window rolled down.

"There's the birthday boy!"

Firas stooped to see the driver, whose presence outside his house, punctuated by a bright, goofy smile, twisted Firas's stomach.

"Howie, what are you doing here?" he asked. "Didn't you get my email?"

"What email?"

And with that, the memory of tucking away his phone without hitting Send on his email revealed itself in a terror-specked blur that dizzied him. He leaned on Howie's polished, expensive hood for balance.

"Are you okay, Fear-az?"

Firas rushed the remaining few feet to his house, burst inside, and saw, to his nauseating horror, that most of his party guests had arrived.

And they were eating mousse.

"I've never been to a party where dessert is served first!" his former co-worker Adaku said to him. "And am I tasting cayenne? It really gives it a kick!"

So far twenty of the expected twenty-four had arrived, all scattered throughout the living room, either standing around or sitting on the folding chairs, which Maysa had rearranged once they started to show. The peach English roll-arm, having once again cracked under the weight of its occupants, now bore its shame up against the far wall. Among the guests were the cousins and Mr. Lindstrom, who had returned with Suhad from their pizza outing.

"It's good we got pizza first," said his second cousin Youssef. "This mousse is great, but it wouldn't've filled me up!"

Suhad, who was the only one not indulging in the dessert, nodded along as though to vindicate her abandonment of his party.

As he locked eyes with his sister, Firas began to trace the evolution of her face, from its pensive stillness to its resolute tilt, to the crinkling of her brow, to the eventual narrowing of her eyes. He gauged the potential success of a distraction, a wry comeback to Youssef's innocuous remark, or an overtly humble plea for it to be repeated as though he hadn't heard it and could not, as the focal point of the evening, afford such negligence. But her face had frozen while her eyes displayed a rapid boost in suspicion and he knew that no distraction could deter the fated question.

"Where's Mazen?"

The perfect distraction came only then, in the form of a large stack of pizzas saddling the feeble arms of a delivery boy entering the house. Howie, entering right behind him, took out his wallet.

"I love Rudy's pizza!" he said. Adaku and Firas's high school friend Ted each took one half of the stack while Howie paid the delivery boy. "That's your congratulations present. And here . . . is your b-day present!" He handed Firas a gift bag and patted him on the shoulder. "Happy birthday. Again."

As the guests indulged in the pizza, he glanced at Maysa, who was amassing empty mousse cups onto a tray. Before heading into the kitchen, she leaned over to whisper to him: "I try texting you."

Firas had turned off his phone to avoid his parents. Upon turning it back on, he noticed, aside from the half dozen warnings of accumulating guests sent by Maysa, he had received one text message from each guest who arrived, three from ones who were on their way, and one from Professor Markum saying he couldn't make it after all, though Firas had little interest in reading why. He then read his mother's one and only message: *Having trouble at nursing home. Will arrive late to party.*

When he looked up from his phone, Suhad, as if by a glitch in a computer screen, appeared directly before him. "Where's Mazen?" she asked again. "Maysa said you took him out for ice cream?"

Rather than waging a fruitless effort to find a distraction, Firas instead feigned being distracted himself. To an extent, he was, by the precise number of minutes it had been since his mother had sent her text, and the presumed number of minutes, now appearing to be nearer to seconds, before the death of his brother finally had to be disclosed.

Footsteps approached from the front door, which nobody had bothered to close.

"Hey," muttered a devastatingly familiar voice. "Happy birthday . . ."

Suhad's facial contortions smoothed themselves out, and her eyes studied the dashing man before her as though he held the answer to her question. "Who's this?" she asked, immediately sensing, based on his lowered gaze and Firas's deep inhale, that this strange man she'd never met was not supposed to be here.

Before Firas could ask him what he was doing here, or how he'd even obtained the address, Tyrese spoke: "I got a text telling me to come over right away." He showed him the message on his phone; it came from a number Firas did not recognize, yet instantly deduced.

Amid Firas's shock, Tyrese turned to Suhad and held out his hand. "Hi. I'm Tyrese."

"Suhad. Nice to meet you."

And then the standard party question: "So how do you know Firas?" What surprised Firas, however, was that it came not from his sister, whose study of his boyfriend grew more intense by the second, but from Tyrese, who was studying her in return.

"Oh . . ." came Tyrese's reply to her answer. He had rushed over, figuring something had gone terribly wrong, only to find that the party was in full swing and his first impression on Firas's family was marked by denim shorts and Old Spice. He glanced at Firas, who could see in his eyes a glimmer of what looked vaguely like annoyance. Never having seen it from

Tyrese before, even when the circumstances unequivocally called for it, it was difficult for him to be sure and to know how best to react.

"And how do *you* know Firas?" It was inevitable, of course, for its omission from the proceeding would have been considered rude. But the added emphasis on the word *you* suggested a different motive altogether. Firas now studied Tyrese, expecting him to fumble through a toothy grin and one-word explanation (*College!*) with so much unwarranted zeal it would do anything but convince her.

"Hey, Firas," interrupted Ibtisam, her tongue struggling to trail the grease sliding down her forearm. "When you said you were serving food, we didn't realize you meant pizza! If we'd known we would've gone for tacos instead!" This did not deter her from devouring some more. "I was actually kinda worried you'd have one of those elaborate feasts you always liked. So glad I was wrong! This is awesome!"

Neither the cousins nor Mr. Lindstrom seemed even to notice that the decorations and place settings he'd arranged just a little while earlier were now entirely absent. They were eating off the paper plates left over from his parents' barbecue the year before, unbothered by the scorching grease seeping through.

"So how do you know Firas?" Ibtisam asked Tyrese after the introduction was made.

"Tyrese!" Celeste shouted from across the room. She hurried over and ensnared his boyfriend in her sinewy arms. Firas began to sweat. The three of them had attended the same college, so he figured a mutual connection was possible. But he hadn't figured the connection would be made public this soon.

"I didn't realize you guys knew each other!" Celeste said, her eyes darting back and forth from one to the other, their swipes reducing in speed and enhancing in precision as the answer to the question everyone kept asking now crystallized. Tyrese was a Stage 6, after all, and Firas, whom all the firm's interns knew hated being the center of attention yet for some mysterious reason decided to throw himself a party, was now standing conspicuously close to him. There was no evidence to validate Celeste's winsome smirk, no smoking gun in Firas's quivering hand, but that is the beauty and beastliness of the closet: it has shutters, but they're thin.

"I think you should take my job," Firas blurted.

". . . What?"

"Yeah, you'd be great at it."

"I can't take your promotion."

"I don't want it."

"How could you not want it?"

"I just don't."

"That's crazy! This is your whole future you're talking about. What do you plan to do instead?"

"I—"

"Wait," Tyrese interrupted. "When did you get a promotion? And why didn't you tell me?"

Celeste's gaze turned back to Tyrese, and with it, half her focus. She looked ready to divert the conversation back to his relationship with Firas, until—

"You still haven't told me where Mazen is," Suhad said. Another distraction, but one immediately demanding another distraction.

"Hey, Fy-russ!" shouted Bethany, the single mother from his cooking class. "This is great pizza! But we're already running low. We need more!" As her eyes shifted to Tyrese, she gulped the morsels in her mouth. "H-hi there." She giggled, and Firas saw that this insatiable homemaker wanted to fuck his boyfriend.

"Thanks for the update, Bethany."

She giggled again and went back for another slice, still glancing over her shoulder at Tyrese. Firas never counted on her libido posing a problem, yet here it was. He had invited Bethany not for himself (she often showed up to classes stoned and made for a terrible cooking partner) but for his mother. With children of her own, two of whom were at the age of raging hormones, Bethany could provide the comfort his own mother was sure to need by the end of the night. Firas wanted this very much, understanding that, while this was his coming-out party, he was not the only one who would be affected by it.

"So where's Mazen?"

"Hey, birthday boy!" Ted shouted. His limbs were entangled so convolutedly with those of his girlfriend Rochelle that no one could ever guess where one lover began and the other one ended. Firas was generally indifferent towards Ted, but his blatant heterosexuality was necessary to dispel his parents' belief that unabashed promiscuity was exclusive to gays. "You got any party games planned? If not, we have a few ideas. Naughty ideas!" He and Rochelle said this last part simultaneously, as though to let the world know they did everything simultaneously.

The swift turn of a knob whipped Firas's head towards the front door, and he began to wonder if these distractions were swatting inconveniences away or merely birthing new ones.

"Marhaba," came his mother's croaky whimper as she plodded in.

"We finally got Jido back into the nursing home," added his father right behind her. They were hunched from the weight of the day but cracking a faint smile as though assuming they'd suffered the worst of it.

Abdullah approached Firas. "Hey, cuz, where's my Bluetooth speaker? I wanted to play some DJ Shiv!"

Mr. Lindstrom approached: "Hey, the coffee cake I brought goes great with mousse. Should we bring it out?"

"You still haven't told me where Mazen is."

"You still haven't told me why you're turning down your promotion."

"You still haven't told us which games we're gonna play."

"Fy-russ, have you ordered more pizza yet?"

"Fear-az, have you opened my present yet?"

"Firas, what on earth am I doing at your party?!"

"LET'S GET DIRTYYYYYYYY!!!"

The music blared incongruously from a quartet of phones, though nobody seemed to mind but Firas. It was a party, after all, and it had a morbid obligation to be discordant, to be messy and wild and crazy. Firas understood this now, but he resented this discovery, for it had come too late and cost too much. He couldn't hear the words pouring out of his sister's mouth, which looked ready to leap off her face, but she—and every other person in the house—would hear the blast that followed.

"MAZEN IS FUCKING DEAD!"

The blaring music stopped. All across the room, chattering mouths snapped shut, but it was hardly another second before some of the weaker ones reopened, gasping, moaning, giggling nervously. Firas had expected the monster to reemerge, but not so soon. Not so openly.

"Habibi, what are you talking about?" asked Abdullah.

"You shouldn't joke like that, cuz," added Samira.

The cousins never knew about Mazen's attempt. Nobody knew, not even his schoolmates and teachers. Mazen had never spoken of it to anyone, and his parents turned away any friend (or teacher, as was once the case) who showed up at their door to find out why he had suddenly stopped being his wonderful self. Firas hadn't accounted for the effect the news would have in the absence of this context.

"Fear-az, you seem a bit crabby today," said Howie. "Is everything okay?"

Firas ignored all questions, even as they were repeated over and over, growing louder and more intense, the space between them shrinking the more they went unanswered. Instead he shifted his eyes back and forth between his mother, his father, and his sister, all of whom he noticed had no reaction. No curve of the lip nor tilt of the head nor an accidental portal into their inscrutable eyes. Only as his sister and parents turned to one another, then back to Firas, and so on and so forth like a directionless stage play, did he understand that none of them was sure exactly *how* they were supposed to react. Every conceivable emotion collided with every other and died in the wreckage, but slowly, so that even numbness and indifference lagged. Eventually Suhad and his parents settled their eyes on him, as though he were the savviest on this matter. But he wasn't. Mazen was, a fact that began to form as clearly as his face did the closer Firas got to the end of the road on his map. Within his brother's face, he saw foreign features: round eyes and pinkish lips that he had seen on another boy less than one hour ago, the late Mohammed Abu Khdeir, whose murder by Israeli settlers was soon followed by the assault on Gaza two years prior, right before Mazen canceled his birthday party, because naturally he couldn't go through with any kind of celebration then. Naturally he had to try to take his own life.

Suddenly tears were streaming from Suhad's eyes. A button had spontaneously been pushed inside her by a svelte torso enveloping hers. If Firas was surprised by the effect of his boyfriend's touch, it was by the realization that it was not bespoke, seeming to hold the same level of significance for anyone who received it. Tyrese was a restrained lover, but a passionate cuddler, which made for a reassuring contrast that often promised something more. And here was the fulfillment of that promise, delivered to his sister, for whom Firas was willing to spare it. Suhad's bluish-pink eyeshadow smudged Tyrese's shirt, while his hands traversed her back, exploring the grounds for more wells to pump. Firas's parents began to cry, too, and wrapped their arms around their daughter so tightly that Tyrese could not escape their grasp to give them the intimacy they deserved.

The sight of the embrace sparked a memory in Firas. Shortly after Mazen's birth, he had begged his parents, incessantly as only children can, to let him hold his baby brother. After several staunch refusals, his Teta once again intervened in his defense and his parents eventually conceded. They let Firas hold his brother, his father crouching before him by the bed Firas was sitting on, supporting baby Mazen discreetly and letting Firas gush at the perceived strength of his own arms. Then another memory flickered in his mind. One of Mazen begging Firas to push their beds together in their shared bedroom in the Dareers' first apartment in Dearborn. He'd been having nightmares from a horror film Firas watched the week before, and which Firas let him watch, too, that collusion of brothers that produces both the bond's harshest punishments and its fondest memories. They pushed their beds together for a few nights, then stopped when Mazen kept rolling too close to the middle, sliding the beds back apart and falling through the crack. For years, Firas believed this apartment to be the place that Mazen relentlessly referred to as "home." For years he had been blind and foolish.

The party guests stopped asking questions. They stopped talking altogether, except to offer Firas their condolences, or to brief the remaining three guests who had just arrived, or to ask one another for help in securing more food, which they stopped eating themselves and instead offered to their host. He hated himself for getting angry at these people, at their denseness throughout the day. He had tried to plan the perfect party to facilitate his coming out, and he expected everyone to play along with a secret they weren't privy to. How lucky he was to have each and every one of them.

He watched the embrace between his family and Tyrese and smiled, knowing that after all his efforts he would not come out on this day after all. Not merely because of Mazen's death, but because that death birthed a new life. Firas had planned his coming out around an arbitrary deadline, like some postcollegiate mission to secure an elusive future, with no regard for whether he was even ready. But Time did regard his readiness. Time observed how he wore his veil so tightly he could no longer see himself. He, like everyone around him, was kept out. Time was considerate and calculating, as he always believed himself to be, but unlike Firas, it was malleable, as much as humanity's sense of it. It is true that it heals all wounds, not as a saint graced with some magic touch, but as a surgeon tasked with a deliberate hand and utmost precision; it heals them at the rate the mind is able to process them, so that it may develop the necessary tools to prevent others of its kind. Firas could always hear the ticking clock, but what he lacked more than Time was the most powerful of those tools: truth. Tonight was intended to be a night of truth, but it was doomed to fail, for truth cannot be shared until it is first examined. Sharing an unexamined truth was no different from sharing an untested cure: too many potential outcomes, too few contingency plans. He knew he couldn't run away with Kashif. Kashif was a firecracker, a 5K marathon that took Firas's breath away when now more than ever he needed to breathe. He needed to breathe and to sleep. With more hunger than years, Kashif would inevitably come to devour him. In a way, Kashif, too, was on an arbitrary deadline. Firas thought of the eight stages of coming out and saw in it the journey of Palestine. He knew not what stage of Palestinianism he was at, but he understood now how the process was one not of progression but of fluctuation, veering back and forth depending on the willingness of the world to move out of the way, and the willingness of the self to push past it when it doesn't. Mazen tried to push past it, and the rest of the Dareers numbed him with pills so that he lost all his strength. It was true that Firas killed his little brother, but he had done so long before this day.

From within the tight embrace, Tyrese's arm protruded and began flailing, calling for Firas to join in where he belonged. To think Firas mistook this man's ungodly patience for casual indifference. That Tyrese had laughed at his proposal, like everything else in his life, suddenly made perfect sense. Tyrese had lost his roots, had had his roots stolen from him since before he was even born, but he managed to find his truth, and would keep on finding it as he continued to float, waiting all the while for the day Firas finally joined him. He tamed his lovemaking so that Firas understood there was no rush to the finish line. He gave Firas an architecture badge for his birthday because it was a practical gift for a practical man, an all-access pass to a conference ten weeks away for the man who was always ten steps ahead. It truly was the perfect gift, for it meant that he was *known*. And even with that knowledge, Tyrese stayed. He didn't burn hot the way Kashif did. The heat that arises in queer people after so many years in a suffocating hole had settled into a more soothing temperature. Tyrese was warm like a blanket, like a hand to a cheek, as love was meant to be.

His flailing arm accidentally knocked against Firas's mother's leg, and she lifted her head, her face drenched in tears that showed no sign of stopping but were forced to stop when she finally noticed this stranger. She had a look of wonder, but there was no introduction, no *How do you know Firas?*, because when Tyrese stepped aside to let him take his place, Firas wrapped his arms around him for all that he had done, not least of which was stand guard over him rather than pull him upward and onward by force. And in that hug, his mother, his father, and his sister tapped into what they had always, on one level or another, sensed about him.

Maysa, who had led Tyrese to this house, who had first known of his presence in Firas's life from those evanescent moments of joy she glimpsed over the last few months—a sigh of relief at the arrival of text, a faint smile at the reading of it—now led Tyrese aside, so that Firas may join his family. Her cunning was something Firas detested about her, but it was necessary, for she too saw the disaster ahead, ever since that night she caught him with Kashif, and she tried to use her cunning on this day to stop it from happening. Now she was setting the stage for another crucial scene, yet she did not fade too far into the background, for she would someday share in their grief. There were many times throughout her life when Maysa found herself resenting families like the Dareers because they got to grow up in Palestine. It was occupied Palestine, but a heap of terrible was, to her, better than a hint of wonderful quickly snatched away. She had tasted freedom only to be forced to spit it back out. The Nakba was a worse version of widowhood; with people, it was better to have loved and lost than never to have loved at all; but with one's land, it was different. Land was not like a person, of whom there were billions, born every minute of every day in every corner of the world, many of them wholly interchangeable. It was not a cog that could be replaced or duplicated. It was a rare, custom-made jewel to be dug up out of one's soul, and Maysa, now in her eighth decade, had long believed her soul was a bottomless pit.

As his family's crying amplified in sound and texture, Firas had yet to cry. For now he was still the dutiful son, the bearer of shoulders on which others may cry, and he was honored to fulfill this duty. But later he would do it, and do it publicly, to remind the world around him that he had had enough. This is what his grandfather wanted and expected of him. He wanted to see the pain, and to see it churned into glorious power. He wanted to see rebirth of a family that died along the border. Like Maysa, Jido was unlikely to see a free Palestine ever again, unlikely even to get to visit it now, which made his family's indifference to it all the more wrenching. Kashif also had this fear deep down, of never seeing a free Palestine in his lifetime. For someone so young to be so afraid . . . Firas often scoffed at the way Kashif claimed a greater connection to the land, given that he'd never once set foot on it. It was cruel, this dismissiveness. It was nonsensical. A connection like that stemmed from something so much greater and truer than geography, than jeeps, than bulldozers and missiles and checkpoints and walls. Mazen understood this better than anyone, and had been robbed more than anyone, for he had no idea what he'd lost, and could therefore never find it. In the end, he went back to Palestine the only way he knew how. And in doing so he brought the rest of his family one step closer to it.

A third memory of Mazen flickered across Firas's mind, from just that afternoon as he was helping Firas prepare the food, and he took a moment to assure his older brother that today would be a wonderful day. He had thanked Mazen for those words, hadn't he? Yes. Yes, he had thanked him.

There were so many more memories to rekindle, of Mazen and of everything else. Firas had severed himself from them, these burdens weighing him down on his march into the future. But a past ignored (for it could never truly be severed) is less a burden than it is an elastic band around one's waist: when one marches forward, the band stretches as far as it can before snapping right back into place; the farther away from its starting point, the harder and harsher the snap. Firas had to stay in the present moment, with his family who needed his shoulders; but when he finished comforting them on this fateful night, he would turn and look back. Yes, by God, he would finally look back! He would remember how his family managed to flee. He would remember his Teta's last words to him before her murder. He would remember all the names and faces of the friends he left behind, and then imagine what those faces looked like now. He would search for them, reach out to them when he found them, reminisce, thank the ones who managed to survive and mourn the ones who didn't. He would remember all of it, bathe in the tragedies, the absurdities, the madness, let it all wash over him, a baptism necessary to avoid drowning in it altogether and drifting down into the cold, boundless sea. But this would not be a blow to Time, for Time would kindly stop to let the past catch up, kiss its secrets across his cheek until they reached his lips and he could speak them. And then, after all that needs to be said is said, after the bandage begins to slide gently off his heart to reveal that the wound had healed and left but the mildest scar, Time would proceed. Time, like an old friend, would guide him Home.

ACKNOWLEDGMENTS

My biggest debt is to Palestine, both for what it is and for what it represents. Among its scattered ashes lie hope, resilience, tenacity, and above all, a defiant sense of joy. There could be no words on my pages without it.

My family, for their continued support and faith in my talent.

My agent, Mariah Stovall, who championed this novel from the very beginning and remained undeterred even as the roadblocks multiplied and the uphill climbs became steeper.

My editor, David Ross, who chipped away the parts of my work that weighed it down and helped me sculpt something beautiful.

My copy editor, Shaun Oakey, whose diligent work reminded me that the literary devil is in the details.

My book designer, Emma Dolan, whose gorgeous design evokes what my words never could.

My friend and mentor Omar El Akkad, whose grace, humility, and passion have made me a better writer and a better person.

My friend and colleague Saeed Teebi, whose unapologetically Palestinian voice has helped me hone my own.

BIPOC Writers Connect, who accepted me into their program and reminded me that there is indeed space for Palestinian stories.

To all the members of the CanLit community who have shown remarkable solidarity with the Palestinian people despite intense pressure and backlash, and who have refused to forget what the art of writing is truly about.

And to Taghreed Halawa, who every day makes me feel one step closer to the homeland.